Praise

"Smiley kicks off a hard-boiled series with a bang in this ... novel that sweeps readers along quickly."

—*Library Journal*

"An excellent book about the emotions that drive some of the best policemen and –women to go after their own justice, no matter the cost."

—*Suspense Magazine*

"Terrific! The classic cop story goes contemporary in this suspenseful, riveting thriller. Instantly cinematic and completely authentic—LAPD's tough and savvy Davie Richards will capture your heart. It's a page-turner from moment one."

—Hank Phillippi Ryan, Agatha-, Anthony- and
Mary Higgins Clark Award–winning author

"In *Pacific Homicide,* Patricia Smiley, at the top of her form in this multi-layered thriller, investigates the grisly murder of a young Russian beauty found in the 6,500 miles of sewer pipelines under Los Angeles. Smiley knows the LAPD from the inside out and writes with the authenticity of Joseph Wambaugh. This is the first of a series featuring the tough-gal detective Davie Richards. I can't wait for the second one."

—Paul Levine, bestselling author of *Bum Rap*

"With a taut style, unfailing ear, and unflinching honesty, Patricia Smiley's *Pacific Homicide* puts a fresh, deeply emotional spin on the police procedural."

—Craig Faustus Buck, author of *Go Down Hard*

PATRICIA SMILEY

OUTSIDE THE WIRE

A PACIFIC HOMICIDE NOVEL

MIDNIGHT INK
WOODBURY, MINNESOTA

FIRST EDITION
First Printing, 2017

Book format by Bob Gaul
Cover design and photo by Ellen Lawson
Editing by Nicole Nugent

Midnight Ink, an imprint of Llewellyn Worldwide Ltd.

Library of Congress Cataloging-in-Publication Data
Names: Smiley, Patricia, author.
Title: Outside the wire: a mystery / Patricia Smiley.
Description: First edition. | Woodbury, Minnesota: Midnight Ink, 2017. |
 Series: A Pacific homicide mystery; #2
Identifiers: LCCN 2017021256 (print) | LCCN 2017025057 (ebook) | ISBN
 9780738753089 (ebook) | ISBN 9780738752358 (print)
Subjects: | GSAFD: Mystery fiction.
Classification: LCC PS3619.M49 (ebook) | LCC PS3619.M49 O98 2017 (print) |
 DDC 813/.6—dc23
LC record available at https://lccn.loc.gov/2017021256

Midnight Ink
Llewellyn Worldwide Ltd.
2143 Wooddale Drive
Woodbury, MN 55125-2989
www.midnightinkbooks.com

Printed in the United States of America

Dedicated to
My great uncle Julius, US Army 91st Infantry Division,
who gave "the last full measure of devotion"
in France on October 9, 1918

———————

Other Books by Patricia Smiley

Pacific Homicide
(Midnight Ink, 2016)

Tucker Sinclair Mysteries
False Profits
Cover Your Assets
Short Change
Cool Cache

Acknowledgments

I'm grateful for the astute literary analysts who read my pages and provided insightful feedback, including Ramona Long; my wise and talented agent, Sandy Harding; and as always, the members of my beloved writing group—The Oxnardians. Thanks also to the team at Midnight Ink—Nicole Nugent, Katie Mickschl, and Terri Bischoff—and to fellow sailor Scott Jarema for suggesting the title. Much credit goes to Detective Michael D. DePasquale for setting me straight on the possibilities and limitations of police powers. I take full responsibility for occasionally ignoring his sage advice.

While researching this novel, I interviewed a number of veterans who shared their experiences from Vietnam and other wars. I offer my heartfelt appreciation for their candor and their sacrifice.

1

DAVIE RICHARDS WOKE UP at four a.m. as she had most mornings for the past few months: drenched in sweat, throat raw from crying out in her sleep. Flashbacks. The shrink had told her to expect them. A symptom of post-traumatic stress, he'd said. For what seemed like the millionth time, her mind played back the response.

"Soldiers in Kandahar have PTSD," she'd said. "I don't have PTSD."

"Other traumas trigger symptoms. For example, people who've survived a car accident or an earthquake. They have nightmares and trouble sleeping, too."

"I do not have PTSD."

He had picked up his pen and scribbled some words on a note pad. She imagined it read something like *Patient in denial and resistant to therapy. Prognosis hopeless.*

She had told him early on how often she thought about the shooting—the sound of gunfire, the sight of blood pooled around the man's head. True, she was going through a rough spell. For the past three months whenever she went to qualify at the firing range the smell of burnt gunpowder sent her heart racing. Loud noises made her flinch. But those reactions would fade over time. She just had to park the bad memories in an inaccessible compartment of her brain, same as she had always done.

Davie got out of bed, letting her coppery red hair tumble down her back. Her oversized white T-shirt had absorbed some of the sweat, but the sheets were damp. She examined them for a moment, wondering if she'd reached The Limit. It was a cop term for the number of dead people you could see before it was beyond your ability to cope. She'd seen her share of bodies during her nine-plus years as an LAPD patrol officer and in the past year as a detective. She'd known other Homicide detectives who'd investigated hundreds of murders and never reached The Limit, but none of them had killed two men in the line of duty. She had.

Sometimes she felt overwhelmed with guilt, thinking about the families that had been left to mourn, but she never questioned her decision to fire her weapon. The shootings were righteous. Her actions had saved innocent lives. But there was a price to pay for taking the life of another human being, and she was only beginning to understand that cost.

The department required everybody who'd been connected with an officer-involved shooting to be evaluated by a shrink. Following the first shooting, she'd been released after only one visit. Her relief was palpable, because extended therapy might have damaged her career. After the second shooting, she continued seeing the shrink because he hadn't released her for duty right away … and because a part of her didn't want him to.

Davie pulled the sheets away from the mattress before heading toward the kitchen to make coffee, hoping her workday would be uneventful.

DAVIE HEARD THE SOUND of jet engines roaring overhead and the long, impatient honk of a car horn. Warm, stale air blasted through the open window of the detective car as she drove up the corkscrew ramp of the parking facility adjacent to Tom Bradley International Terminal at LAX. An hour after arriving at work, she and her partner, Det. Jason Vaughn, had been called out to investigate a body found on the second floor. Davie disliked the closed-in feeling of parking garages. Lately they made her feel claustrophobic.

Vaughn ended his phone conversation. "Communications Division didn't get any calls about a disturbance before the body was found."

"Probably no witnesses then. Just our luck."

He looked at her and smiled. "Another opportunity to use our superpowers."

Davie had known Vaughn since their academy days but had only worked with him for the past several months at Pacific Area Homicide. They didn't always agree on how to approach the work, but they hashed out their differences without any permanent damage to the friendship.

After Davie parked, she stepped out of the car, inhaling the acrid odor of motor oil and tire rubber. Pacific patrol officers had already established the crime scene perimeter to protect any evidence and marked it off with yellow tape that read POLICE LINE—DO NOT CROSS. She instructed them to cordon off all entrances to the garage and list the make, model, and license plate numbers of nearby vehicles. She also assigned one officer to maintain the crime scene log and another to canvass the area for witnesses.

Davie and Vaughn always followed the same routine. They studied the area from different angles and compared notes later, because the truth was, sometimes you *couldn't* see the forest for the trees. Davie jotted down their arrival time and the weather conditions—57 degrees and overcast—and noted that the lights in the garage provided limited visibility.

Normally she and Vaughn agreed on a path that everyone would use to enter and exit the crime scene to keep contamination at a minimum, but she was annoyed to see their protocol had already been breached. An officer and a sergeant from the Airport Police had walked through the crime scene and were standing near the victim. Before approaching them, she made a sketch in her notebook, including the position of the parked cars relative to the body on the pavement. She was no artist, but the diagram had to be completed before calling in the criminalists. Sometimes things got moved or disturbed and she had to know exactly how the scene looked when she arrived.

The Airport Police had a stormy history with the LAPD, so when she introduced herself to the sergeant, she wasn't surprised that his greeting was short and curt. The sergeant's chin tilted upward in a gesture of defiance. "I called the coroner's office. They're on their way."

Davie could almost feel her blood pressure spike, but she wasn't going to give him the satisfaction of knowing that. What he'd done

4

was improper and he knew it. This was Pacific Homicide's crime scene, not his. The sergeant was just leg lifting, marking his territory.

No ambulance had been called to the scene, so it would be the coroner's job to determine time of death and later to check the victim's body for hair or fiber evidence. She had an hour to make the first call to the coroner's office but that was only to give them a heads up about the body. The investigator wouldn't respond to the scene until Davie called the second time, because once he arrived the corpse belonged to him. Between the two calls, detectives and criminalists had a chance to take photographs, collect fingerprints, and gather other evidence without having everybody and his brother tramping through the area.

Her tone was low but firm. "Stand down, sergeant, before you piss off the wrong people."

The sergeant's stony expression told her he was unmoved by her warning. "Just trying to speed things up."

Vaughn shot him a hard stare as he pressed numbers on his cell keypad. "I'll call Dr. Death. Tell him to put us on the list but not to roll out until we phone again." He turned his back on the sergeant and walked a few feet away to talk in private.

Davie was petite—five-one, just over a hundred pounds. Men often used their bulk to intimidate her. It never worked. "We only have one chance at a crime scene. You screw that up and a killer goes free. You want that on your conscience?"

The sergeant glanced at the officer by his side and then answered in a matter-of-fact tone. "You're preaching to the choir, Detective."

Davie thought about pressing her point but suspected any attempt to change his attitude would be unproductive. Instead, she jotted down his name, serial number, and rank. "Who found the body?"

"A schoolteacher," the sergeant said. "She came back from a wedding in Jerusalem. On her way to the car, she saw him slumped on the ground." He pointed to the body lying by the trunk of a four-door Audi A6. "Over there."

"Where's the witness now?" Vaughn said.

Davie flinched at the sound of her partner's voice. He'd obviously completed his call to the coroner's office, but she hadn't heard him creep up behind her.

"In the back of our patrol car," the sergeant said. "She's pretty freaked out."

"I'll grab the tape recorder from our Murder Kit and have a talk with her," Vaughn said. "Maybe she saw the hit go down."

As soon as her partner left, Davie squatted next to the victim. He was a white male with muscular arms and a trim waist. Judging by the wrinkles on his face and loose skin on his neck, she estimated his age as somewhere in his early sixties. Still, he looked unusually fit. None of his clothing was torn. There were no visible defensive wounds, so the victim hadn't put up a fight. He was in the fetal position, which was often a reaction to pain. Rigor mortis hadn't yet set in, so it was unlikely he'd been dead for long.

A pool of blood from a perforating bullet wound on the right front side of his skull had saturated the victim's black leather jacket and white polo shirt. She was no forensics expert, but the shot looked like it had been taken at fairly close range. The neat hole on the back of his head was smaller, which told her the bullet entered from the front and exited in the back. She flashed back three months to the suspect she'd killed with a similar shot and then forced her eyes closed to keep the memory at bay.

When she opened them again, she saw that a dog tag, wound loosely with black electrician's tape, was attached to a ball chain around the victim's neck. The tag lay near his left ear. The placement seemed unnatural, as if it had been staged.

She glared at the sergeant. "Anybody touch the body before we got here?"

"I moved the dog tag, ma'am. I was hoping to identify him, but I gloved up first."

Davie turned toward the voice. The name on the Airport Police uniform pocket read LUNA. The officer had wide-set eyes and full lips. Close-cropped hair made his ears look like wings. Stitch marks were still visible on a jagged scar that stretched from his right ear to his chin.

"Nobody touches the body until the coroner gets here," she said, recording his name and serial number in her notes. "You should know that."

The sergeant crossed his arms over his chest to convey his disapproval. "He *told* you, Detective. He didn't touch the body."

Luna's expression was impassive. "I served two tours in Afghanistan, ma'am. Army infantry. I saw the dog tag. I thought he might be a bro."

Davie studied Luna's scar and wondered if it was a battle wound. Then she pointed to the victim. "This guy looks at least thirty years your senior. It seems unlikely he's still on active duty."

"That doesn't matter. He's still my bro."

"How do you know he's Army?"

Luna returned her stare without blinking. "You can tell by the dog tag. Each branch of the military uses different information. That's why I know this guy was Army, like me."

"Is that printed on the tag?" Luna shook his head, so Davie continued. "What else can you tell me about it?"

"It's painted black. Since Vietnam, the Army requires soldiers who operate behind enemy lines to blacken all insignia."

"You think he served in Vietnam?" she said.

"Hard to say, but the tag looks old. This one has a social security number on it. The Army doesn't use those anymore."

Davie sat on her heels next to the body for a closer look. "Why is it wrapped with tape?"

Luna hunkered down across from her and pointed. "See that plastic bumper around the tag? It's called a silencer. It's supposed to keep the tags from making noise when you're on the move. Sometimes that isn't enough. The enemy can still hear you coming. So, some guys tape the tags together to keep them from jangling."

"You keep saying *tags*. I only see one."

"There's usually a second one attached by a short chain. When a soldier dies in battle, one tag is removed and taken back to headquarters. The other stays on the body for identification purposes."

Davie pulled a pen from her notebook and slipped it inside the finger of a latex glove. She lifted the tape, exposing five lines of information stamped into the metal: WOODROW, ZEKE C., followed by a social security number, O POS, and NO REL PREF. She assumed the last two lines represented his blood type and his religious preference—none.

"The tape looks like it was torn," Davie said. "The edges are still clean, so I'm guessing it was recent."

"Yes, ma'am. That's what I thought, too."

"You think whoever tore the tape stole the second tag?"

"Could be."

Davie rose to her feet. "You think the victim could still be on active duty?"

Luna stared at the body. "I doubt it. The Army makes you retire at sixty. He looks a few years older than that."

"If he's retired, why was he wearing dog tags?"

A haunted look settled on Luna's expression as he stood to meet her gaze. "I don't know, ma'am. Most retirees don't wear their tags, but you get close to people when you're in the military. Soldiers are trained to get everybody out alive. Sometimes you fail. The victim might be honoring a buddy who died in combat. It's hard to explain to civilians. It's a brotherhood stronger than anything, even family."

Davie didn't know what it was like to be a soldier, but she'd been a cop for almost ten years, so she understood the bonds between people who were responsible for keeping you safe. She made a 360-degree turn, studying the garage. The murder had been committed in a secluded area in the early morning hours when it was likely still dark and no one would be around. There was no place for the victim to escape an attacker unless he jumped two floors to the street. Robbery might have been the motive for the attack, but it seemed unusual that a killer would find value in old military ID tags. She would know more about what was missing when she searched the car.

A car-key remote lay near the body. It couldn't be moved until it had been photographed, but Davie wanted to know if it belonged to the Audi. She gloved up, walked toward the car, and discovered that the driver's side front door wasn't locked. That told her the victim hadn't had time to secure the car before he was killed. Since he fell near the trunk, he may have been heading to get his suitcase.

She made notes and then returned to the body. Without disturbing the position of the remote, she pressed the lock button. The Audi's lights flashed. The victim had likely driven the car to the airport, but that couldn't be confirmed until she ran the license plate. Once she viewed the garage surveillance footage, she hoped to see who fired the shot. She pressed the remote again to return the vehicle to its unlocked state.

A cursory search of the car's interior revealed no obvious evidence. Davie swept her hand under the seats but found nothing. Travelers used this garage because it was across the street from the international terminal. Either the man—Zeke Woodrow, presumably—had come to the airport to meet somebody or he was taking a flight himself. If the latter was true, he must have a passport in his pocket or in a suitcase.

During her police academy training, instructors had taught her to write only what she saw and heard at a crime scene, not her hunches or conclusions. But she was a Homicide detective now so theorizing was part of her job. She flipped open the trunk using the release lever inside the car but saw no luggage there, boosting the theory that Woodrow had come to pick up a returning passenger. On the other hand, Davie already suspected the shooter removed the dog tag; maybe he'd taken the victim's luggage, as well.

She heard footsteps and turned to see Vaughn walking toward her. "Did you learn anything from the schoolteacher?"

He pulled her aside so the sergeant couldn't hear the conversation. "She heard tires squealing when she stepped out of the elevator and then a car barreled around the corner. The windows were tinted, so she couldn't see the driver, but she believes the car was a BMW, one of the bigger models. She doesn't think the driver saw her but she's scared. I checked the area for tire marks. The garage is full of them. I'll have the techs take some photos, but I doubt they'll lead anywhere."

"We need a copy of the garage security tapes."

Vaughn gestured toward the sergeant. "We aren't going to get any love from Darth Vader over there. I'll call the substation and ask one of the detectives to get them."

"Maybe Luna can help. He seems like a decent guy."

He nodded. "The photographer and the crime scene peeps are on the way. I'll corner Luna."

A short time later, the criminalists, latent print techs, and the police photographer from the Scientific Investigation Division arrived. Vaughn had also contacted Pacific's official towing service. The truck driver would take the Audi to a sterile location, where techs would search for trace evidence.

Davie made the second call to the coroner's office. While she waited for the investigator to arrive, she asked the SID photographer to take two sets of photographs of the body—one in color for her and one in black-and-white to spare future jurors from looking at death in full color.

She turned when she heard the coroner's investigator call her name.

3

DAVIE WATCHED AS THE coroner's investigator searched the body. He found no passport, cell phone, or wallet in the victim's pockets. Davie told him what time the body had been found and when she and Vaughn had arrived at the garage. With that information, he checked the victim's liver temperature and estimated the death had occurred somewhere between 5:00 a.m. and 6:30 a.m. A search on her cell revealed that sunrise had been at 6:35 that morning, so the attack had likely not happened in full daylight.

Two hours into the investigation, the most concrete information Davie had about Zeke Woodrow was the social security number stamped on his military dog tag. From past investigations, she knew the first three numbers were associated with the state where a person was born. A search on her cell revealed Woodrow was likely born in Iowa. She wasn't sure how that information could help her investigation, but she made a note of it anyway.

Davie hunched over the coroner's investigator, watching him work. "How soon can you schedule the post?"

He rolled his eyes. "You're joking, right? We have at least a hundred fifty bodies stacked up waiting for autopsies. Even if we give you priority, you're still behind other homicide cases that came in before yours."

"So ... tomorrow?"

He chuckled. "Ain't gonna happen, Richards. Not even for you."

It was after ten o'clock when the coroner removed the body and the Audi was towed from the garage. Davie and her partner closed the crime scene and headed to the car.

Vaughn removed his jacket and placed it neatly folded on the back-seat.

"New suit?" she said.

Vaughn beamed. "A beauty, isn't it? Half price sale at Barney's."

Her partner had a tall, slim build that was perfect for designer suits and silk pocket squares. His fashion gene had been passed down from a Northern Italian mother who was also responsible for his sandy hair and soft-brown eyes. Davie called him George Clooney's better-looking cousin, a tease he didn't seem to mind.

She started the car and made a U-turn. "If you were any more of a clotheshorse, Jason, you'd have to list your height in hands."

He settled into the passenger seat. "Funny. At least it beats your lame Yogi-phobia jokes."

The tires squealed as she negotiated the city ride down the ramp. "You shouldn't have told me bears were your Kryptonite."

"Trust me, that won't happen again."

Her partner's bear phobia was a running joke dating back to their police academy days. One night over drinks he told her about a camping trip with a group of friends and a baby black bear that had wandered into their campsite looking for food. He'd overdramatized the incident to make her laugh, probably not expecting she'd still be kidding him about it all these years later.

Davie drove on surface streets toward the station where she and Vaughn were assigned to the Homicide table. Pacific Division was number fourteen of twenty-one decentralized police stations. It was a small piece of the Los Angeles pie—25.74 square miles of the city's 468—and included 200,000 of the approximately three million residents. Its western border was the Pacific Ocean with Culver City to the east, the Los Angeles International Airport to the south, and National Boulevard to the north, and included the neighborhoods of Venice Beach, Oakwood, Mar Vista, Playa del Rey, Playa Vista, Palms, and Westchester.

As Davie drove, she noted how the years of drought had made neighborhoods look like dusty brown outposts in some third-world country. It was striking how much she missed the greenery. The landscape would change once you entered neighboring West L.A. Division, where affluent residents could afford the cost of second– and third-tier water usage to keep their lawns lush.

When they arrived at the Culver Boulevard gate, Davie pressed her ID to the security sensor and parked in the area designated for detective cars, just steps away from the back door of the two-story brick station. Once inside, she and Vaughn turned right into the squad room. Her boss, Det. Frank Giordano, was sitting in his workstation cubicle. She could almost hear the crinkle of his starched white shirt as he waved to acknowledge her presence.

Giordano was bent over the phone, speaking in a low voice, which was unusual because he was a big man with an even bigger personality. His retirement was a couple of months away and she wasn't looking forward to the day. She hoped he was quietly lobbying to postpone the inevitable. Giordano had lobbied the brass after the second shooting until they returned her to Pacific. His loyalty and support meant everything to her.

Giordano ended the call and peered over the gray cubicle wall that separated their desks. "How did it go, kid?"

She filled him in on the homicide. "So far, we don't know why the victim was at the airport this morning. You think the airlines will tell us if his name was on a passenger list?"

"They might," Giordano said. "Call and ask. If he was at Bradley terminal, he was probably flying international. That narrows the field. If anybody asks for a search warrant, you can write up a boilerplate and get a judge to sign all of them at once."

"I'll make some calls," Vaughn said. "I can type up a warrant if we need one. In the meantime, Luna is working on getting us the garage surveillance video."

"Keep me posted," Giordano said.

Vaughn sat at his desk across from hers and logged onto his computer. A moment later, he called to her. "Look at this. Luna already came through with the surveillance footage."

Davie grabbed her notebook. She and Giordano stepped to Vaughn's workstation, hovering over his shoulder to see the screen. Luna had included the video feed from two hours before the murder until an hour after the body was found. There wasn't much happening in those early hours, so Vaughn fast-forwarded until the Audi came into view. Davie noted the time Woodrow's car entered the garage and pulled into the parking spot. A moment later, Vaughn jammed his finger on the pause button. "There's the BMW. Looks like a black 740i."

Davie noted the make and model of the car and that it had entered the garage a couple of minutes behind the Audi. The BMW's windows were tinted so it was difficult to see inside the car, but the driver appeared to be alone and wearing a ball cap pulled low over his face.

She couldn't make out the license plate number because both front and rear plates were obscured.

"Hard to see the guy's features," Vaughn said. "I'm not even sure it's a male."

The BMW drove to the second floor and rolled slowly forward. Vaughn adjusted the screen so they could see several views at once. Woodrow got out of the Audi, walked to the trunk, and opened it. He jerked upright when the BMW stopped next to him. There was a muzzle flash and Woodrow disappeared from sight. The BMW's tinted windows blocked some of the action, but it was clear the shooter got out of the car and ran toward the body, perhaps grabbing a wallet, passport, and the dog tag. The man then reached inside the trunk, pulled out a black carry-on bag, and ran back to the BMW. After that, the car made a U-turn and raced down the ramp. The schoolteacher appeared on screen less than a minute later. Vaughn switched to the camera shot of the exit kiosk. A woman collected the parking fee from the BMW's driver and then he casually drove into the night.

"I'll talk to the cashier," Vaughn said. "Maybe we can get an artist to meet with her and come up with a composite."

"Forget it," Giordano said. "All we can see is he's male, probably white, medium build, agile, dressed in dark clothes, but the guy's face is obscured by a ball cap. My guess is he knew there'd be cameras in the garage, so he probably disguised himself in other ways, too. If the cashier didn't get a good look at him, she might guess and your composite won't be worth shit. You put a sketch on TV that looks like half the US male population and offer a reward, a million people will call in to say, 'Hey, I know that guy.' Where does that leave you? Nowhere."

Davie leaned forward with her elbows on her knees. "At least we know why we didn't find a suitcase in the victim's car. The shooter took it."

"He didn't seem to care if the victim was identified," Vaughn said. "Otherwise, he wouldn't have left the second dog tag. We still don't know why Woodrow was wearing it."

Davie thought again about the single dog tag. Luna had told her the two were separated when a soldier died in combat. She wondered if that missing tag was symbolic to the killer. Maybe he was in the military and familiar with battlefield protocol, or perhaps he'd killed before and this was another trophy to add to his collection.

Davie rolled the chair back and got up. "I'll run the Audi plates. See if I can find the victim's address. He might have a family member who could tell us why he was at the airport."

Vaughn closed the video file. "I'll start calling airlines, see if they'll provide intel about his travel plans without a warrant."

Davie sat at her computer, searching the Department of Motor Vehicles database. Zeke Woodrow had no vehicle registered to him, but he might have listed it under the name of a spouse or a business. The Audi was registered to a rental agency in Carpinteria, but when she called to speak to a representative, she got a message that the office was closed for the day.

She found Woodrow's California driver's license in DMV records but the information was restricted. It showed his photo but not his address. That often meant the driver was a law enforcement officer, but there was no LEO note on the file. Luna had told her that Woodrow's blackened dog tag likely meant he'd operated behind enemy lines. Perhaps his address was hidden because of that past military service. She continued searching until she was able to access his residential address from a non–law enforcement database.

Woodrow was leasing a house in Topanga managed by a local real estate company. A few minutes later, Davie located the agent's name, Amber Johnson. The woman sounded surprised when Davie called with the news of Woodrow's death and offered obligatory condolences. She told Davie that, as far as she knew, the victim lived in the house alone. She agreed to meet them at the address with a key.

Davie leaned toward the half-wall partition that separated her workstation from Jason Vaughn's. "I found Woodrow's address."

"At least one of us has good news. I just got off the phone with a buddy in the DA's office. To get information about Woodrow's military record we have to send a subpoena and cover letter to the headquarters for military records in St. Louis, Missouri. She said they take at least ten weeks to respond, that is, *if* they respond."

"We're investigating a homicide."

"The military doesn't give a rat's patootie about that. Their mission is to protect the privacy of their personnel."

"Maybe Luna knows a back door into the database."

"I'll ask him."

Giordano was on the telephone again. He didn't even look up when Davie opened his desk drawer and grabbed the keys to a detective car. She and Vaughn logged out of the building and headed for the parking lot.

4

TOPANGA WAS A NARROW mountain canyon between Santa Monica and Malibu, accessed by a two-lane road with 25 mph curves. Just beyond the shoulder, the hills were covered with sagebrush, sycamore trees, cacti, and a few token palms. Davie had always thought of the place as a haven for artists, musicians, aging hippies, and people who just wanted to be left the hell alone. She wondered if Zeke Woodrow fell into any of those categories.

As they neared the summit, a smattering of small businesses and a few claptrap houses lined the road. Davie turned left near the Fernwood Fire Station and continued up a narrow road to the top of a hill that ended at a gated driveway.

Vaughn scanned the terrain. "It's isolated up here."

"Looks like there's only one way in—and out."

"I'll check the gate."

He got out of the car but stopped a few feet away, leaning over to pick up a metal object from the dirt shoulder. Davie rolled down the window as he walked toward her.

He held out a damaged lock for her to inspect. "Looks like somebody cut it off the gate. You think it was the real estate agent?"

"Not likely. If she has a key to the house, she probably has one for the gate, too. If somebody broke in, they were sloppy to leave evidence behind."

Vaughn pushed open the metal barrier and returned to the car, setting the lock on the floor mat. "Or maybe they didn't care if we found it."

The driveway led to a modest two-story stucco house. Morning glory vines snaked around the trunks of three maple trees that obscured the front façade. If someone was looking for privacy, they had come to the right place.

No cars were parked in the driveway, which meant the agent hadn't arrived. Davie knocked but no one came to the door. She and Vaughn walked along the side yard to see if the house had an alarm system. If it did, it was well hidden. After ten minutes of waiting for the agent, Davie grew impatient. She climbed the three flagstone steps to the front entrance, pulled a pair of latex gloves from her pocket, and reached for the doorknob. It turned with no resistance.

Before she could open the door, Vaughn grabbed her arm. "Whoa, partner. We can't just barge inside. What if this is a secondary crime scene?"

"There's only one way to find out."

She drew her Smith & Wesson from its holster. As she eased open the door, the aroma of wax and ammonia hit her like a wrecking ball. "Smells like cleaning products," she whispered.

Vaughn drew his Glock and followed her inside, his shoes echoing on the hardwood floors. He stopped with a jerk. "What the hell—"

The space was what designers called an open floor plan—nothing blocking the view from the living room to the kitchen to the dining room to the outside. On the back wall, French doors led to a flagstone patio with a panoramic view of the mountains. That scene was unobstructed because the house was empty—no furniture, no artwork, no magazines on a coffee table, no coffee table, no nothing. The stripped interior had Davie feeling uneasy about what else she might find.

She pulled a flashlight from her belt. The smell of wax grew stronger as she bent down, aiming the beam obliquely over the floor, knowing that the angle of light would show any small item that wasn't otherwise visible—maybe something that had inadvertently been left behind.

"See anything?" Vaughn said.

"Not even a dust bunny."

"Maybe Woodrow moved out and the management company already cleaned it for the next tenant."

"Seems like the agent would have told us that. All she said was he lived here alone."

She and Vaughn climbed the stairs to the second floor and found two bedrooms, both stripped of furniture, and a bathroom that was so spotless it beamed like a Maine lighthouse. Once they'd cleared the house, Davie returned her weapon to its holster.

"Hello. Anybody here?"

The voice was female and came from the first floor. Vaughn kept his weapon ready as they walked down the stairs and saw a tall, willowy woman wearing baggy cut-off jeans rolled to mid-thigh and an oversized man's plaid shirt. Her brown hair was shoulder-length and tangled. The sun had blanketed her face with a healthy glow and a crop of fine wrinkles.

"Sorry I'm late. I had to deliver a goat."

Vaughn shot Davie a wide-eyed stare. She'd seen that look before: *We're not in Kansas anymore, Toto.*

Davie didn't know if Amber Johnson was a cab driver or a midwife but decided to let the truth come out organically.

"No problem," she said. "The door was unlocked so, we decided to wait inside."

Amber's hiking boots left dusty footprints on the polished floor as she walked toward them. "That's weird. The door should have been locked, and how did you get through the gate?"

"Somebody cut the lock," Davie said.

The woman frowned as her gaze swept the room. "Where are Mr. Woodrow's things?" Her expression turned to alarm. "Somebody must have broken in. They stole everything."

"Is it possible that Mr. Woodrow moved out?" Vaughn said.

"If he did, nobody told me."

Vaughn moved toward her. "Were his rent payments current?"

Amber wandered into the kitchen, perhaps to make sure the emptiness wasn't an aberration. "He paid for a year in advance. There were still three months left on the lease."

"How did he pay?" Davie said.

The woman opened a kitchen drawer but found it empty. Davie should have cautioned her not to touch anything, but her fingerprints probably didn't matter. The place had not only been stripped of Woodrow's possessions, it appeared to have been sanitized.

"I didn't handle the money. I was told Mr. Woodrow wired funds directly to the owner's account."

"Who hired you to look after the place?"

Amber turned toward Davie, still dazed by the condition of the house. "A lawyer who worked for the owner."

"He hired you because you're in real estate?"

"I got my license but I've never actually sold anything. My kids and I run a small organic farm, so that takes up most of my time."

"Do you manage other properties?"

"Just this one." Amber must have realized how odd that sounded. "The lawyer called out of the blue. Said he found my name on an Internet site about local Topanga businesses. He told me Mr. Woodrow traveled a lot and the owners wanted somebody local to watch the place in case of wildfires. He offered to pay me a lot of money, so I said sure."

Davie hadn't been able to locate the property owner, so this was good news. "I'll need the name and number of that attorney."

Amber opened her phone and called out the information. Davie recorded it in her chrono notes. The attorney's name was Alden Brink, and the area code wasn't local. Davie did a quick search and found his number registered to a cell in Virginia, which meant he could be anywhere. Amber also gave her Zeke Woodrow's cell number.

Amber moved into the dining room and made a 360-degree turn. "Everything is gone, even the curtains." She opened the French doors and disappeared around the side of the house.

Davie followed as far as the patio, where she and Vaughn stood on the flagstones, inhaling the fragrance of sage that drifted up from the canyon. A coyote howled in the distance. A hawk flew overhead, searching for lunch. She scanned the area for anything that looked out of place but saw nothing suspicious.

The sun was high in the sky, casting shadows on the landscape. Davie thought of Zeke Woodrow, ambushed in that airport parking garage, and wondered why he had been there and who had wanted him dead. Even if he had left clues in the house that pointed to his killer, somebody had swept them away, along with all of his possessions. So far, nothing about this case made sense.

Vaughn was holding his nose. "Smells organic out here."

"Imagine sitting on a deck chair with your morning coffee, looking at nothing but unspoiled wilderness."

"I'd rather be playing volleyball at the beach."

Amber Johnson reappeared and walked over to join them. "Everything looks okay in the side yard."

Before Davie could respond, her eye caught a flash of light on the slope below. She squinted against the sun and saw two eyes staring at her from inside a drainage pipe that had been cut into the soil midway down the hillside.

Davie poked Vaughn's arm and pointed toward the light. "Did you see that? Looks like some kind of animal."

"I hope it's not a skunk," Vaughn said. "I'd have to burn my new suit."

Amber walked to the edge of the patio, raising her hand to her forehead to shield her eyes from the sun. "That's Mr. Woodrow's cat, Hootch."

"What kind of a name is that?" Vaughn said.

Amber sat on her heels at the edge of the hillside. "It's a hillbilly term for alcohol, I think."

Davie rummaged in her pocket for her sunglasses. "Would Mr. Woodrow move and leave his cat behind?"

"I can't image him doing that," she said. "He loved that cat. Besides, we don't let our pets run free up here because of the coyotes."

"Sounds like you and Mr. Woodrow were tight," Vaughn said.

"Actually, I never met him. Like I told you before, he traveled a lot. When he went out of town, I came over once a day to feed the cat and clean his box."

Davie squatted next to her. "Did he ask you to cat sit in the last couple of days?"

Amber reached out and snapped her fingers to get the cat's attention. "He texted a couple of days ago to let me know he was leaving again—today, in fact. I assumed he'd be here this morning to take care of Hootch, so I wasn't planning to drop by until tonight. I can't imagine what happened. Maybe the movers accidentally let Hootch out and Mr. Woodrow didn't notice. Except, why didn't he tell me he was leaving before the lease expired, and why would he need a cat sitter if he was moving out?"

Hootch must have recognized Amber's voice, because he crawled out from the drainage pipe and slowly crept up the hillside. He appeared to be a large longhaired tabby, charcoal gray and beige. He reached the edge of the patio and froze, staring at Davie with suspicious pistachio-green eyes.

Davie held out her hand. "Hey, buddy, why are you out here all alone?"

The cat must have hoped there was food in that outstretched hand, because he slinked forward. When he got close enough, Davie petted his coat. It was matted with dirt and twigs. Hootch brushed his body against her arm, leaving a smear of cat hair on the sleeve of her black polyester jacket.

"Poor baby," Amber said. "Now that Mr. Woodrow has passed, I could ask a friend of mine to take Hootch. She runs a no-kill shelter and I'm sure she'd find him a good home."

Davie remembered the call of that coyote and knew the cat wasn't safe living outside. She could let Amber take Hootch to her friend's shelter, but she hadn't yet located Woodrow's next of kin. Maybe someone in the family wanted the cat.

"I'll take charge of him for now."

Vaughn flashed her a look that said, *What the hell?* She ignored his silent warning but wrote the name of the shelter in her notebook just in case.

Hootch didn't protest when Davie gathered him in her arms. He was heavy, about twelve pounds, she guessed. She moved toward the door, trailed by her partner, unsure about taking the cat into custody. She'd never owned a pet and didn't know how to care for this one, even temporarily. Homicide detectives spoke for the dead, standing alone in the victim's shoes and protecting their interests against those of all others. Maybe that also held true for their cats. Hootch's destiny was in her hands now, and she would do whatever it took to make sure he landed on his feet.

5

DAVIE AND VAUGHN HAD just left Zeke Woodrow's empty house and were sitting in the detective car. She could tell her partner's irritation had faded when he agreed to drive while Davie held Hootch on her lap in the passenger seat. The sun had spiked the temperature in the car to sauna level, but opening a window created a potential escape route for Hootch. Instead, Davie cranked up the A/C.

"I've never arrested a cat before," Vaughn said.

"You should broaden your horizons, Jason."

"What are you going to do with him?"

"I'll figure it out. First, we need to talk to Alden Brink. If we're lucky, his office is nearby so we can interview him. Otherwise, we'll head back to the station."

Hootch seemed content to sit in Davie's lap, so she used the car's computer to search for Alden Brink. The name was unusual but even so, she got a few hits. None seemed like a plausible match, but because it was always wise to know as much as possible about a potential witness, she ran the limited information through law enforcement databases.

Vaughn glanced at the screen of her cell. "What did you find?"

"Nothing." She keyed in Brink's telephone number and waited for somebody to answer.

"Law offices." The woman's voice was nasally and hollow, like it came from some distant galaxy. Davie identified herself and asked to speak to Brink.

"He isn't available. Would you like to leave a message?"

Davie checked her watch and scrawled the time on her chrono notes. "Where are you located?"

There was a long silence. "I'm not sure what you mean."

The woman's response struck Davie as odd. "What's your address?"

"Please hold."

Vaughn was no longer content to listen to her side of the conversation. "What's happening?"

"Stonewalling." She held the receiver to her ear for at least a minute before she heard a man's voice on the line. That surprised her.

"This is Alden Brink. How can I help you, Detective?"

"I got your name from Amber Johnson. She said you represent the owner of a property in Topanga Canyon. Is that correct?"

"What can I do for you?"

His tone was self-assured, but Davie noted he hadn't answered her question. "I'm investigating the murder of the tenant who was leasing the property—Zeke Woodrow."

There was a long silence before he responded. "Murdered? Sorry to hear it. What happened?"

"We're still investigating."

"Of course." There was a sound of papers rustling. "I was just processing Mr. Woodrow's paperwork. He did live in the house, but according to my records, he moved out this past weekend."

"I guess you forgot to tell Amber Johnson about the move."

"It was on my things-to-do list." His tone was smooth and confident, like he was playing a mind game he had already won.

"The house looked sanitized. Who did the cleanup?"

He cleared his throat before answering. "That would have been the tenant's responsibility. I don't know who he hired, but I'm glad to hear they did a good job."

Davie ran her fingers over Hootch's matted hair. "Does the lease list Mr. Woodrow's next of kin or somebody to call in case of emergency?"

There was more shuffling of paper. "I don't see anything like that here."

"Did Mr. Woodrow leave a forwarding address?"

"We didn't need one. He left before the lease expired, so there was no refund. We consider the matter closed."

"Your cell has a Virginia area code. Is that where your office is located?"

Davie heard the receptionist's voice in the background. "Just a minute," Brink said. "I have to take another call." His next words were muffled as if he were talking to somebody standing next to him. "Here, hold this," he continued. "Just don't touch this button—" The call was disconnected. Davie redialed but nobody answered.

"What happened?" Vaughn said.

She looked at her partner. "I'm not sure. Either Alden Brink runs the most dysfunctional law office on the planet or it's time to up our game."

———————

The cat seemed calm until Vaughn put the car in drive. The noise must have triggered a flashback, because Hootch clawed his way up to Davie's shoulder and launched his body into the back of the car, leaving her skin burning with pain. She turned in time to see him burrow into the space beneath the seat.

"We'll have to dismantle the ride to get him out of there," Vaughn said, clearly irritated.

"Chill, Jason. One of the garage mechanics can remove the backseat if it comes to that."

"You need to get him out of there," Vaughn said. "What if he freaks out again and causes an accident?"

Her partner had a point. Hootch had already snagged her jacket and clawed her shoulder. Who knew the extent of his fury?

"I can try to coax him out, but I'll need the universal persuader—food. Let's find a pet store."

She used her cell to locate a retail outlet a short distance away. Davie dashed inside while her partner stayed in the car to call Officer Luna at the Airport Police station to ask about a backdoor into Woodrow's military records.

When Davie came out of the store, she had a shopping cart full of essential supplies, including a litter box, food, a large airplane crate, and a credit card receipt for $105.96. Vaughn watched as she loaded part of the supplies into the trunk. Davie climbed into the back with the crate and the food, knelt on the floor, and peered into the dark space beneath the seat. A pair of pistachio-green eyes glared back at her. She popped the tab on a can of salmon cat food and peeled off the lid.

"Jeez, Davie. What kind of crap are you feeding him? It's stinking up the car."

She slid the can toward Hootch's hiding place. "Turn up the air conditioner."

"It's already cranked up to Polar Vortex."

"Did you talk to Luna?"

Vaughn shifted and backed out of the parking spot. "He doesn't know how to access Woodrow's records, but he's an active Reserve, so he's going to use his ID to get into the system. If he finds anything, he'll let us know."

Hootch wasn't responding to the bait, so Davie scooped some salmon onto her finger and shoved her hand under the seat.

Vaughn merged into traffic. "At least it beats getting a court order and waiting ten weeks for a response."

"Any other alternatives?"

"He said we could contact the Army's personnel office. They might at least give us the name of a relative."

As the car accelerated onto the freeway, Davie felt something like sandpaper scrape across her finger. She pulled her hand from under the seat to inspect for injuries. The food was gone. She reloaded her finger with salmon and pushed it toward the cat. It took fifteen more minutes to lure Hootch out from under the seat. As she coaxed him into the crate, her fingers felt something small and hard between his shoulder blades.

"The cat has a lump on his neck."

"How big is it?"

She probed Hootch's skin. "Hard to say. About a millimeter long and half as wide."

"That's what he gets for sleeping rough in the wilds of Topanga Canyon."

She nudged Hootch into the crate and closed the door. "I think we should take him to a vet."

Vaughn lowered the visor to block the sun. "I told you not to bring him with us. We're trying to solve a homicide, Davie. We don't have time for a sick cat."

"He's the victim's cat. That makes me responsible for his well-being. There's a clinic on Sepulveda near Santa Monica Boulevard. It's open 24/7 and it's on our way to the station. It shouldn't take long. I'll tell them it's an emergency."

"A vet in West L.A.? Are you kidding me? It'll cost a fortune. Just don't ask me to chip in on the bill."

"You spend more than that every day on lattes."

"Yeah, whatever. Check back with me when they cut off your credit."

6

VAUGHN PARKED THE CAR on the bottom floor of the veterinary clinic garage in a spot that allowed Davie to see the street, an accommodation her partner made without comment.

He opened the windows to rid the car of cat food odor. "I'll stay here and make a few more calls."

Davie horsed the heavy crate to the elevator and pushed the button for the second floor. A set of double doors opened into a well-lit lobby where the fragrance of flowery disinfectant hovered in the air. She assumed the strong chemical smell was an attempt to reassure pets and their owners that microbes or flesh-eating viruses need not apply.

A middle-aged woman sat on a couch, sharing a sloppy kiss with her little black dog. A man and woman who looked like two investment bankers sat on the opposite side of the room talking on their cell phones and completely ignoring their apricot poodle. She wondered if there was a happy medium when it came to pet owners. At least she heard no sobbing. She wasn't sure she could handle that.

Hootch howled as they sat together on one of the couches, waiting for the next available veterinarian. She poked her finger inside the crate and stroked his nose, but the gesture didn't comfort him.

A few minutes later, a man in his mid-thirties walked toward her. His brown eyes were engaged and focused completely on her as he introduced himself as Dr. Dimetri. His short beard and flowing mahogany hair reminded her of a Russian orchestra conductor—a bit mad but in an appealing sort of way.

He smiled warmly. "Come with me, please."

He motioned for her to follow him down a long aisle. Hootch continued to meow as Dimetri ushered her into one of several examining rooms. She lifted the crate onto a stainless steel table and told the doctor about the lump on the cat's neck.

"Let's take a look," he said.

As soon as Dr. Dimetri removed Hootch from the crate, the cat stopped howling. He remained docile as the doctor looked inside his ears and mouth and poked at his stomach. After finding nothing suspicious, he kneaded the bump on Hootch's neck.

"Is he okay?" Davie said.

He smiled. "It's nothing to worry about. It's just a microchip. It's inserted under the skin and programmed with information to help return Hootch to his owner in case he gets lost."

She knew about microchips, but she'd never had a pet so the mechanics were unclear to her. "What sort of information?"

The doctor pulled a small white instrument from a bank of drawers. "This is a universal scanner. It reads the chip's radio frequencies. In a minute we'll see which pet registry the owner used."

Dimetri swept the scanner over the cat's neck. He frowned and repeated the maneuver a second time. Hootch froze, stiff and wild-eyed, staring into space like a zombie waiting for the apocalypse.

"Something wrong?" Davie said.

"I'm not sure. The chip usually lists a phone number for the pet recovery agency plus the owner's personal identification number. This one looks different." He held up the scanner so she could read the narrow display panel.

He pointed to a series of numbers. "The first few digits might be the agency's phone number, but the other information looks like gibberish. Maybe the chip is defective."

Davie studied the display. There were ten numbers. They weren't separated by dashes but appeared to be a telephone number in the 310 area code. If so, the pet recovery agency was located somewhere on L.A.'s Westside. The other entry read: A 1 € > ? 2 ¥ $ * > €. Davie had no idea what it meant. In fact, she didn't recognize several of the symbols in the sequence.

Dr. Dimetri ran his hand over Hootch's coat. "I would normally call the registry to let them know the cat is here and ask them to contact the owner, but since you said the man is dead—"

"I'll handle the notifications, but thanks for your help."

Davie wasn't sure she could accurately transcribe the strange sequence into her notebook so she snapped a cell photo of the display panel while Dr. Dimetri guided Hootch inside the crate and escorted them out to the lobby. On the way, he grabbed a brush from a display of pet supplies and handed it to Davie.

"Your boy has some mats. You should brush them out. He can groom himself, of course, but you don't want him to swallow all that hair or you'll be stepping on hairballs in the middle of the night."

She'd heard a million jokes about hairballs but had never actually seen one, nor did she want to. "Thanks. Where do I pay?"

"The brush and the visit are on the house," he said. "It's our way of saying thanks for the work you do. Next time you bring him back, you pay."

He smiled again and shook her hand. She appreciated the gesture, but didn't have the heart to tell him there would be no next time for her and Hootch. As soon as she located Zeke's family, the cat was moving on.

Back at the car, she strapped the crate into the back seatbelt and slid into the passenger side next to Vaughn.

"What's the verdict?" he said. "Is the cat out of lives?"

She pulled a bottle of sanitizer from her pocket. "The lump was a microchip with some sort of code and the number to a pet recovery service. I'm going to call to see if Zeke filled out an application with actual information. If so, Hootch just gave us the first break in the case."

"Seriously?" His tone was skeptical. "So, what's next?"

She squirted a dab of sanitizer onto the palm of her hand and rubbed it in. "The lieutenant's adjutant loves animals. Maybe she can babysit while we follow up on the lead."

"April Hayes?" His tone was skeptical. "She's cool but what makes you think she'll do it?"

"Because she has a framed picture on her desk of her pug sitting on Santa's lap."

Vaughn smiled. "Perfect."

Her partner maneuvered out of the parking garage and headed toward the station. Without Dr. Dimetri's gentle touch, Hootch's howling resumed until it reached a dangerous decibel level. The cat was still protesting his incarceration when Vaughn finally turned into the station's driveway.

Once Hayes had taken charge of Hootch and all his supplies, Davie hurried back to her desk, brushing cat hair off her black pants and rubbing the welts on her shoulder. She used her desk phone to punch in the telephone number for the pet recovery agency listed on the microchip.

"Hello." It was a woman's voice. She sounded anxious. The woman hadn't mentioned the name of the pet recovery agency as businesses usually do, so Davie checked the number to make sure she hadn't misdialed.

"This is Detective Richards from the Los Angeles Police Department. Who am I speaking to?"

There was a moment of silence before the woman answered with a sob. "Shannon Woodrow. Is this about my father? He's dead, isn't he?"

7

IT WAS TECHNICALLY THE coroner's job to notify a decedent's next of kin if they lived outside the city of Los Angeles. Santa Monica was an upscale beach town that bordered L.A. but still a separate city. It was hair-splitting but nonetheless Davie made a courtesy call to let the coroner's office know she and her partner were on their way to interview Zeke's daughter. Twenty minutes later they parked the detective car at Shannon Woodrow's condominium in the downtown area, three blocks from the palisades overlooking the Pacific Ocean.

An elevator lifted them to her fourth-floor unit. A middle-aged Filipina in a colorful nurse's uniform met them at the door with eyes that were swollen and red. The woman ushered them across travertine marble tiles into a living room bathed in light from two large windows flanking a gas fireplace. Soft blue paint on the walls made the space seem serene. The art was modern and the carefully placed sculptures on the fireplace mantel suggested Shannon Woodrow either had a gift for decorating or the money to pay someone who did.

The nurse nodded toward the couch. "Please sit. I'll get Miss Shannon."

Before the woman left the room, Vaughn said, "Mind if I look around?"

Even during interviews with cooperative witnesses, detectives had to stay alert. Until they'd cleared the house, they didn't know if anybody else was inside the residence or have any clue to their state of mind.

The woman nodded her consent and disappeared down the hall. Davie walked toward an off-white chair that matched the couch, inhaling the aroma of roses in a vase on the coffee table. A moment later, Vaughn reappeared.

"Dining room leads to the kitchen, but nobody's in there."

"Take a look at that," Davie said, pointing to an end table next to the couch.

On it was a photograph of a bare-chested young man wearing olive green military fatigues and hugging an M-16 rifle. He was standing alone in a field, a skinny kid with a mop of dark hair and a cocky grin. Behind him was a mountain range, the peaks brushed by a swath of dark clouds.

"You think it's her old man?"

"That's my guess," she said.

The photo had been taken in Vietnam. Davie was sure of that. There had been a similar shot of her uncle Rob in a silver frame on the fireplace mantel at her parents' old house. He wore those same military fatigues draped over his thin frame. A cigarette dangled from his lips as he grinned at the camera. Not long after the photo was taken, her uncle had been killed in the battle of Duc Lap, near the Cambodian border. Her brother Robbie had been named after him. The conflict ended long before she was born, but even after all these years, her mother and grandmother were still hollowed out by her uncle's death.

Davie heard sounds coming from the hallway. She saw a woman in her early thirties sitting in a wheelchair, rolling herself toward them. Hot-pink sweatpants could not hide her withered legs. Whatever had happened to her, Davie guessed it hadn't been recent. The nurse followed a discreet distance behind her.

Shannon Woodrow's skin was pale but her nose looked red and swollen from crying. Her facial features and the cloud of short dark hair confirmed that the man in the photo was her father. Shannon stopped the chair near the coffee table. The nurse set the brakes with her foot and walked toward the dining room. Vaughn leaned against the fireplace mantel as the afternoon sun blazed through the window.

Shannon clenched a wilted tissue in her fist. "You told me on the phone my father had been shot, but I didn't think to ask for details."

Davie flashed back to the gunshot wound in Zeke Woodrow's head and felt a familiar sense of guilt. "His body was found in a parking garage at LAX. Was your father planning a trip?"

Shannon shook her head. "He traveled a lot, but he always told me when he was going out of town."

Davie heard dishes rattling. She looked up to see the nurse carrying a silver tea set and a plate of cookies on a large tray. She set it on the coffee table, squeezed Shannon Woodrow's hand, and left the room. Shannon poured tea into one of three dainty china cups and offered it to Davie.

"It's Darjeeling," she said. "I think you'll like it. It's my favorite."

Davie usually didn't drink anything offered by citizens because there was no guarantee it was safe to drink, but she accepted the cup anyway, because she appreciated what it must have taken Shannon Woodrow to serve tea and cookies after just learning of her father's death.

"When was the last time you heard from your dad?" Davie said.

"He called me yesterday afternoon."

"What did you talk about?"

Shannon gestured toward the plate of cookies on the tray but both Davie and Vaughn declined. "He had something to tell me, but he didn't want to discuss it on the phone. He said he'd drop by later that night, but he never showed up. I kept texting and calling him but he didn't respond. That's when I knew something was wrong."

That explained why Shannon had seemed upset when she answered Davie's call. She had been expecting bad news. No phone had been found on the victim's body, which meant the killer had likely taken it from the scene.

"Any guess what he wanted to talk about?"

Shannon closed her eyes, searching for strength. "I thought he might tell me he planned to retire and how that would impact me."

Vaughn shifted his gaze toward Shannon. "Why would his retirement make a difference to you?"

She poured herself a cup of tea. "I publish online newsletters for a couple of clients. It doesn't pay much but I can work from home. My dad still insists on paying all my expenses and that adds up. Once he retires, he'll be living on a fixed income. I love Lita, but I've told him a million times I don't need a caregiver."

If Zeke had driven to the airport to take a flight somewhere, it seemed odd he hadn't told his daughter. Maybe he intended to tell her when he dropped by the day before he died, but why not just tell her over the phone? Obviously there was something more consequential about the trip that he needed to explain face-to-face and Davie guessed it had nothing to do with his retirement.

"He's always been my protector," Shannon continued, "even more so after this." She pointed to her legs.

Vaughn walked to the couch and sat on the arm. "What happened?"

"A drunk driver crossed the centerline and hit me head on. I was in the hospital for months and in rehab for months more after that. When I got out, my father bought this condo for me so I could be close to my mom without actually having to live with her."

Davie noted the hint of dysfunctional family dynamics in her comment. "I assume your parents are divorced."

Shannon nodded and reached for the pot to refresh Davie's tea, but she put it down when she saw that the cup was still full. "I stayed with Mom for a while after I got out of rehab, but she and her husband entertain a lot. My disability was difficult for them to manage."

"We went to your dad's house in Topanga Canyon," Vaughn said. "It was empty. Did he tell you he was moving?"

"No, but that wasn't really his home," she said. "He leased the place from his employer. They kept the cost low because they wanted him to be close to a major airport. Even the furniture was rented."

A respectable time had passed, so Davie drank a courtesy sip of tea and set the cup on the coffee table. "Then where *did* he live?"

"He split his time between the house in Topanga and a small cottage in Santa Barbara that's been in the family for years. It's in my name, but it was his place. I never lived there."

Davie had no idea the military was such a lucrative profession. She wondered how Zeke Woodrow had accumulated enough money to buy real estate in Santa Monica and Santa Barbara, two of the priciest cities in Southern California. Even if the Santa Barbara house had been in the family for decades, real estate there had never been cheap.

"When did your father retire from the military?" she said.

"The Army forced him out when he turned sixty. That was three years ago. After that he went to work for a private sector business."

Davie leaned forward. "What's the name of the company?"

Shannon dabbed at her eyes with the tissue. "TidePool Security Consultants, but he never talked about his work. My impression was he didn't like the job much. That's why I thought he was going to retire. He loved Santa Barbara, and he loved his little cottage. He called it his hootch. That's what soldiers in Vietnam called the bamboo shelters they made in the jungle." Her face drained of color as if she'd just remembered the cat and felt guilty about that. "Where's Hootch?"

At least Davie knew how the cat had come by his name. "He's fine. Someone is watching out for him at the police station. Would you like us to drop him by later?"

She rested her head in her hands. "I'm so sorry but I have asthma. The doctor won't allow me to have pets. Maybe my mom ..."

Davie didn't want to compound Shannon's grief by pressing her about Hootch's future. She would have to figure that out later. "Don't worry. We'll find him a good home." She pulled out her cell and held up the photo she'd taken at Dr. Dimetri's clinic. "I found this on Hootch's microchip. It looks like some sort of code. Do you have any idea what it means?"

Shannon studied the symbols for a moment and shrugged. "I've never seen it before. Do you think it's important?"

Davie returned the cell to her jacket pocket. "Maybe. Did your father ever mention a man named Alden Brink?"

"Not that I remember. Who is he?"

Davie wondered if the Topanga house had been cleared out and sanitized in order to remove evidence of something. If her hunch was right, she had to prevent that from happening to Zeke's other residence.

"He's the lawyer that managed the Topanga lease," Davie said. "Does anybody else know about your dad's Santa Barbara place?"

Shannon sipped her tea. "We've owned it for years so my mother knows, but I doubt he told many other people. My father guarded his privacy."

41

Vaughn was staring at the cookies, probably wondering what kind of caffeine rush he could get from the chocolate chips.

"Did you know any of your father's associates?" Davie said.

"He didn't have many close friends, except for a few guys from his military days. My mother could probably tell you more about them. I'll give you her phone number, but just so you know, she doesn't like to talk about my father."

She sensed Shannon had a difficult relationship with her mother, possibly because of the divorce and her mother's new husband. Davie hesitated to project her feelings onto Shannon but if that was the case, she could identify. Her mother had left her father for another man during a particularly dark time in her dad's life. Davie and her brother were just kids at the time, but they'd split their loyalties—she'd gone with Bear, her brother stayed with their mother. Even after all those years, Davie still wasn't close to her mom or brother.

"What about enemies?" Vaughn said. "Was there anybody who'd want to hurt your father?"

Shannon stared at the tissue in her hand. "No."

"We'd like to have a look inside the Santa Barbara house," Davie said. "Do you have a key?"

"It's in my bedroom. I'll get it."

Vaughn went out to the car to get a Consent to Search form. After Shannon had signed it, she reached back to unlock the brakes of her wheelchair. Davie got up to help but Shannon brushed away her hand. She felt embarrassed by her misplaced assumptions. To change the subject, she gestured toward the photo on the end table.

"Your dad was a handsome man," she said, realizing immediately how inadequate those words were as tools of comfort.

Grief had etched lines across Shannon Woodrow's forehead. She spoke softly, almost to herself. "My father was a strong man, physically and mentally. He would expect no less of me."

Davie's training and years as a cop had taught her to control outward displays of emotion. So she did the only thing she could do to comfort Shannon Woodrow in the only way she knew how.

"I promise you," she said, "I'll find the person who murdered your father." In her mind she added, *however long it takes and wherever it leads*. Right now, it led to Shannon Woodrow's mother. Davie suspected that interview might not come with tea and cookies.

8

"**WHAT ARE YOU GOING** to do now that Shannon can't take the cat?" Vaughn said as he closed the car door.

Davie steered into traffic. "I'll just have to find him a home with somebody else."

"Just don't pawn him off on Woodrow's ex. From the sound of things Hootch would be better off at the pound."

"I'll ask Hayes if she can take him home until I figure it out," she said. "She and Hootch seem to have a groovy kind of love. For now, let's drive to Beverly Hills and talk to Zeke's ex."

"Here's a better idea. You go. Take me back to the station. I have a friend who works CCD. She might be able to help us find information on TidePool Security Consultants."

The Commercial Crimes Division investigated everything from white-collar crime to complex bunco cases like embezzlement, blackmail, and extortion. Davie agreed they might have access to information that could help them close the Woodrow investigation, so she dropped her partner off at the station and went east to interview Zeke's ex-wife.

Lynda Morrow lived in a long, low ranch-style house in the flats of Beverly Hills just north of Santa Monica Boulevard. The property sat on a wide, palm-lined street next to other upscale houses that had so far dodged the tear-down-and-rebuild craze.

Davie parked on the street just beyond the circular driveway and made her way to the doublewide front door, which was made of etched glass and varnished wood. Two planters filled with spring flowers flanked the entrance.

A woman opened the door, accompanied by a large designer dog. *Not a Saint Bernard*, Davie thought, *but the other mountain dog, the one that sounded like a sauce—Bernese.*

Davie had called in advance, but when Lynda saw her standing on the doorstep, she seemed taken aback. Even the dog looked startled. Maybe it was Davie's five-one frame or her hair—a mix of bright red and orange-brown that she labeled rust. She had once read that only 1 or 2 percent of people in the world had red hair. It's uncommon, so folks notice. She had learned over time that either you allow the attention to annoy you or you own it. She had decided long ago to own it.

Lynda Morrow looked youthful and fit with only a few fine lines around her blue eyes and full lips. Her artfully cut blonde hair, cherry red manicure, and silk pantsuit cemented her image as a woman who lived a healthy and affluent lifestyle.

Lynda led Davie to the kitchen through a sitting room that had a fireplace edged by bookcases. The books were all hardbacks and mostly nonfiction from what she could see. Outside the French doors a young man in khaki shorts and a black T-shirt used a long-handled net to scoop leaves from a swimming pool. The dog flopped near the door to watch him.

"I don't have much time to talk," Lynda said. "We're having people over for cocktails tonight and I'm behind schedule."

"I just have a few questions."

45

Three cucumbers sat on the counter. Lynda picked up a knife, sliced each one in half and scraped out the seeds. "Yes, that's what you said on the phone. I guess this is where I should say I'm surprised and deeply saddened by the news of Zeke's death, but he's not my problem and hasn't been for many years."

Her unnecessarily harsh comment made Davie wonder what had broken the marriage apart. As she said, Zeke hadn't been her problem for many years so the resentment must have been festering for a long time.

"When did you last see him?" Davie said.

"A couple of years ago. We've had to communicate because of Shannon's disability and the care she needs, but that's mostly done through email. My current husband is an attorney, so he usually handles the details."

Lynda picked up a pastry tube and squirted a zig-zag line of what looked like cream cheese on each cucumber half. From somewhere in the house, Davie heard the drone of a vacuum cleaner.

"Zeke was career Army," she continued. "Did you know that? He enlisted toward the end of the war in Vietnam."

"Your daughter told me."

"Shannon." She said the name like an indictment. "Zeke babied her. She romanticized everything about him and refused to accept any alternate version, even when it was the truth."

Davie found the bond between Shannon and her father touching, but she didn't know the full dynamics of this family and decided to reserve judgment for now. "What did Zeke do during Vietnam?"

Lynda picked up a jar of caviar on the counter and twisted off the lid. "He killed people. Lots of them, I assume. Isn't that what soldiers do in war?"

"How long were you together?"

"We got married just after high school, 1971. He'd already joined the Army. We both knew he'd be sent to Vietnam, so we didn't want to wait. Our parents were against it. They thought we were too young. It seems ridiculous now, but I guess we were in love."

"Eighteen *is* young."

Lynda used a small knife to spread caviar on top of the cream cheese. "And stupid. But Zeke was hard to resist back then—tall, handsome, and muscular from working on his dad's farm. All the girls in school thought he was a hunk and he was, especially in his uniform."

"How long before he went to Vietnam?"

"He left for basic training a week after the wedding. Fort Benning."

"Did you go with him?"

"I couldn't afford to follow him to Georgia. I wanted to stay with my mom and dad, but Zeke insisted I move in with his parents to help them on the farm. They lived in the boondocks, but a girl didn't challenge her husband in small-town Iowa back then—at least, I didn't. I raised Shannon to be more assertive, for all the good it did. She idolized her father. Everything he said and did was gold to her."

Davie watched Lynda, still assessing the level of her pique. At least it seemed she had allowed Shannon to believe the best about her dad without tarnishing his image, which earned her a few points in Davie's book. "What happened when he came home from the war?"

Lynda cut the cucumbers into small diagonal slices. "He was intense, secretive, cold, and addicted to Dexedrine. I thought he'd heal and we'd start our life together. Instead, he told me he planned to make the Army his career. I was devastated. Wars didn't end with Vietnam, you know. There were others."

"Where did he go after that?"

"We lived on Army bases in a lot of places. He was a Ranger, so he was away a lot on assignment. When the first Gulf war broke out, he left for the Middle East. Shannon and I went back to Iowa to stay with my parents."

"Sounds like a lonely life."

She held the knife underhanded like a street fighter. "You have no idea what it's like for a military wife. I spent days, months, years taking care of a household and a child on an enlisted man's paycheck. I was alone night after night, wondering where he was, if he was in danger, if at dawn I'd get a knock on the door and find two men in uniform telling me my husband was dead. The worst part was he loved being a soldier. Loved the brotherhood, the idea of serving his country, fighting for liberty and the so-called American Way."

The blowback from Lynda's anger threatened to set Davie's hair on fire, but she continued lobbing questions. "Sounds like he was an Army recruiter's poster child."

Lynda slammed the knife on the counter. "The Army doesn't take you out to dinner on your anniversary or comfort a baby with colic. The military was more important to Zeke than anything, including me. When that finally sank in, I left him."

Davie felt she was witnessing some sort of confession. Shannon had said her mother didn't like to talk about Zeke, so she probably hadn't shared her negative feelings with her daughter. While Zeke was off fighting wars, Lynda had been home raising their daughter and hoping he'd come back to them alive. She seemed to have kept her frustrations bottled up for years, waiting for the right moment to unload on anyone who'd listen about the challenges faced by military wives.

Davie waited for Lynda to remind her that she was too busy getting ready for a party to answer questions, but that never happened. Zeke's ex was giving Davie the sort of emotional information dump the department shrink had hoped to get from her but never did. Lynda's memories might be cathartic and helpful to the investigation, so she let the woman talk, occasionally slipping in another question.

"Did he have any enemies who may have wanted to kill him?" she said. "Or was there any specific incident that might have made him a target?"

"Soldiers do things in war they don't talk about to outsiders. I suspect there may be a long list of people who'd be glad to see him dead."

Davie wondered if Lynda Morrow might be one of them. "Did he ever mention names?"

Lynda set the cucumber slices on a doily-lined tray. Her mood had turned reflective, almost sad. "After a while he stopped talking to me about his work. Since he worked all the time, we effectively stopped communicating."

"Are his parents still alive?"

"They're both dead. Zeke was an only child so Shannon was all the family he had—except for me, of course."

Davie noted Lynda spoke of herself as an afterthought. She moved closer and leaned against the counter. "What about his friends?"

"I wouldn't know about his current friends. Back in the day, Zeke was close to three guys from his Ranger unit. When they came home from Vietnam, they all reenlisted together. They were like brothers. All Ranger, all the time."

"Do you remember their names?"

After having just ranted about her ex, her gentle smile was surprising. "How could I forget? They were always hanging around our house, drinking beer, and laughing at their corny jokes."

The drone of the vacuum cleaner had stopped. The house was quiet except for the sound of Lynda Morrow calling out the names of Zeke's Army buddies like taps playing at a military funeral: Harlan Cormack, Dag Lunds, and Juno Karst.

Davie recorded all three names in her notebook—Zeke Woodrow's closest friends, his band of brothers.

Davie poised her pen over the notebook, prepared to make another entry. "Do you know where they are now?"

Lynda shook her head as she covered the cucumber slices with plastic wrap and slid them into the refrigerator. When she turned to face Davie, her eyes were moist and her tone raw. "All I can tell you is that one was originally from somewhere in the South. One was from Oregon. The other was a Midwesterner. Why do you keep asking me about Zeke's war buddies? Nobody cares anymore."

"Mr. Woodrow was wearing his Army dog tags when he died. His killer removed one of them. That made me think the murder might be related to his military service."

Lynda blinked, sending a tear rolling down her cheek. "I find that hard to believe."

"Truth often hides in the most unlikely places." Davie thanked her and turned to go.

"Wait." Lynda walked out of the kitchen. A short time later, she reappeared with a photograph, which she handed to Davie. It was an image of four young men, lounging on a worn couch and grinning at the camera. "It's all of them, taken in our living room," she said. "I'm not sure why I kept it all these years."

"I'll make a copy and return it," Davie said.

Lynda stared at the photo, her lips trembling. Sometimes people reacted to grief with anger. If so, Lynda's seemed to have died somewhere during the search for that picture and was now replaced by memories of a man she'd once loved.

"Keep it," she said. "I don't need it anymore."

Davie nodded and set out toward the front door. As she entered the living room she noticed the carpet, newly vacuumed for Lynda's party that night. She paused for a moment and then stepped around the edge, like she would at a crime scene.

Davie returned to the station and entered through the back door. As she made her way through the squad room to her workstation in the Homicide area, she noticed a half-eaten birthday cake on the table near the printer and remembered she'd chipped in a few bucks to buy it for a civilian clerk in Records. None of the other Homicide detectives was in the squad room, including her partner. A subpoena sat near her computer, ordering her to testify in an old theft case she'd worked at Southeast Division.

She pulled Zeke Woodrow's Murder Book off the shelf above her desk and felt the smooth stainless steel of the bookends, a gift from Detective Giordano. Each one formed the numbers 187, the penal code number for homicide. She squeezed them together to hold the other manuals in place and opened the blue three-ring binder to Section 11, Victim Information. The photo of Zeke and his Army buddies slid easily into the plastic sleeve. Finding them after all these years wouldn't be easy, but she logged onto her desk computer and started searching.

9

SHE FOUND JUNO KARST first.

Juno Karst's death notice was posted online in a Tonopah, Nevada, newspaper. *William "Juno" Karst died on March 29. Mr. Karst was born February 11, 1952, in Macon, Georgia. He was a US Army veteran. Arrangements by Birch & Birch Mortuary.*

It wasn't much information. Nothing about survivors. Nothing about how he died. Nothing specific about his military career. Lynda Morrow claimed all four of the men in Zeke's Ranger unit had reenlisted after Vietnam and stayed together, at least, Davie assumed, for the next several years. There was no indication of what had happened after that. Karst may have retired years ago and lost touch with the others. But somebody must have known enough about him to fill out the death certificate. Whoever that was might know the rest of his story or, if not, might know others who did.

Davie printed a copy of the article about Karst's death and looked up the telephone number for the mortuary. She opened the Murder

Book to a page in Section 1, noting that the interview with Birch & Birch would be conducted by telephone in the Pacific detective squad room. She initialed the entry and called the number. A woman answered. The voice had the quivery timber of someone who was elderly. Davie identified herself and asked if she remembered Juno Karst.

"Sure, I remember him. We handled his cremation."

"How did he die?"

"Suicide. Bless his heart. Shot himself in the head. What a mess that was. My nephew's the sheriff over at Goldfield. He told me the man was found in a rental car just off Highway 95 in Esmeralda County. Not many services in Goldfield. We're about thirty miles away, so they brought the body here."

Dread settled in Davie's chest. "I'd like to talk to his next of kin if you have their contact information."

"We didn't deal with the family, so I can't help with that. Some attorney paid for the arrangements. Told us to put him in a nice urn and he'd foot the bill. We left a message for him when the ashes were ready for pickup. That was almost a week ago, but so far he hasn't called back. They're still on the shelf in the storage room."

Davie kept her tone steady, even though her heart was pounding. "Do you remember the attorney's name?"

"Not off the top of my head. It was unusual, though. I can look it up if you'd like."

"I'd appreciate that."

Davie heard the receiver clunk against something hard and a chair scrape the floor. She waited on the line for a couple of minutes before she heard papers rustling.

"Here it is," the woman said. "His name's Alden Brink. He wired the money direct to our bank account. I've never had that happen before. Had to call the bank to find out how it's done. My husband and

I were suspicious at first, so the next day I called the bank again. The money was there, all right."

Davie leaned forward, elbows on her desk, staring at the computer screen but seeing nothing. Alden Brink was the attorney who represented the owners of Zeke Woodrow's leased Topanga Canyon house. Now she was learning Brink was also connected to Zeke's military buddy Juno Karst. Davie jotted his name on the interview sheet followed by an exclamation mark.

She tried to swallow but her throat was too dry. "Did the money come from a law office or some other company?"

"Says here it came from TidePool Security Consultants. The deceased was an employee."

Given that the attorney paid for the cremation, it made sense that Karst also worked with Zeke at TidePool. "Did your nephew investigate Karst's death?"

"Like I said, honey, it was a suicide. He'd have told me if it was more than that."

Davie wasn't so sure. She heard someone call her name. She looked toward the door of the squad room and saw Jason Vaughn striding toward her with both thumbs pointed up. He stopped when he saw she was on the phone.

"Was there a police report?" Davie said.

"You'd have to ask my nephew about that."

Vaughn sat on a chair next to her desk.

Davie held up her hand to stop him from interrupting. "Was anything else found with the body?"

"Mr. Karst came to us with only the clothes on his back," she said. "The sheriff's office kept the gun. I think there was a wallet, probably a rental agreement for the car. That's how they identified him. My nephew might have kept other property, but you'd have to ask him about that. I can tell you for sure, Mr. Karst wasn't from around here. Is there anything about him I should know?"

"What will you do with the ashes?" Davie said.

"Hold 'em for a month or two. If nobody picks 'em up, we'll scatter him in a pit the cemetery uses for the unclaimed."

"Can you hold the ashes until you hear from me?"

Silence and then a sigh. "I will until I need space on the shelf."

"I can send you an official Preservation Letter signed by the Chief of Police," Davie said, "ordering you to—"

"That's not necessary." Her tone had grown testy. "I'll hold the ashes."

Davie ended the call quickly after that. Zeke Woodrow had died of a gunshot wound to the head. A military dog tag had been found on Zeke's body; the other was missing. Now Juno Karst, his friend and TidePool coworker, was also dead. Like most cops, Davie didn't believe in coincidences. It was possible the two deaths were linked. The cause might be workplace violence associated with TidePool or some unrelated dispute. If the motive was connected to their military service, the question was, what new event had occurred since they'd retired to prompt the killer to take action now?

To understand the murder, Davie had to investigate the victims. To do that, she had to find the other two Ranger buddies.

10

DAVIE TURNED TOWARD VAUGHN.

He studied her expression and frowned. "You look like crap. Who were you talking to?"

"Juno Karst is dead."

He rolled his chair closer. "That's one of the Army friends you texted me about. What the hell? How?"

"They found him a few days ago in a rental car in the Nevada desert with a bullet hole in his head. The local sheriff ruled it a suicide, but I'm not convinced."

"You think his death is related to Zeke's?"

"Shannon Woodrow told us her dad retired three years ago. Zeke and Juno were friends and about the same age. Each died by a gunshot wound to the head. Both worked for TidePool, so yes, their deaths might be related."

Loud voices and laughter erupted from the hallway outside the squad room. Four Burglary detectives, wearing blue nylon raid jackets with POLICE stamped in white on the back and a handful of patrol officers were laughing and talking like cowboys spinning tall tales around a campfire.

Vaughn gestured for her to follow him toward the hallway. "I have something important to tell you. Let's go somewhere quiet where we can talk."

Davie walked behind her partner up the stairs to the second-floor lunchroom, where a civilian Records clerk was eating a sandwich from the vending machine and reading a newspaper. Vaughn poured himself a cup of coffee before setting out for the roof deck above the squad room. A strong breeze whipped the branches of the nearby trees and loosened wisps of Davie's red hair from the bun knotted at the nape of her neck.

Vaughn stopped at the far corner of the deck next to the parapet wall. Across the parking lot below, a dozen tarps had been thrown on the pavement and were topped with piles of clothing. She saw Burglary's Det. Spencer Hall following a group of people dressed in street clothes as they inspected the items. Hall wore a raid jacket tucked into his jeans and a pair of sunglasses perched on top of his short blond hair. His chest looked bulky from the Kevlar vest he wore. Underneath that vest, she assumed his muscles were still as lean and toned as they had been the last time she'd seen them.

Davie gestured toward the scene below. "What's going on?"

"Burglary served a search warrant this morning and recovered a bunch of stolen merchandise. Those people walking around are buyers from local department stores, trying to identify their stuff. It won't be hard. The knucklehead gangbangers didn't even bother to cut off the tags." He paused a beat before adding, "Hall's going to be loud and proud for the rest of the day."

She and Spencer Hall had been an item when she worked Burglary and he was assigned to the Major Assault Crimes table at Southeast Division. One day his partner had been unavailable, so she'd gone with him on a follow-up call for a domestic violence case and found the victim's husband beating her again. As Hall struggled with the suspect, the man grabbed his service weapon. Davie shot and killed the man. Later, the suspect's wife falsely accused her of lying on the police report. Davie had been relieved of duty. The fallout nearly ended her career.

After the incident, rumors swirled that Hall was in control of the situation and Davie had panicked. It wasn't true. Her supporters, including her current partner, believed Hall was responsible for the rumors. As it turned out, he wasn't the source, but Vaughn still didn't trust him. Davie just wanted to put the turmoil behind her.

"It's his case, Jason. He deserves to celebrate. What did you find out at CCD?"

Vaughn folded his arms over his chest. "My contact told me Tide-Pool Security Consultants is registered as a limited liability company in Delaware, a state that has more LLCs than people. They make a bundle peddling secret tax havens to everybody from corporations to organized crime syndicates."

Davie leaned in closer. "Who's behind TidePool?"

"That's the beauty of an LLC. The companies don't have to tell you. They operate in total secrecy. All I know is they're a global security contractor. They have a website but it doesn't tell you much. Lots of vague words like 'logistics management.' My friend says they don't advertise. Their clients come to them by referral only. Employees are all former CIA and military types—Special Forces, Rangers, Navy SEALS."

"Who are its clients?"

"Anybody who can pay the fees, including the US government. Ever hear of Blackwater?"

58

"As in the Iraq War Blackwater?"

"According to the detective at CCD, Blackwater provided services to the CIA and other government agencies to the tune of a billion dollars or more. Employees all had top-secret clearances. A ton of them were former SEALS or Rangers just like Zeke Woodrow. Then several contractors killed a bunch of civilians in Baghdad. Twenty more were injured. Some of their people died, too. The scandal forced them to change their name and regroup. And by the way, CCD told me Blackwater was also registered as an LLC in Delaware."

"Just like thousands of other companies."

Vaughn drank coffee from his cup. "Right, but it's still interesting. Both Zeke Woodrow and Juno Karst had decades of experience in covert and clandestine operations and both were TidePool employees."

"And both are dead," Davie said. "How does your contact know so much about this?"

"After 9/11 she was loaned to the FBI to work on a counterterrorism task force. She knows a lot about terror networks in the Middle East and private security contractors."

Davie mulled over the implications. "You know what's weird about this case?"

"Everything. Are you adding to the list?"

"Both Zeke and Juno were trained for things like rescuing hostages behind enemy lines and all that shock-and-awe hype."

Vaughn swirled the dregs of his coffee around in the cup, like a medium divining someone's fortune. "Yeah. So what?"

"I'd guess guys like that are paranoid and suspicious as hell. So, if it turns out they were both murdered, why did they let someone get close enough to put a bullet through their heads?"

"Because they knew the killer and trusted him?"

"Yeah," Davie said. "The daughter and the ex both claimed Zeke was close to friends from his military days, but that can't be the extent of his social life. I mean, did he pal around with coworkers, a girl-friend, a trainer, a hair stylist? Somebody else had to be in his life."

"The daughter also said Zeke didn't like working for TidePool. We don't know why yet but maybe he had a beef with somebody there. Except, we don't know if the same person killed both men. We don't even know if Karst was murdered."

Davie stared at the buyers milling around the parking lot. "The dog tag might mean the hits were related to his military service, but that spans a lot of years and a lot of wars—everything from Vietnam to the Gulf Wars, possibly even to Afghanistan. If that's the motive, why would the killer wait until now?"

"To pull off two hits like that, the person must have had some kind of special training, either military or police. He also had to have time and money."

Davie felt a quiet dread as she caught her partner's gaze and held it. "We don't know that it's just one person. It could be two, or ten. We have to search Zeke's house in Santa Barbara."

"It's late. It'll be dark soon. We won't be able to see anything. Let's use the rest of the day to follow up on other leads, like getting that crime report from Nevada."

Davie knew he was right, but it didn't make her any less edgy. "I'll search for contact information on Woodrow's other two buddies, but first thing in the morning we'll head to Santa Barbara."

Vaughn gave her the thumbs-up sign. "I'll call TidePool. See what they have to say."

Vaughn lingered in the break room to make a fresh pot of coffee, but Davie headed back to the squad room. She nearly ran into Spencer Hall as he entered the back door.

"Hey, Spence," she said. "Congratulations. Looks like you cracked a major theft ring."

He grinned as he unsnapped his raid jacket and slipped it off, exposing the Kevlar vest. "Thanks, Davie. It was a lot of work, but we got a couple of lucky breaks toward the end."

They studied each other in silence as several patrol officers hustled through the door and navigated around them. Finally Davie broke the uncomfortable stalemate. "So ... good work." She turned and walked into the squad room followed by the fading sound of Hall's voice.

"Thanks."

11

DAVIE RETURNED TO THE squad room and saw Autos Det. Joss Page with a telephone receiver held to her ear, motioning Davie toward her desk. Joss had transferred to Pacific from Devonshire Division at the beginning of the last deployment period. She was a willowy blue-eyed blonde with perfect skin and the healthy glow of a yoga instructor. Despite this, Davie liked her. The first time Davie and Joss had gone to the gun range together to qualify, they discovered each of them had been crack shots since the first time they'd picked up a weapon. In the early days, Davie thought her ability to hit the bulls-eye nearly every time was dumb luck, but as time passed she realized it was a gift. Joss felt the same way, but neither could explain how they did it.

Joss hung up the receiver. "Davie, I wanted to catch you before you got busy. I'm recruiting people for the Baker-to-Vegas Challenge Cup. Interested?"

Baker–Vegas was an annual twenty-five-mile foot race through the desert that was meant to promote fitness and a sense of community among law enforcement personnel. LAPD officers competed every year, but she'd never thought about participating, mainly because she hadn't run distances since her academy days.

"Didn't the race just happen last month?"

"Yeah, but we're already gearing up for next year. The first planning meeting isn't until October, but we'd love to have you join us."

Davie shook her head. "I don't run anymore ... unless I'm chasing bad guys."

"Come train with me. You're in good shape. It won't take long to get past the pain."

"You make it sound like so much fun."

Joss laughed, a warm lilting tone that explained why her chronic volunteerism sucked everybody into its vortex. "Good. I'll put you on the list. And don't forget tomorrow is Blue Shirt Tuesday."

Davie spent a few more minutes chatting with Joss. Then she waved and returned to her desk to find that Vaughn had reached the Goldfield County sheriff. The man was out on a call but promised to fax the Juno Karst death report as soon as he got back to the station. Vaughn had also called TidePool to inform them of Zeke's murder. The CEO was on assignment in Istanbul but the HR director verified that both Zeke and Juno were employees and provided basic information, most of which they already had.

"Did you ask if Cormack or Lunds worked there, too?"

"Yeah, but the guy didn't want to give up the information at first. I kept pressuring him until he finally told me Cormack didn't work for them but Lunds did. He said for security reasons he couldn't give me any more information without checking with his boss."

"Let's wait for the CEO to call back. If we don't hear from him by the end of the day, we'll go to plan B."

After that they called a few airlines to see if Woodrow was on their passenger list, but they were met with enough resistance to force Vaughn to write a boilerplate search warrant, as Giordano had suggested.

While Vaughn was busy getting a judge to sign the warrants, Davie looked for any trace of Zeke's Army buddy Harlan Cormack. She searched law enforcement databases and public websites but found no information about him. Cormack was a ghost.

She'd been searching for over an hour when she found an entry in the Department of Motor Vehicles database that she'd overlooked because of a spelling error. "Harlen" Cormack had a mobile home registered with an address in Barstow, California, but when she searched a maps program to get a look at the place, it turned out to be a mailbox store.

There was no telephone number listed under Cormack's name. She wanted to find him but other than staking out the mail drop, which would take valuable time she didn't have, she had run out of ideas. From everything she knew about the four men, they'd been best friends, but investigations were not solved by assumptions. Until Cormack and Lunds had been interviewed, she couldn't rule out the possibility that either or both had killed Zeke. As a last resort, she wrote a note on an LAPD contact form that included her name, telephone number, and a short message, asking Cormack to call her about Zeke Woodrow's death. If he killed Zeke, the letter would tip him off that the police were closing in, but that was a risk she had to take.

Davie didn't know how long the letter would sit at the station before it was picked up, so she drove to the post office, slipped it into an overnight mail envelope, and paid for the postage herself. The likelihood that Cormack would respond to her request for an interview seemed slim. All she could do was hope for the best.

She drove back to the station past squatty apartment buildings, strip malls anchored by liquor stores, and nail salons. Above the streets, telephone lines crisscrossed like cat's cradles, throwing spindly shadows on mature trees covered in dust. Even the occasional patch of fake grass seemed less like landscape and more like a bad dye job on an old man's toupee.

When she returned to the station, she continued the search for the last of Zeke's friends, Dag Lunds, but had no luck finding him. Privacy was practically nonexistent these days, but for people who worked in intelligence and law enforcement there were ways to live off the grid.

Davie always worked her cases until she ran out of leads to investigate, sometimes going for days barely eating, sleeping, or showering because she had long ago accepted the reality that a good Homicide detective had no life. It wasn't a job for people who wanted to eat dinner with their family every night, but she'd known that going in and she loved her job. Zeke had chosen a similar path, a career in the Army, and that made her feel closer to him.

By midnight she had already dozed off twice at her desk. She considered crashing in the second-floor cot room but rejected the idea. There was no way to determine how many sweaty bodies had tossed and turned on that lumpy mattress since the sheets were last washed. She planned to go home to rest for an hour or two, but on her way, she stopped to see her father.

William "Bear" Richards owned a dive bar called the Lucky Duck in an area of Culver City that Davie considered hip adjacent. The neon sign above the door illuminated the boxy façade and dark wood exterior. While much of the city was on the path to gentrification, the Duck had remained mostly unchanged since the 1970s. It was once a hangout for cops and neighborhood drunks, but over the years the clientele had become more upscale. Not that Bear was happy about that.

The front door of the Duck was locked. Bear must have closed early. The light was on, so she assumed her dad was still inside. Davie walked through the alley and tapped on the back door before using her key. Rusty hinges groaned as she nudged it open with her shoulder. Inside, cold air blunted the odor of spilled beer soaked into ancient carpet.

Her father was hunched over several liquor cartons stacked on the floor in the middle of the room. His brown XXL leather jacket stretched across his broad back as he guided the blade of a box cutter along the seam of a carton of Hornitos Reposado.

Without looking up, he said, "Hey, Ace. Just in time to help."

Davie surveyed the room and the boxes of liquor. "Where's PJ?"

Bear looked up and sighed. "Sick. I sent her home early and closed the bar."

PJ had been a bartender at the Lucky Duck long before Bear had bought the place. She had agreed to stay on, but just until she told him how to run the business. That was ten years ago and she was still telling him what to do. Davie had half expected them to hook up, but Bear continued to resist her charms and Davie guessed that wasn't about to change.

"What brings you here so late?" he said.

"I'm working a case. It's not much fun."

"None of them are."

Cold air snaked up Davy's spine as she remembered Zeke Woodrow's body curled up on the ground of the parking garage. Bear was a former LAPD detective, so she laid out the generalities of her investigation so far. "The victim was a retired US Army Ranger who was working for a private security contractor."

The box-cutter made a clicking sound as Bear ratcheted up the blade from inside its plastic case. Davy could tell by his frown he was disturbed by the information.

"Pisses me off. A man gives his sweat and blood fighting for his country. Then he comes home and gets lit up by some asshole."

Davie grabbed a couple of bottles of tequila and set them on the shelf. "Just curious. Did anybody in the family keep Uncle Rob's dog tag after he died?"

Bear raked his hand through the stubble of his self-inflicted crew cut. "He was your mother's brother. Why are you asking me?"

"Just thought you might know, that's all. Maybe Grammy has it. I'll call her when she gets back from Ojai."

Normally Davie called or visited her grandmother every day at her assisted living apartment, but her grandmother was staying with a relative for a couple of weeks, enjoying the country atmosphere and the fresh air. Davie knew she would phone if she got lonely or just wanted to talk. So far, there had only been one call to let her know she was having fun.

Bear opened another box. "You could check with Robbie."

It seemed unlikely her brother would have anything that belonged to their dead uncle. Robbie wasn't the sentimental type. He had a law degree and thought he was Atticus Finch, even though he was a contracts attorney for a high-profile entertainment law firm, not a trial lawyer fighting for the wrongly accused.

Her father pulled four bottles of tequila from the box, two in each hand, and resettled them on a wooden shelf bracketed to the wall. "Why do you want to look at Rob's tags anyway?"

"I don't know. Maybe if I touch them I can get into Zeke's head, get a sense of why he died."

"You've been watching too many episodes of *L.A. Psychic.*" He paused and looked at her. "Call your mother. If anybody has Rob's dog tags, it would be her."

Davie studied the curled edges of the yellowed posters hanging on the walls, government rules about employee breaks and wages that Bear had probably never read. Nobody took a break at the Lucky Duck, at least that she'd ever seen.

"The tags aren't important to my case," she said.

"Look, Ace, I forgave your mother for cheating on me a long time ago. You should, too. She's been married to that Cross guy for years. At some point you'll have to rip the Band-Aid off and be friends again."

"We don't have much in common and besides, she doesn't seem interested." Davie paused by the door before leaving. "Bear, I've been thinking. You've lived alone for a long time. Have you ever thought about getting a pet? Maybe a cat?"

He bent over to open a box of Maker's Mark. "No."

"They're independent and they don't need much care."

He opened the seam and pulled out a couple of bottles. "Like I said—no."

"Okay. Just though you'd enjoy the company."

He put the bottles on the shelf then moved his hands to his hips. "Let me guess. You found some stray and now you want to pawn it off on me?"

"My victim had a cat. He's a good-looking male with charcoal gray hair."

"Sounds just like what you've been looking for."

"I can't keep a pet. I work all the time."

He gestured broadly to indicate the bar. "You think this is a hobby?"

"Forget it. It was just an idea."

As she got into her car, her head felt like it was stuck in a vise. Most cases were solved through old-fashioned police work—interviewing people who saw or heard something and were willing to talk about it. She had to focus her energy on finding Harlan Cormack and Dag Lunds and forget about looking for a home for Hootch. Her plan was to get a couple hours of sleep and then go back to the station to continue tracking down leads.

Twenty minutes later, she punched in the gate code and aimed her Camaro up the long driveway to the guest cottage she rented in the affluent neighborhood of Bel Air. The place would have been out of her price range if it hadn't been for the largess of her landlord, Alex Camden.

Alex was an international art dealer whose clientele included billionaires, politicians, and movie stars. He'd been instrumental in helping her solve a Grand Theft case in Southeast Division after she first made detective. Over the course of the investigation, they'd become friends. When he found out she was looking for a place to live, he offered her the furnished guesthouse adjacent to his mansion.

The property was tranquil, secluded, and—best of all—it had a swimming pool. Alex liked having a cop around to guard the valuable antiques and art he parked in the house. The tradeoff for reduced rent was furnishings that changed periodically when he found buyers. It wasn't a problem for her. It just made her life more interesting.

She parked in the carport behind her cottage. The place had no back door. If she lived in any area other than behind fortress-like walls and a security gate she would have found the limited access a cause for concern, but she had long ago acclimated to any inconvenience.

A wood and wrought-iron door opened to the living room. The cottage was small—581 square feet total, with 449 on the main floor and 132 on the upper floor loft, accessed by a spiral staircase. The place had only one bedroom and one bathroom, so adding a roommate wasn't an option. Not that she cared about that. She liked living alone.

The light from the lamp bathed the walls in muted colors that blended together like a spring bouquet. Alex called the shades wisteria, indigo, and sea-foam green. She called them comforting, so much that she could almost smell the fragrance of the lilac bush in the front yard of her grandparents' old house.

For the past few weeks, the walls had been covered with contemporary art, lots of bold lines and circles she found hard to appreciate. She couldn't understand why anyone would pay twenty grand for a red line on a white canvas, but she didn't judge how rich people spent their money.

At first it had felt uncomfortable to settle in among Alex's possessions. From the age of fifteen, she'd lived with her father in an apartment he'd rented after her parents' divorce. Neither she nor Bear had the decorator gene, so the place had been a chaotic jumble of threadbare furniture, mismatched pots and pans, and stacks of crime novels he read to escape the real world. It was anything but posh, but at least nobody complained if her friends put their feet on the coffee table.

Even after a year, she still worried about damaging the antique furniture and exotic rugs but she was grateful to learn about Alex's gift for color and design. Maybe someday when she saved enough money she would buy her own house and have the skills to decorate it.

She walked across the hardwood floor of the living room to the bedroom, where she sat in her grandmother's old rocking chair and removed her Oakley boots. She'd rescued the rocker from a yard sale her mother staged after Grammy moved into assisted living. Davie called the chair Celeste because it was still draped in the original French silk upholstery dating back to the 1920s. Celeste's arms were hand-carved in the shape of swans' necks. At some point, the chair's life made an awkward turn. The right arm was broken and pasted back together with a lack of finesse. There were other scars, covered by makeup that fooled no one. Davie had loved Celeste from the moment she saw the photo of Grammy rocking her in that chair as a newborn.

She stored her gun and badge in the top drawer of the bedside table, as she always did, and checked the closet for her running shoes. They were serviceable but worn. If she were serious about training with Joss, she'd have to invest in a new pair.

After a quick shower and an application of antibiotic cream to the cat scratches, she fell into bed, stretching her limbs across the polished cotton sheets, searching for the last patch of coolness.

She tried to doze off, but her mind kept churning out thoughts and theories about Zeke Woodrow's murder. She was still thinking of possible theories when she finally drifted off to sleep.

12

DAVIE DIDN'T AWAKEN UNTIL six a.m. the following morning. She bolted out of bed, surprised that she'd slept so long. Maybe focusing on the case had distracted her from her ever-present feelings of guilt. She checked her cell. Vaughn had left three messages. She dressed, grabbed an apple, and darted out the door to her car. When she got to the station, a group of detectives were standing against the wall near the kit room, all wearing blue shirts.

Joss held a camera ready to take the shot. "Davie, hurry. Get in the picture."

Davie had forgotten it was Blue Shirt Tuesday. She held up her hands, palms up. "Sorry."

Joss grabbed her elbow and guided her to the group. "Doesn't matter. Just say cheese."

The camera flash was still blurring Davie's vision as she entered the squad room and found Vaughn sitting at his desk.

She threw the apple core into a wastebasket. "What's up?"

He made a drama of looking at his watch in a faux gesture of disapproval. "I found more information on TidePool Security Consultants. They have an office in Delaware, but it looks like the headquarters is in Fairfax County, Virginia."

She rolled a chair to her partner's desk and sat. "Isn't that where the CIA is?"

"You got it." He held up a set of car keys. "I put gas in the green Crown Vic and let Giordano know we'd be driving to Santa Barbara this morning. Ready for a road trip?"

Giordano knew they planned to search Zeke Woodrow's house with the consent of his daughter, but he was still obligated to notify the Detective Bureau at the Police Administration Building downtown that two of his detectives were leaving the county. Giordano was away from his desk. She and Vaughn signed out and left the station.

Davie steered the car toward Santa Barbara along the coast highway, shifting her view from the ocean to her left and the bone-dry mountains to her right.

"We'd get there in half the time if you took the freeway," Vaughn said.

Driving the 101 was tedious, so she always chose an alternate route if possible. She could have reminded Vaughn about her affinity for sand and sea air, but he already knew that. Instead, she said, "Relax. Enjoy the scenery."

Santa Barbara hugged the meandering Pacific Ocean coastline with the steep Santa Ynez Mountains as a backdrop. Every neighborhood they passed looked like a vintage postcard—blue skies, white Spanish-style buildings with terra cotta tile roofs, palm trees, and well-kept landscaping despite the drought.

Zeke Woodrow's cottage was no more than a thousand square feet nestled in a quiet, secluded neighborhood. It was the perfect location for somebody who valued his privacy. Two large windows, covered by shutters, flanked the entrance. A driveway on the left led to a one-car garage. Davie parked on the side of the road. She and Vaughn circled the property and found that the cottage was built on a small embankment just above the beach. To the right was a wooden staircase that descended to the sand below. The place was so close to the water she could smell the aroma of brine and decomposing kelp and hear the waves lashing the shore. Shannon said the property had been in the family for decades. It must be worth a fortune now.

"You think Zeke chose this place because it has an escape route to the water?" Vaughn said.

"Not likely. There's no place down there to keep a boat."

"He was a Ranger. You don't think the Army taught him how to swim?"

He had a point, except the water was cold. Not even a former Ranger could survive for long without a wetsuit.

Davie turned away from the shoreline. "Let's check out the house."

They made their way through the gate of a white picket fence. The house had no alarm system. That seemed unusual for a security-minded guy like Zeke, even if he didn't live in the place full-time. Once inside, she and Vaughn split up and checked each room until they'd cleared the house. Nothing looked disturbed. In any event, whoever had sanitized the Topanga Canyon place had not been here.

The furniture in the living room had clean lines with accent colors that reminded Davie of Shannon's Santa Monica condo. She figured the same decorator designed both places.

"Let's split up," Vaughn said. "You search the house. I'll take the garage and maybe talk to the neighbors. Somebody must have known Zeke."

After Vaughn left, Davie searched the living room but found nothing of evidentiary value, so she proceeded down a short hallway to the master bedroom. The bed was made with crisps folds and bed linens stretched taut. A small bookcase was positioned near the bed. Davie opened each volume but found no cryptic notes or telltale receipts. A wicker basket at the foot of the bed held only extra blankets.

Davie pulled a chair over to the ceiling fan. She felt along the blades but found nothing taped to the surfaces and surprisingly little dust. Either he had a housekeeper or he was a neatnik. She searched all drawers in the bedroom and attached bathroom, as well as the closet. Zeke's clothes were mostly jeans and polo shirts, but there were a few ties and a couple of dark suits. The pockets were empty. She also checked the toilet tank and under the mattress.

A second bedroom had been converted into an office. There was a desk that held a laptop computer. She tried to boot it up but was stymied when a login box appeared on the screen, asking for a password. Since she had no idea how to get into Zeke's files, she would book the laptop as evidence at SID. If Shannon didn't know the code, the computer specialists would be able to figure it out.

Davie looked through the desk drawers and the closet but found no utility bills or mortgage statements. Zeke might have used online billing, but his cell phone hadn't been found on his body and the information on the laptop was inaccessible at the moment.

French doors led from the office to a patio, which was blocked off from the neighbor's yard by a high fence. Someone had added an additional two feet of wood lattice pieces for privacy. There was nothing in the yard except for two empty trash bins so she returned to the office and closed the door. She sat at the desk for a few minutes, wondering where Zeke Woodrow kept his personal information. Most people banked online, so she was unlikely to find cancelled checks or statements. But employment records were different. Those had to be somewhere. It was possible he scanned the paper forms onto a computer file and shredded the paper.

Next she went to the kitchen. The cupboards were old but well preserved. The rest of the room didn't appear to have been updated since the house was built. The windows were all locked. The lights weren't turned on. There was no food prepared and waiting on the table that might indicate Zeke had left in a hurry.

She thought of all the hiding places she'd uncovered while serving search warrants. Most people weren't all that original. She herself had once hidden a stash of emergency earthquake money in a sack of peas in the freezer. Zeke worked for a security contractor, so maybe he'd be cleverer. Just to make sure, she checked the refrigerator. It was mostly empty except for several bottles of cola and enough mustard to throw a hot dog party for the entire city.

It was clear that a man lived here alone. There were no cosmetics in the bathroom, no matching table linens, and no leftover canapés in the refrigerator from last evening's cocktail party with the neighbors. Other than one placemat left on the kitchen table, the house was organized with military precision. Zeke lived a solitary life but in a peaceful place with a cat he loved. At least he had a daughter and three friends who cared about him. It seemed like a good life until it ended in violence.

She was about to rummage through the pots and pans when she noticed the adjacent laundry room. A cat box and a sack of food confirmed this had been Hootch's home as well. Hootch's microchip had led Davie to his daughter. Maybe Zeke had hidden something in the cat food. She found a pot in one of the kitchen cupboards and emptied the kibble into it but was disappointed to find nothing. She stared at the litter box. A moment later, she lifted the lid. It looked clean. There were diagonal slash marks through the surface, somebody's attempt at a Zen garden.

She pulled a vinyl glove from her pocket and squatted next to the box. The litter was the consistency of sand. Her hand sifted through it until the hash marks were obliterated. There was something small and hard in one corner of the box, maybe a parting gift from Hootch. She removed the object and brushed it off. It was a USB drive.

Her heart hammered with the discovery. She had intended to run outside to look for her partner but as she pivoted, she knocked over a can of cola that sat opened on the counter next to a laundry basket. She flinched at the sound of the metal hitting the tile floor. Zeke had likely set it there and forgot about it.

Davie stared at the brown bubbles, wondering where Zeke kept his paper towels. That's when she felt a jolt of electricity moving down her spine. Bubbles. She bent over, stripped off the gloves, and touched the liquid. It was cold. Zeke had been murdered yesterday morning. If this had been his cola it would have been flat and warm by now. Somebody else had been in the house. Maybe was still in the house.

She heard the creaking of hinges. It wasn't her partner making that noise. Vaughn was out interviewing neighbors. She slid the USB drive into her pocket and slowly, silently removed her gun from its holster.

Davie checked the kitchen. No one there. She peered around the corner to the hallway but saw no movement. The rubber soles of her boots were silent as she inched down the hall, keeping her body close to the wall. When she got to the master bedroom, she stopped. Looked inside. Empty.

She continued down the hall to the office. With her back pressed to the wall she turned her head just enough to look inside the room. The French doors were wide open, not closed as she had left them. She stepped over the threshold and swept the aim of her weapon from wall to wall, looking for an intruder. That's when she saw the laptop was gone.

Footsteps echoed in the hallway. Her heart pounded as she moved into a shooting position, her gun trained toward the threat. As the footsteps came closer, she slid her finger from the barrel to the trigger, ready to shoot.

"Davie, you in there?"

Her hands trembled as her finger slid back to the barrel. Her breathing was labored. Fear and guilt washed over her. She didn't want to think about how close she'd come to shooting her partner. Vaughn stepped into the office just as Davie bolted out the French doors.

"What's going on?" he shouted.

"Somebody was just in the house. Zeke's computer is gone."

He broke leather and followed her out the door.

Davie heard a car engine start and tires squeal. She ran toward the sound but by the time she got there, the car had disappeared. She kept running through the streets of the neighborhood, hoping to catch a glimpse of the suspect, while Vaughn jogged back to the house for the car. She was out of breath when her partner finally pulled up next to her.

"Get in," he yelled. "He may still be in the area."

She shook her head. "It's no use. I heard the engine start, but I didn't see the car. I don't know the make or model or even the color."

"You want to call Santa Barbara PD or should I?"

She put her hands on her thighs and dropped her head to catch her breath. Maybe training with Joss Page wasn't such a bad idea after all. "You call."

She got in the car and Vaughn drove back to Zeke's cottage to wait for patrol officers to take the burglary report.

"What did you find in the garage?" she said.

"A bunch of old paint cans and a few tools."

"What about the neighbors?"

"Only one person answered the door. She didn't know anything. She and her husband just rented the place for a week on one of those online house-sharing sites."

Davie made it as far as the entryway of the house before her legs could no longer support her weight. She pressed her back against the wall and slid to the floor. Her body trembled and her breathing became shallow and fast.

Vaughn reached out his hand and pulled her up from the floor. "You okay?"

"Yeah, just out of breath."

A moment later Davie hauled herself the rest of the way to her feet. She went back to the kitchen to finish the search she'd begun when she'd been distracted by the litter box. Now she found crowbar-like marks on the back door and splintered wood around the lock. There was a bench against the wall on one side of the kitchen table. Davie tugged on the seat cushion and found that it opened for storage.

"Hey, Jason," she said. "Look at this."

Vaughn walked over to join her. "Looks sort of cramped in there but I guess there's enough room to hide as long as the guy wasn't a linebacker."

When the officers arrived, Davie directed them to the laundry room to collect the can of soda in case there was enough saliva for DNA testing. When they finished, they dusted for prints on the bench and then moved to the French doors. That's when she saw a small piece of black cloth caught in the lock's strike plate. Somebody had snagged his clothing, maybe in a rush to get away. Next to the cloth was what looked like blood splatter.

The officers didn't have a bloodstain collection kit, so Davie got one from the trunk of the Crown Victoria. At her direction, the officer opened the wrapper on one of the sterile cotton swabs and pulled the attached cap from its protective tube. She directed him to drop a small amount of distilled water on the tip of the swab and use a circular motion to collect the blood. There was enough for a second swab so she had him collect that as well. Then he broke off part of the stick so the swab and the protective cap fit into a coin envelope. When he was finished, he closed it with an official seal and had Davie sign for it. With the chain of evidence clear, he officially turned it over to the LAPD.

The USB drive was useless for the time being. They no longer had a computer to open it, so she slipped it into an evidence bag, too. When she and Vaughn were finished, they locked the house and returned to the station.

13

THE SHRINK WAS IN his forties, pasty white and balding. Sitting in the brown leather wingchair—worn and cracked, its brass tacks tarnished— he looked like a softball nestled into an old catcher's mitt. He wasn't old enough to have worn out the chair. Either he had scoured yard sales and used furniture stores until he found it or it had been donated to the department by a well-meaning citizen who'd just cleaned out the garage. The shrink steepled his fingers and waited for Davie to speak.

"I almost shot my partner today," she said.

"And how did that make you feel?"

Davie figured shrink school hadn't taught him to avoid psychiatry clichés. "What kind of a question is that?"

He leaned forward, resting his forearms on the desk. The sleeves of his plaid shirt were rolled up to the elbows, which made him look like a camp counselor, not somebody responsible for mending broken minds.

"Perhaps this will help you decide," he said. "There's disagreement among professionals, but let's just say there are six basic human emotions: happiness, sadness, fear, anger, surprise, and disgust. Which one of those most closely resembled your feelings at the time?"

She thought about the question before answering. "None of them and all of them."

He caught her gaze and held it. "Perhaps you should ask yourself why it's so difficult for you to pinpoint your feelings. You can speak freely. Our conversations are confidential."

Davie wasn't so sure about that and she wasn't the only one. There were many cops who worried that sensitive personal information would make its way from a shrink's notebook to the Chief's desk.

The shrink paused to judge her mood. "You're frowning. What are you feeling at this moment?"

"I'm feeling irritated that you keep needling me about how I feel. I told you I could have killed my partner. I think you can imagine how I felt."

He set his pen on the desk. From the grim look on his face, she didn't have to wonder how *he* was feeling at the moment—frustrated. She wondered why that emotion wasn't on his official list.

"That's not how this works," he said. "It's not my job to project my emotions onto your experiences. I need to hear them from you. Don't be a martyr."

She felt wounded by his accusation but gave it a fair hearing before deciding the label didn't fit her at all. "If you think I'm suffering or withholding my feelings to get attention, you're wrong. I love my job. I care about my cases. That's why I need to get back to work."

He glanced up at the wall clock. "We have fifteen minutes left in the session." He sat back in the chair and studied her face. "You look tired. Are you still having trouble sleeping? I can prescribe medication if you need it."

"I don't do drugs."

"Stoicism is often associated with control issues. Are you afraid medication will cause you to lose your edge?" He waited for her to answer. When she didn't, he wrote some words in his notebook. "If not drugs, perhaps you might consider yoga or meditation. When you're awake at night, try counting to one hundred. Start again and again. Keep counting until you fall asleep."

Downward Facing Dog and numbers games were not on her agenda, but she'd agree if it meant getting out of the session early. "I'll try it."

Expressing emotions was not her strong suit. Vaughn called her a machine. He was teasing but he had a point. Perhaps events in her past had used up her allotment of pain and drama, or maybe it was because her police training had taught her to compartmentalize. The worst thing she could do was become emotional, particularly on the witness stand or when interviewing a distraught family member whose loved one had just been murdered. Being stoic might make her a difficult friend, but it also made her a good detective. Life was full of trade-offs.

He crossed his hands on his lap. "Darwin believed that emotions actually aid in human survival."

"I'm guessing Darwin never worked as a cop." She leaned toward him. "My dad was a detective, too. Ever since I was a kid, he's drummed into me that wearing the badge means you have power over people. When you combine power and emotions, somebody is likely to get hurt. Maybe holding back my feelings is what's saved my bacon for all these years."

He gave her an impassive stare and closed his notebook. "Try counting and see if it helps you sleep."

Twenty minutes later Davie sat at her desk at the station, filling out the serology form to request blood analysis. As she filed a copy in the

Murder Book, she thumbed through the pages, reviewing her notes until she came across the data on Hootch's microchip.

Dr. Dimetri had told her the information was unusual. Standard practice was to include the phone number of the pet recovery agency and the owner's private code. Hootch's chip held Shannon's telephone number and a line of gibberish that Dimetri considered computer garbage. Davie checked the screen shot on her cell and again stared at the combination of letters, numbers, and symbols: A 1 € > ? 2 ¥ $ * > €

Some of them didn't even appear on her keyboard. She opened the word processing program on her desk computer and clicked IN-SERT and SYMBOLS on the menu bar, searching the options until she found one symbol and then all of them.

She copied the € first. When she pasted it into her Internet search box and learned it was the currency symbol for the Euro. The ¥ represented the Chinese yuan. The dollar sign was obvious. Maybe they represented the last three places TidePool had sent Zeke. The others she recognized as mathematical symbols. The > meant "greater than" and * meant "multiplication."

The more she thought about it, the more she suspected Zeke had included the sequence for a reason. Amber Johnson said he loved his cat. Hootch's microchip led them to the daughter. The USB drive was hidden in the cat box. Maybe Zeke wanted the code to be accessed in an emergency. Tortured logic to be sure, but it rang true and Hootch was at the center of it all.

She emailed the sequence along with her observations to a computer techie she knew at the Scientific Investigation Division and asked him to determine if it meant anything or if it was just a unique password Zeke had created. Perhaps it was the code that would open Zeke's computer once it was recovered.

Davie was about to plug Zeke's USB drive into her desktop computer when a gust of air swept over her. She looked up to see Jason Vaughn strolling into the squad room.

He dropped his notebook on his desk and peered over the workstation partition. "Where have you been?"

His tone was a mix of curiosity and irritation. Vaughn didn't realize how close he'd come to dying at her hand, and she didn't plan to tell him. As for her schedule, she wasn't obligated to account for every minute of her day, especially her mandatory shrink appointments.

"Just wondering if Hootch's microchip code would have opened Zeke's computer," she said, skirting the question. Her hands felt sweaty as she plugged the drive into the port and hovered her finger above the keyboard. She pressed RETURN. A moment later a folder opened.

"Jason. Come over here. You're not going to believe this."

Vaughn ambled around Giordano's desk to her side of the cubicle and pulled up a chair next to hers. He stared at the computer screen. "What is it?"

"Zeke Woodrow's whole life, including work records."

He leaned in for a better look as Davie opened documents. Zeke had organized his information into folders and subfolders. His monthly bank statements were listed under FINANCES. Under TIDE-POOL SECURITY CONSULTANTS they found a series of files labeled with city names, including Kabul, Paris, and Montevideo. Each file included an expense report with costs—airfare, hotel, food, and transfers to and from the airport, which were marked *Limo*.

Hong Kong appeared to be his most recent trip. Zeke had departed LAX for Asia just shy of two weeks before his death and spent five days there. Listed at the bottom of the document was a separate itinerary that included Juno Karst, confirming that he had accompanied Zeke to Hong Kong on the same flights.

Vaughn pointed toward the screen. "There's a second Hong Kong file."

Her partner was right, but it wasn't under the main TidePool umbrella. She opened it and found several documents, including an Excel worksheet.

"Looks like a list of expenses," she said.

Vaughn pointed to the first item. "He paid just under two grand for a ticket on Cathay Pacific for a trip back to Hong Kong. See that note at the bottom? The flight was scheduled to leave Bradley terminal at nine a.m. yesterday." Vaughn blew out a puff of air. "At least we have the answer to why he was at the airport."

The file had been created three days before Zeke's body was found in the parking garage. He came back from Hong Kong and immediately booked another trip to the same place. If he had additional business there, why not just extend his stay? It was cheaper to pay the airline's change fee than to book a separate trip.

"Why do you think this Hong Kong file wasn't with the others?" Vaughn said.

"Good question. Maybe he decided to go back on his own."

"You mean just for fun? Like he met somebody there?" Vaughn winked and nudged her with his elbow. "You know, like a hot Hong Kong romance."

Her partner was kidding, but the thought gave her a chill. Maybe Zeke *had* met somebody there, somebody who had stalked him to Santa Barbara and broken into his house. That idea was farfetched. The theft of the computer could have been a simple burglary, unrelated to Zeke's murder. Maybe she and Vaughn had surprised an intruder in the midst of drinking cola. He ran, taking the only valuable item he saw—Zeke's laptop.

Davie wondered if Zeke kept sensitive information on the laptop since it was sitting on a desk in plain sight. It was the USB drive that had been hidden in the litter box. The drive contained all sort of personal and business-related information, but nothing on it seemed top secret. Maybe Zeke had another file floating in a cyberspace cloud somewhere.

She pointed to another file labeled NUMBERS. "Could be more financial information."

The file turned out to be an address book, but Davie was disappointed that Zeke hadn't listed the phone numbers for his friends Harlan Cormack and Dag Lunds.

"There's a number for Jade Limousine Service," she said. "Must be the one Zeke used when he traveled."

"Except he didn't ride with them the day he was killed, which suggests it might have been a personal trip. Otherwise, why not take the limo and write it off as a business expense?"

Davie printed everything they'd found on the drive and slipped the copies into the Murder Book. "Let's have a chat with the limo owner. If Zeke was a long-time customer, they might know something helpful."

Vaughn stood. "I'll get a car."

14

Jade Limousine Service was located in Westchester, not far from LAX. It was housed in a small building set in the middle of a parking lot filled with late model cars, SUVs, and stretch limos. Davie followed her partner through the front door and noted that the office was professional but not posh. The décor probably didn't matter. She assumed that most business was done by telephone and over the Internet.

A woman in an orange blazer sat on a stool behind the counter, keying information into a computer. Her DNA was an exotic stew that might have included genes from Asia or possibly Polynesia. Her silky black hair was gathered into a ponytail and held in place with a tortoise-shell clip. She turned when she heard the door open, staring at them through a pair of naughty-librarian glasses, the sort of eyewear that was meant to make beautiful women look studious.

The woman stood and walked from behind the counter to greet them. "Good morning. I'm Jade Chen. How can I help you?"

Chen towered over Davie by seven or eight inches. Davie craned her neck to catch her eye. She flashed her badge and introduced herself and her partner.

"Do you know a man named Zeke Woodrow?" she asked.

Chen smiled, showing her even white teeth. "I've been taking Zeke to one airport or another for the past two or three years. Is something wrong?"

"Do you drive him yourself?" Vaughn asked.

Her smile was replaced by the first hint of concern. "My brother and I own the company. I don't usually drive customers anymore, but Zeke is a long-time client and he's particular about who's behind the wheel. I guess he just got used to me and didn't want to break in somebody new."

Vaughn stepped closer. "When was the last time he used your service?"

The crackle of a radio dispatch interrupted the conversation. Jade unclipped the handheld device from her belt and gave the driver instructions before answering Vaughn's question. "I was supposed to drive him to the airport on Monday but he left a message late Sunday night, cancelling."

Vaughn frowned. "Do you know why?"

"He didn't say. I assumed he decided to drive or take a cab."

Davie picked up a business card from the counter and slipped it into her pocket. "In the past when you picked him up, what kind of vehicle did you use?"

Chen frowned. "Usually one of our Mercedes S models but sometimes an SUV. Zeke never wanted a stretch limo. I got the impression he didn't like to call attention to himself."

Vaughn glanced toward the cars in the parking lot. "Do you have any BMWs in your fleet?"

Chen moved to the counter to tidy a stack of brochures, but Davie sensed it was a diversion. "Mercedes is the only luxury sedan we use." Her expression had turned wary and suspicious. "Why are you asking all these questions? Is Zeke in trouble?"

Davie's stomach clenched as she told her the news. "He was murdered yesterday morning."

Jade Chen's mouth opened, but no words came out.

Davie waited for a couple of beats while the woman regained her composure. "Before that cancelled trip," she continued, "when was the last time you transported Mr. Woodrow?"

Chen turned away and dabbed at her eyes with the sleeve of her jacket. She was the third woman who had cried over Zeke Woodrow's death. That wasn't always the case with murder victims, which told Davie that whatever his shortcomings might have been, people cared about this man.

"A few weeks ago," she said, "but I'll have to check the date to be sure." She went around the counter to the computer and pulled up a new page. "Here it is. I picked him up in Topanga not quite two weeks ago at around five thirty in the morning and dropped him off at LAX for a flight to Hong Kong."

Davie leaned over the counter to read the screen. "Did you ever meet him at the airport when he returned from one of his trips?"

"Not always. Sometimes he called a cab. But I did pick him up when he got back from that trip."

"Was he alone," Vaughn asked, "or with a friend?"

"Alone." She scrolled down the page and called out the date. "I remember because that day was out of the ordinary. Instead of driving him back to Topanga, he asked me to take him to a building on Wilshire Boulevard."

Vaughn stepped closer to Chen. "Do you have the address?"

She read it from the screen and Davie jotted the information in her notebook. The building was near the corner of Westwood and Wilshire Boulevards, not far from UCLA.

"Did you drop him off or wait for him?" he said.

"I waited in the parking garage. According to my log, he was in the building for a little over an hour. He texted me when he was ready to leave, and I drove around to the front of the building to pick him up. I was supposed to drop him off at his house in Topanga Canyon but he changed his mind at the last minute. Instead, he asked me to take him to Santa Barbara."

Davie looked up, surprised. "That's a long trip."

Chen pulled a tissue from a box on the counter and wiped her eyes again. "It's generally out of our service area, but he was such a good customer I said okay. He didn't say boo when I handed him the bill. It was for a lot of money."

Davie continued questioning her. "Did he mention what he was doing in the building or who he was there to see?"

Chen lowered herself onto a chair and stared at the crumpled tissue in her hand. "No, but he seemed upset when he got back to the car. We always had a great rapport. We'd talk about everything from baseball to books. But he didn't say much for the rest of the trip. I even had a hard time getting an address out of him. He told me to just drive and he'd give me directions when I needed them. Actually, he was sort of rude, which was unusual."

Davie handed Chen her business card. "Please call if you remember anything else."

She and Vaughn left the woman to mourn in her own way and returned to the car. As Davie maneuvered through traffic, she processed the new lead Jade Chen had provided. Zeke had just returned from a long, tiring trip to Asia, but instead of going home, he'd taken a detour. It must have been important because otherwise he could have made a phone call.

When Davie got back to the station, she found the cat carrier sitting on her desk with Hootch huddled in a back corner, spring-loaded and ready to fire. His box and a bag of litter were under her desk.

She eyed Vaughn and nodded toward the carrier. "What is that?"

"Looks like a failed attempt to pawn off your cat on April Hayes."

"He's not my cat."

"I'll find out." Vaughn walked toward the lieutenant's office, returning a few minutes later. "April said Hootch attacked her pug, so the feline foster home experiment is over. She sends her regrets. Expect a vet bill."

Davie sat on her chair and stared into the carrier. At least she'd bought one that was roomy enough for Hootch to move around in. "What am I supposed to do with him? Bear doesn't want a cat."

"No surprise there, and don't say I didn't warn you about taking him in the first place."

"He can't stay with me. I'm never home."

Vaughn walked to the coffee pot behind Giordano's desk and poured himself a cup. "The way I see it, you have a few other options—unload him on Woodrow's ex, or the shelter Amber Johnson told us about, or maybe your landlord will take him."

"Alex is out of town or I'd ask him, but I doubt he'd be interested. He already has two dogs."

Vaughn removed his jacket and draped it over the back of the chair. "Well, he can't stay here. That's for sure."

Davie rested her forehead on the carrier's grated door. Hootch stared at her. After a few minutes, he stood and arched his back in an exaggerated stretch. When he stepped toward her, she noticed that he smelled good and all the mats had been brushed out of his hair. He looked presentable, maybe even handsome. She reached through the grates to pet his head. The cat nuzzled its face against her finger and started to purr.

"I'll call Dr. Dimetri," she said to her partner. "Maybe the clinic can board him overnight until I come up with a plan."

"Ka-ching. Ka-ching. Just take him home, Davie. You can figure it out tomorrow."

Despite her partner's phony concerns about her finances, his suggestion seemed reasonable. Zeke traveled a lot for his job, so Hootch must be used to staying alone much of the day with periodic visits from a pet sitter. If he could handle that, then so could she.

"Okay, I'll park Hootch at the guesthouse until I find him a permanent home."

"Good. What's next?"

"Chen said she drove Zeke to a building on Wilshire Boulevard," she said. "He was inside for over an hour. I want to know who he went to see and why. Let's drive over and look around."

"You don't even know what you're looking for. How many offices are in that building? Tons of them, I bet. I'd rather stay here and chase other leads."

"Fine. I have to drop Hootch off at the guesthouse first. I'll be back in an hour or so."

Twenty minutes later, Davie maneuvered the carrier out of the car. It occurred to her that Alex might not appreciate a cat roaming free with his valuable antiques and Persian rugs. Normally, she would ask permission, but he was away for the week in Bali, buying antique furniture for a client's Maui vacation home. Bear had always told her it was easier to beg forgiveness than to ask permission, so she hauled the carrier into the house, resolving that the cat would be in a permanent home by the time Alex returned from his business trip. She just hoped

Hootch didn't damage anything in the meantime. To protect against that, she parked him in the bathroom, along with his food, water, litter box, and a couple of toys left over from his brief stay with April Hayes.

She gripped the bathroom door. "Stay safe." Hootch let out one soft meow. She closed the door, feeling like a jerk.

FIFTEEN MINUTES AFTER DROPPING Hootch at her guesthouse, Davie arrived at the office building where Jade Chen had taken Zeke the day he returned from Hong Kong. Street parking was nonexistent, so Davie left the ride in the bus zone on Westwood Boulevard with a plastic city-parking permit on the dashboard and made her way into the lobby of the building.

Her rubber-soled boots squeaked as she walked across the marble tiles to a bank of elevators. A list of tenants was posted on the wall. The names were in alphabetical order—doctors, lawyers, accountants. None of them were people or companies she'd heard of before. She read the list again, slower this time, until she reached the Ls and stopped. Something was different about one of the listings, a bit of minutia that didn't fit the pattern. She hadn't noticed before, but it read only LAW OFFICES next to a suite number. It was unusual that the name of the firm wasn't included.

Davie ran through the facts she knew so far as she waited for the elevator. Zeke and Juno Karst both worked for TidePool Security Consultants. Alden Brink was associated with Tidepool, but she wasn't sure if he was an employee. Was the generic law office upstairs his?

Time to find out.

The elevator doors closed and the car began its ascent to the fifteenth floor. The hallway was empty as she located the suite number and turned the knob. Locked. She knocked but got no answer. There was an intercom on the wall. The button made a buzzing sound when she pressed it.

An answer came back in a nasally whine. "May I help you?"

Davie recognized the voice. It was the woman who'd answered Alden Brink's telephone when she'd called the day before.

"It's Detective Richards from the Los Angeles Police Department. Open the door. I need to speak to Mr. Brink."

The woman had been less than cooperative during their last conversation, so Davie wasn't sure she'd comply. But a moment later, the door cracked open. The face peering at her belonged to an older woman with a short blunt-cut hairdo and bangs that reminded her of a grayer version of Mo's do from *The Three Stooges*.

The woman held a cell phone in one hand. With the other hand, she pushed her oversized black-framed glasses up the bridge of her nose and tilted her head back to study Davie through her bifocals. "I'm not supposed to let people in without an appointment."

"I'm a Homicide detective investigating the murder of one of your employees. You work for TidePool Security Consultants, right?"

The woman adjusted the jacket of her boxy vintage suit and fingered a string of fat pearls that had to be fake. "I work for Mr. Brink."

Davie noticed her black velvet flats. They had rhinestone cats on the toes. "Is his name on your paycheck?"

"How would I know? I'm a temp. I've only been here a week." The woman must have decided further resistance was futile, because she opened the door.

Davie stepped into a monastic room that was outfitted with only a chair, a desk that held a laptop computer, and a small vase with three wilted carnations. A cardboard box served as a wastebasket. There was a desk phone, but the lines weren't connected to the wall socket. Three shadow boxes were stacked against a wall ready for hanging. The top one was filled with vintage political campaign buttons, including one that read I LIKE IKE. The contents of the other two collections weren't visible to her.

"Are you moving in or out?" Davie asked.

"In, but we're not open for business yet. How did you even know we were here?"

Davie turned toward a door that led to what she assumed was another office. She walked toward it. "Is Mr. Brink in?"

The woman was agile for her age, because she scurried across the room and spread her arms over the door to block Davie from going inside. "He can't be disturbed."

Davie wondered if the woman was a temp from Central Casting, because her reaction was pure drama. "How much does that temp agency pay you?"

"Eleven bucks an hour," she said in her nasally voice.

"You should ask for a raise."

"You been eating donuts?" she asked. "The sugar is making you cranky."

For a small woman, she has a big attitude. "Look, ma'am, unless you want me to arrest you for interfering with a murder investigation, step away from the door."

The woman blinked several times and then lowered one hand. "If I get fired it's on you." She used the other hand to tap on the wood. "Mr. Brink, can you come out here? We have a *situation*."

A man's deep voice boomed from inside the office. "Handle it, Fern."

Davie didn't wait for further discussion. She turned the doorknob and walked into the office. A desk sat parallel to the window, apparently so Brink would see anyone entering the office.

The decor was partially assembled, but there were still boxes on the floor next to several new file cabinets, price stickers plastered on the front of each. Brink stood facing the wall with a tape measure in his hand. He sensed her presence and turned. He was in his early to mid-thirties, tanned, and dressed casually in a pair of cotton chinos, a long-sleeved Oxford shirt, and tan boat shoes—no socks. She guessed his hair was strawberry blond, although it was cut so short it was hard to tell. He looked like a successful corporate lawyer enjoying casual day at the office. Davie expected him to be confrontational when she introduced herself, but he flashed a high-beam smile worthy of any toothpaste commercial.

"Detective," he said with that same commanding tone she recognized from their phone call, the kind used by powerful men or those who aspired to be. "I meant to call back after my receptionist cut you off the other day, but as you can see"—he swept his hand to indicate the mess in the room—"things are chaotic around here. Fern's not exactly up on the latest technology, so there were some mishaps along the way." He followed that statement with a puckered smile.

"Your headquarters are in Virginia. What brought you to California?"

"TidePool is increasing its presence in Asia, so they asked me to open a satellite office here. As you can see, I'm still moving in."

Davie glanced around the room. "The place seems small."

His expression soured, as if he had interpreted her comment as an insult. "This place is temporary, just until I assess the merits of having an L.A. office. If I decide it's the right choice, we'll move to a larger space. If L.A. doesn't work out, I'll relocate the office to someplace that better appreciates our business." Brink set the measuring tape on the desk. "Have a seat." He gestured to the only chair in the room reserved for guests.

Davie waited for him to sit. When he didn't, she remained standing, too. He noticed but didn't respond.

Brink pulled a black-framed diploma and a rag from a cardboard box and wiped fingerprints off the glass. "How can I help you?"

"You can tell me why Zeke Woodrow came to see you last week."

He looked up from his cleaning. If her knowledge surprised him, he didn't show it. "Company business."

"Mr. Woodrow had just come back from a business trip that day. Was that what he wanted to discuss?"

Brink set the diploma on his desk. "I believe he was sent with a team of executives to court a new client. The contract was worth a lot of money, so we showed them the best we had."

Davie noted he didn't answer the question. She wandered over to the desk and picked up the diploma, a JD degree from a law school in Arizona. She didn't recognize the name, but it was definitely not one of the top-tier schools. "Did everything go well?"

He frowned and jerked the diploma from her hands. "As far as I know, yes."

"Is that why you were sending him back? To close the deal?"

He tilted his head toward his shoulder and frowned. "I'm not involved with employee work assignments, but as far as I know, nobody at the company authorized a second trip. That first meeting was just to establish relationships. The next step in the process would be handled by email."

Davie glanced inside the box on the floor. It was full of pens, a stapler, and a hammer. "Mr. Woodrow was booked on a flight on Cathay Pacific scheduled to leave yesterday morning."

"If he went back to Hong Kong, he was going on his own dime."

"Why would he do that? What happened at that first meeting?"

Brink's tone was self-assured but measured. "I'm a lawyer. I acquire and manage TidePool's extensive real estate portfolio. I also write contracts and offer legal opinions. What I don't do is arrange sales meetings with potential clients, and even if I did I couldn't tell you the details. It's confidential company business. Maybe you should speak with someone who runs that division."

Davie stepped closer, hoping to breach his comfort zone. "As I told you on the telephone, Mr. Woodrow never made his flight because somebody killed him. That makes two of your employees who've been murdered within the last few days. If somebody were targeting my people, I'd be concerned."

He seemed taken aback. "Two? How do you figure?"

"Zeke Woodrow and Juno Karst."

Brink paused before responding. "Mr. Karst committed suicide. At least, that's what the local sheriff told me. He had no close family so the company handled the arrangements."

Davie didn't understand why Juno had been killed first, but she would figure it out eventually.

"I doubt it was a suicide. Two similar deaths, so close together. That's odd, wouldn't you agree?"

"Of course, we're all saddened by the loss. They were valuable employees and important members of our training team."

"What was Juno doing in Nevada?" she said. "Did the company send him there on assignment?"

Brink fished in the bottom of the box until he found the hammer and a nail. "As I told you before, I wouldn't know why he was there, but I don't think we sent him."

"Who took possession of his personal property from the car, like his wallet and cell phone?"

Brink walked toward the wall. "I assume the sheriff has all that. He asked about the gun Mr. Karst used to shoot himself. I told him to dispose of it."

"I'll need Juno's home address."

He studied the wall, avoiding her gaze. "He lived in a property owned by the corporation. After he died, I had the place cleaned out. Since he had no family, his possessions were donated to charity."

"That was quick," she said, adding an edge to her tone. "He's been dead less than a week."

He slowly turned toward her. "I have a lot of responsibilities and not much time."

"Is it common in your industry to provide housing for your employees?"

"No, but it's a brilliant idea—at least, the board thought so when I presented it to them. In fact, they were so impressed they asked me to head their new real estate division. We offer housing to employees at a discount, which is especially important in high-priced areas like Southern California. It's a recruiting tool and an important part of our retention strategy. It also adds valuable assets to our balance sheet. Win-win, as they say."

Davie ignored his self-aggrandizing sales pitch. She had interviewed a slew of witnesses in her career. Reactions to her questioning ran the gamut from hostile to heartfelt. Hostility was easy to read.

Brink seemed thin-skinned and full of himself, a clear departure from the businesslike response in their prior telephone conversation. That didn't surprise her. It didn't take much effort to brush off a detective's phone call, but remaining even-tempered during a face-to-face interview required different skills.

She walked toward the window and looked out at the view. In the distance was the Los Angeles National Cemetery—row after row of white headstones like dinosaur teeth bleaching in the sun.

"Ever wonder why military gravestones all look the same?" she said. "No matter how you look at them, they're always lined up in perfect symmetry. You don't see that in civilian cemeteries."

"I'm sure you'll find the answer on Wikipedia," he said.

She ignored his smartass remark. Cops dealt with all kinds of posturing, mostly from people who conned themselves into believing they had the upper hand.

"Maybe it's because they're all equal, all fighting for the same cause," she said. "Did you serve in the military?"

Brink pounded the nail into the wall with more force than needed. "No."

"Who's the client Mr. Woodrow went to see in Hong Kong?"

Brink hung the diploma on the nail and then rocked it back and forth until it was level. "Why should I jeopardize my future with the company by divulging confidential information?"

"Consider what you could jeopardize if you don't talk to me."

He glared at Davie. "I'm not sure what you mean. Is that some sort a threat?"

Davie studied the diploma's placement. It was still crooked. "Why would you think that, Mr. Brink?"

"In case it's not already apparent to you, Detective, TidePool sells security. A lot of what our clients do is proprietary. They don't want their competitors or the public to know their business."

"You think the LAPD is going to use the info to horn in on your deals?"

He rolled his eyes, making it clear he thought her comment was ridiculous. "Of course not."

"I'm going to find out who killed Zeke Woodrow and Juno Karst," she said. "As a company employee, I'd think you'd want to help me."

Alden Brink seemed to bristle at "employee," as if the word devalued his importance. He put his hands on his hips and stared at the floor like he was weighing the pros and cons of giving up the information. He held that pose for several moments before finally looking up. "Guardian Advanced Technologies is a multinational defense contractor based in Hong Kong, but they also have offices in other places—London, Berlin, Istanbul."

"What do they make?"

He looked past her out the window at the cemetery in the distance. "Weapons systems, military satellites, other products I can't mention."

"Who else went on that Hong Kong trip?"

"A couple of executives from our Langley office. Zeke and Juno represented our training division. Both were former Rangers—poster boys for tough and smart. We always hauled them out for clients to see because they were impressive even in their sixties."

She guessed her boss Detective Giordano wouldn't appreciate the ageism crack. "Do you know a man named Harlan Cormack?"

He made a pretense of examining a pen he'd pulled from the box. Its clip was an angular winglike decal that reminded her of a vintage hood ornament. "He used to work for us. He was injured about six months back. We had to let him go."

"Injured on the job?"

Brink set the pen on the desk. "In a motorcycle accident—on his own time."

"I'll need his address."

"I don't know where he is. He was living in a TidePool condo in San Pedro. When he left the company, he moved out."

"What about Dag Lunds?"

"He's on the payroll, but he wasn't on the Hong Kong trip. He won't go to Asia, so we only send him to other arenas like South America, the Middle East, and Europe."

Davie sensed movement. Out of the corner of her eye, she noticed Fern hovering near the doorway, listening. "I need to contact Lunds."

Brink shrugged. "I'll give him your telephone number. If he wants to speak with you, he's free to do so. I assume you'll find him before I do."

Davie stared at Brink. "Just one last question. You told me on the phone that Mr. Woodrow broke his lease. When did he tell you he was moving?"

He seemed to grow uncomfortable with her scrutiny and looked away. "The day he dropped by. He'd decided to retire. Normally he'd fill out the paperwork and send it to our HR department back in Virginia, but since I manage all the company's real estate, he wanted to give me the key to the house. He said he didn't plan to go back there."

"Seems odd," she said. "If Mr. Woodrow moved out, why didn't he take his cat?"

Brink's eyes darted toward the door, but Fern was no longer there. "I'm sure it was inadvertent. No need to read anything sinister into it."

There was no way Zeke forgot about Hootch. She kept her tone even and calm. "Recognizing sinister is why I'm good at my job, Mr. Brink."

16

IT WAS AFTER THREE p.m. when Davie left Alden Brink's office. She couldn't remember how long it had been since she'd eaten a real meal. Instead of returning to the station, she detoured to Tia Juana's. Law enforcement personnel were discouraged from eating at restaurants outside their division while on duty in case there was a tactical alert that required a quick response. Tia's was always her go-to place. It was a small family-owned operation run by Guillermo and Maria Sanchez with help from their four children who waited tables and worked in the kitchen on the weekends. They were a model family in Davie's view, unlike her own, and she felt welcome whenever she walked through the door.

Guillermo Sanchez greeted her in a green apron embroidered with the restaurant's name and logo—a smiling cartoon tortilla with grates of cheesy hair sprouting beneath its sombrero. Mr. Sanchez was short and stocky with gray hair combed back and held in place with some kind of beauty product. His wife, Maria, was hunched over a hot grill in the front of the store, making fresh tortillas by hand. The fragrance was familiar and comforting.

Mrs. Sanchez nodded hello as her husband ushered Davie to a back table in the dining room. He held out a menu. "What can I get for you today, Detective?"

The restaurant was scrupulously clean, but Davie didn't like to touch menus. The plastic covers always seemed greasy. "Huevos Rancheros."

"With flour or corn?"

"Flour."

He nodded and disappeared around the corner to the kitchen, returning a moment later with a glass of ice water and a basket of chips and salsa. Canned mariachi music flowed from speakers strategically placed around the room. As she waited for her food to arrive, her cell phone pinged with an incoming text. It was from her partner.

Where are you?

Tia's.

Stay put. I'll be there in 5.

It was more like ten minutes before Jason Vaughn arrived. Her food had just been placed on the table in front of her when he barreled through the door and hurried toward her. Mr. Sanchez followed him with a menu.

Vaughn brushed it aside. "No thanks. I'm not hungry."

"What's going on?" she said.

"I finally got Juno Karst's death report from Nevada. You're not going to believe what's on it."

He handed it to her. It was only two pages. She'd written longer grocery lists than that. She read the narrative and then looked at her partner.

"There was a suicide note?" she said.

"That's what it says. And it was short and sweet—'Sorry.'"

Sorry to whom and for what? she wondered.

"Did anybody verify that the handwriting was Karst's?"

"Nope. And they didn't test his hands for GSR, either."

Preserving gunshot residue on the victim's hands would have been a simple procedure to follow as long as they were tested within six hours of death. After that, it was almost impossible to get a reading. All first responders would have had to do was slip clean evidence bags over Karst's hands and secure them with flex-cuffs for testing later. Davie examined the report again. The gun that killed Karst was a Glock 19, 9mm—a typical weapon used by law enforcement and thousands of other people.

"So the sheriff found a gun, a note, and a body and didn't bother to look any further," she said. "You think Karst killed himself?"

Vaughn unfolded the napkin covering the fresh tortillas and pulled one out. "If somebody murdered Karst, they knew how to set up the scene to confuse law enforcement. The hit happened in a remote area. The killer must have known that would delay first responders."

"Who found the body?"

Vaughn reached across the table and picked up Davie's knife. "The report says they got an anonymous call at the sheriff's office." He swiped a pat of butter across the warm tortilla. "It was a man's voice but he wouldn't leave his name. Just said he was driving by and saw the car parked along the shoulder. He stopped to see if Karst was having car trouble, saw the blood, and called it in. The sheriff didn't consider that odd. Not everybody wants to get involved."

A disquieting calm settled into her chest. "The man called the sheriff's office directly?"

Vaughn used Davie's spoon to scoop a load of refried beans from her plate and dump it on the tortilla in his hand. "That's what the report says."

"So how did the guy get the number? He was out in the middle of nowhere. He would have to know what county and law enforcement jurisdiction he was in, and then look up the number on his cell or call information. That's a lot of effort for a guy who just happened on a dead body. Why not just call 911?"

"I thought it might be a local guy who already knew the number," he said, "but I contacted the sheriff's office to see if they could find him through the call history. I got a civilian employee who checked for me."

"And ... "

Vaughn seemed introspective as he studied his handmade burrito. "And ... I called the number. A man answered. Turns out he owns a gas station a few miles up the road from where the body was found. The call was made from a pay phone a few feet from the pumps."

"I didn't know they still had pay phones. Did the owner see who made the call?"

Vaughn bit into the burrito. His words were muffled as he chewed. "Seems like business is slow in his neck of the woods. He spends a lot of time sitting outside on a chair, watching cars go by. He claims a man used the pay phone the day the sheriff's office got that call."

Davie pulled a tortilla chip from the basket. "Did he give a description?"

Vaughn had finished the burrito and was eyeing the basket again. "Yeah, but it was too vague to be useful—medium height and in good shape. The guy was wearing a ball cap so the owner couldn't see his face. But he's seen a lot of license plates in his day and he noticed these were from Washington State. He didn't pay attention to the numbers but he remembered the make and model of the car."

Davie nibbled on a chip as her partner pulled a second tortilla from the basket. "I thought you said you weren't hungry?"

"You've hardly touched the food. I hate to see it go to waste."

Davie pushed her plate to his side of the table. "So, the car?"

Vaughn tucked into the eggs with Davie's fork. "The guy was driving a black BMW 740i. Sound familiar?"

She felt the skin on her neck tingle. That was the same model car they'd seen on the surveillance video, speeding out of the LAX parking garage just before Zeke Woodrow's body was found.

"So there's our link between the two deaths," she said.

Vaughn nodded. "The area where Karst died is remote. We're probably not going to find any actual witnesses to the murder."

"We're not sure Juno was killed at that location," Davie said. "Why was he out there in the middle of nowhere, and why did he stop along that particular stretch of highway? What happened to the car?"

"I asked the civilian employee. She said Alden Brink had somebody from the rental agency pick up the car at impound. The woman said it was a mess. She was sure the front seat, carpet, and side window all had to be replaced. I'm guessing since TidePool paid for Karst's cremation, their insurance company also paid for repairs to his rental car."

Davie sat up straight in her chair, as she focused on Vaughn's words. "The side window?"

"Yeah, I guess the shot blew it out."

She put her elbows on the table and leaned toward her partner. "But nobody analyzed the direction of the flying glass."

"If you mean, did anybody check to see if the gun was fired from inside or outside of the car, the answer is no, but I asked the sheriff to send us all his photos."

17

DAVIE LEFT VAUGHN AT the restaurant and returned to the station. She was disappointed to see that Cormack hadn't responded to the letter she'd sent the day before. While she waited to hear from him, she continued her efforts to locate Dag Lunds, the fourth man in Zeke's band of brothers.

Woodrow's ex-wife had told her one of his three friends was from somewhere in the South. That was Karst, whose obituary confirmed he came from Georgia. Another was a Midwesterner. The fourth was from Oregon. The Midwest encompassed a lot of territory but Oregon was manageable. For the next few hours, Davie searched every database at her disposal, including out-of-state vehicle, firearms, and drivers license registrations, arrest warrants, criminal history, and data from the National Crime Information Center, specifically targeting Oregon. Lunds's name was unusual, so she couldn't understand why it didn't come up in any search she attempted. It appeared the guy was living off the grid.

Frustrated from so many dead ends, she walked toward the vending machine in the hallway near the kit room to buy some water. The drinking fountain wasn't an option. The city claimed the water was safe to drink, but until they vouched for the ancient pipes that carried it into the building, she'd stick with bottled.

Everything was quiet in the station except for the sound of her coins jangling down the slot of the vending machine. Davie thought about the four men who had served and sacrificed for their country for so many years and the toll it had taken on their personal lives—Zeke Woodrow, divorced, and Juno Karst with no close family to even take possession of his remains. She wondered if Dag Lunds also had an angry ex-wife.

Davie punched in the vending machine code and watched as an arm grabbed the water bottle. She remembered listening to Lynda Morrow's tortured memories about Zeke's absence, caring for their child alone, and her ex's emotional remoteness. Those issues weren't limited to military families. Plenty of cops had marriages that fell apart because of irregular work hours and the stress of the job. Spencer Hall was one of them. Her father was another.

The bottle thudded into the tray. She grabbed it and returned to her desk to continue her search. After another fifteen minutes online, she stumbled across a site of archived Oregon State marriage and divorce records from 1965 and after. The listings were by county, so she had to search each one. It seemed to take forever but when she finally got to the Washington County file, she found a divorce decree for Dag and Christina Lunds that had been finalized in 2010. Unlike her ex-husband, Christina Lunds was easy to find. Within minutes Davie had the woman's telephone number and an address in the city of Beaverton.

She called Christina from her desk phone, not expecting to reach the woman on the first try. To her surprise, Christina answered.

Davie introduced herself before firing off the first question. "I see you two are divorced, but are you still in touch with Dag?"

"Not often, but yes. We have a son together, so we've stayed on friendly terms for his sake. Is anything wrong?"

Davie cradled the receiver against her shoulder as she twisted off the cap on the water bottle. "I need to ask him a few questions about a homicide case I'm working."

Christina's tone now sounded curious. "You think it was somebody Dag knew? Who is it?"

Davie didn't want to tell her about Juno Karst. That wasn't her case and she didn't want to alarm the woman more than necessary, especially since the cause of Karst's death was still just a theory. "His name is Zeke Woodrow."

Christina's sharp intake of air was audible. Then words started spilling out. "Zeke? Oh my god, that's horrible. He was like family. Dag will be devastated. What happened?" Her voice was husky, like she was fighting back emotions. "Would you like me to break the news to Dag? He was a mess after the first Gulf War—PTSD. I'm concerned how he'll react."

Davie preferred to tell Lunds about Zeke's death to judge his reaction firsthand, because until he was cleared, he was a suspect. On the other hand, if Lunds was innocent, the humane thing to do was let Christina handle it. "You can but I still need to speak with him."

Christina must have found a tissue nearby because she blew her nose. "Before I call, maybe you could just give me a little more information."

"I'm sorry. I can't discuss the details of an open case."

"Of course, Detective," she said. "Dag lives in a condo in California, in San Pedro. But you should call before you go there. He travels a lot on business and may not be home."

"Are there any other places he hangs out, like at a bar or gym?"

"He's not the gym type. As for bars, he prefers to drink at home. There's another place you might check. We used to own a cabin in Kern County by the Kings River. It was his retreat from the world. When we divorced, I moved back to Oregon but he kept the cabin. I'm not sure if he still uses it, but if he's there, the cell service is iffy. And as I said, he travels a lot, so if he's in a place where reception isn't great, you'll have to leave a message. He'll call you when he can."

Davie wrote down Dag Lunds's contact information in her notebook. San Pedro was only twenty-five miles from the station so going there to interview him wouldn't be a problem. If she and Vaughn had to drive to a cabin in Kern County, however, it would be a major time commitment. She hoped Lunds would be available to meet her at the station.

"Does Lynda know about Zeke?" Christina's tone seemed tentative.

"Zeke Woodrow's ex? Yes, she knows."

"How did she take it?" She didn't wait for Davie's response. "Not exactly devastated, I'd guess. Such a shame she's still so angry. Will there be a service for Zeke? I'd like to be there."

Davie didn't know, but the mention of a funeral made his death seem real in a new way. "I suggest you check with his daughter."

Davie ended the call and put the water bottle to her temple. It was still cool but it didn't relieve the pounding in her head or her sense of loss. She punched in Lunds's cell number.

He didn't answer so she left a message asking him to contact her as soon as possible. She wrote a report summarizing her conversation with Christina Lunds and filed it in the Murder Book.

Davie stayed at her desk for hours, waiting for a callback that never came. It was late. She was tired and on edge. She had followed all leads, at least for now, so she would go home for a few hours to get some sleep. She locked her desk, grabbed her purse, and headed toward her Camaro.

"Davie?"

She turned to see Jason Vaughn jogging across the parking lot toward her. "Where have you been? I thought you went home already."

"I had to go out for a while," he said. "Personal stuff. Going home?"

She fished in her purse for the car keys. "Yeah, I'm going to crash for a couple of hours then come back and start over again."

He smiled. "The cot room is open. Perez just rolled out of the sack. He worked a double shift so I'm sure he had a shower a couple of days ago, at least."

"I'd rather sleep in the Jetta," she said.

"That ride is a breeding ground for drug-resistant hooker bacteria. Your chances of survival are better in the cot room. At least the bugs are cop bugs."

Vaughn accused her of being a germophobe. She wasn't, but in police work it was wise to be cautious about what you touched, especially in the Jetta. The car was a junker used by Vice detectives for undercover assignments and was the butt of a lot of jokes at the station.

"You're probably right." She turned and walked toward her car. "See you tomorrow."

"Davie," he said, matching her stride. "You want to go out for a drink? Some teambuilding. A glass of wine. We can talk about the case or what's happening in our lives or whatever."

She opened her mouth to say no, but his expression seemed so earnest. "Okay. One drink. Then I have to go home and get some sleep."

"How about that place in Malibu you like? Near the beach."

The beach was a place of refuge for her, but Malibu was too far away. "Let's go to the Lucky Duck. It's close by."

He stared at her, as if uncertain how to respond. "Your dad's place?"

"It's a nickname, Jason. He's not a real bear."

He rolled his eyes. "I know that. You've just never taken me there before."

"Meet me in the Duck's parking lot in ten minutes," she said. "I promise not to mention the *B* word again tonight. I'll just call him Dad."

Bear must have oiled the bar's front door hinges so they wouldn't creak, because the only thing she heard as she walked into the bar was the low murmur of voices and the crack of a stick against a billiard ball. The place smelled of popcorn and beer. For luck, she touched the sign at the entrance: WAS A WOMAN WHO LED ME DOWN THE ROAD TO DRINK. I NEVER WROTE TO THANK HER.

Bear nodded when he saw Davie. She introduced him to Vaughn before settling at the only table available, which was located toward the back of the bar near the restrooms. Hearing toilets flush all night was a small price to pay for privacy. It didn't take long for PJ to saunter over with two glasses of ice water. Tonight she was dressed in a tight aqua jumpsuit, a holdover from the 1980s.

She set a piece of paper in front of Davie and tapped it with her blood-red acrylic fingernail. It wasn't a menu. The Duck didn't serve real food. It was an Avon price list. PJ sold makeup on the side and was always trying to get Davie to buy the latest products. She had on occasion, just to keep the peace, but PJ's heavy face paint created the wrong sort of testimonial.

PJ patted her bouffant blonde hairdo, which had always reminded Davie of a Jetson's space helmet. "Hey, sweetie. What can I get for you and your hunky beau?"

PJ could be sharp-tongued when the situation called for it, but she could also turn on the charm. Most customers loved her. At the moment, that didn't include Davie. "He's my partner, not my boyfriend."

"My bad, sweetie."

Vaughn swept his hand toward Davie in a grand gesture. "You first, *dear*."

"Don't encourage her," Davie whispered. She planned on returning to work in a few hours, so she decided to forego alcohol. "Club soda on the rocks with a squeeze."

PJ never wrote down an order. Her memory was legend. "The usual for Davie. What about you, honey?" she said to Vaughn.

"MGD. No glass."

She looked toward the bar. "We might be out of Miller. You got a second choice?"

"Anything but lite."

After PJ left to get the drinks, Vaughn leaned on the table with his hands clasped in front of him. "Your dad seems like a nice guy."

Davie studied his expression. "You sound surprised."

"No, not at all." He hesitated before speaking again. "I saw you talking to Spencer Hall at the station."

Davie brushed condensation from the water glass. "I was congratulating him on the bust."

"Is that a good idea? He might think you're still interested."

"His desk is fifteen feet from mine. I can't avoid talking to him. Don't worry, I'm totally focused on our case."

Vaughn leaned back and crossed his arms. "Do you ever think about anything but the job?"

Davie stared at the Avon price list to avoid her partner's scrutiny. "What kind of a question is that? Of course I do." She gestured toward the brochure. "Don't you see me thinking about eyeliner?"

"It just seems like you live and breathe work. I don't feel that way. I want to have a social life, maybe find somebody, get married, have a couple kids."

Davie was taken aback as she paused to consider his comment. "As long as we've known each other, Jason, I've never seen you date the same woman longer than six months. You seem happy enough. And by the way, police work and family aren't mutually exclusive."

PJ delivered their drinks and a bowl of popcorn. She observed Davie and then Vaughn. Whatever she saw in their expressions made her decide to leave them alone.

Vaughn stared at the popcorn with a skeptical expression. "Maybe I need to mix things up, do something different."

His words alarmed her. She'd known her share of cops who couldn't take the stress. The smart ones got out before the department forced them out, but that didn't apply to her partner. Jason had always used his trademark humor—sometime inappropriately—to get through his day. He didn't seem to be joking at the moment. He seemed conflicted.

"Mix it up how?" she said. "Personally or professionally?"

He laid a single popcorn kernel onto his tongue. "I'm not sure yet. Just tossing around a few ideas."

A woman on her way to the restroom bumped against their table, sloshing club soda from Davie's glass. Vaughn saw the rivulet flowing toward his suit pants and caught it with a napkin.

"What's wrong, Jason? Is there a problem? What can I do?"

"Nothing right now."

"You can't leave the division. You'd miss me too much." Davie knew that would make him smile and it did.

"You're right. You were a training nightmare. I wasn't sure I'd ever survive."

They talked for a while longer. Davie filled him in on her grandmother's trip to Ojai. Vaughn confessed that his mother was pressuring him to learn Italian for a planned family vacation to visit her relatives in Milan. Half an hour later the beer bottle was empty. He checked his watch. "I have to go. See you tomorrow." He rose from the chair and walked toward the door, leaving her to nurse her club soda alone.

Davie wasn't sure what had just happened. She and Vaughn had gone out for drinks numerous times before. This time was different. Something was off. The only thing that lowered her blood pressure was her belief that Jason would have told her if he was leaving Homicide or Pacific.

Bear must have been watching them, because as soon as Vaughn left, he came out from behind the bar and slipped into the vacant chair. "Your partner seems like a decent guy. Why haven't you brought him in before?"

Davie swirled the melting ice cubes in her glass. "I know him from the academy, but we've only been working together for a few months."

"It would make me happier if next time you brought a date—but not a cop. Or if you decide to date a cop, pick somebody from another division ... or another agency. Better yet, don't date a cop."

She leaned back and crossed her arms. "Bear, I'm thirty-one. You don't get to organize my social life."

He jabbed his index finger at her to emphasize his point. "I'm your father. That privilege never expires."

The same woman staggered out of the restroom and careened past the table. Davie noticed she had a piece of toilet paper stuck to her shoe.

Bear frowned as he used his hand as a fender. "By the way, what did you do about that cat?"

The cat.

18

DAVIE RACED HOME AND bolted through the door of the guest-house. She jogged into her bedroom, threw open the door to the bathroom, and got slammed by a wave of toxic air. Hootch's food bowl was empty, his cat box was full, and he'd splashed water from his bowl all over the tile floor. He'd also pulled a bath towel from the rack and was curled up in a ball, eying her with distrust.

She cleaned the box, but when she bent down to pet him, he bolted through the door and disappeared into the living room. She was too exhausted to chase after him now. After cleaning the bathroom, she moved the food and water bowls into the kitchen and re-settled the cat box near the front door. If Hootch got hungry enough, he'd find the bowl. She just hoped he'd find the box.

The poor little guy had been marooned alone in the bathroom for hours and she was overwhelmed with guilt. She'd have to do better by him. After her shower she dropped into bed and counted to one hundred at least six times, until she eventually drifted off. At some point during the night, Davie heard rumbling in her ear. She opened one eye and found Hootch curled up next to her, purring. Too groggy to shoo him away, she fell back into a restless sleep.

The next morning the cat was gone from the bed. When she stumbled into the kitchen for coffee, she found him sitting on the counter near the sink, looking out the window at a squirrel leaping between branches of a sycamore tree.

She didn't have time to think about finding him a permanent home at the moment, so he'd have to stay for at least another day. After a thorough search of the cottage, she found no damage to any of the rugs or furniture. Pangs of conscience kept her from locking him in the bathroom again. This time she left him out to explore the house. Her place was small. What could go wrong?

As she walked out the door for work, she heard a scratching sound, like mice in the attic. But when she turned to look, it was only Hootch batting a paperclip across the hardwood floor like a star forward on a kitty soccer team.

———————

When Davie arrived at her desk in the squad room, the message button on her phone was flashing. Harlan Cormack had called. He didn't mention anything about Alden Brink, only that he'd picked up her letter that morning at his mailbox and wanted to know more about Zeke Woodrow's death. He left no telephone number but she found it anyway, in the phone's call history. She pressed the numbers on the keypad and waited.

A man answered, "Yo," in a voice that was craggy and hoarse.

"Mr. Cormack. It's Detective Richards from the Los Angeles Police Department."

"Yeah. I got your letter. How'd Zeke die?"

She opened her notebook and jotted down the date and time of the call. "He was shot. His body was found at LAX. But I'm afraid that's not all. Juno Karst was also found dead several days ago on the side of a highway in Nevada. The local sheriff ruled it a suicide."

"Juno would never kill himself. It's not in his nature." His tone was low and stripped of emotion.

She heard the static of the dispatcher broadcasting a 459 Burglary and plugged her ear to block the sound. "My partner and I are doing everything in our power to solve this case, but we need your help. Can you come to the station for an interview?"

"My back's screwed up from a motorcycle accident. I can hardly walk. Sitting isn't much easier. I can't drive to L.A. for a thirty-minute chat, even for Zeke." There was another long silence. "Look, I don't like talking on the phone. I'll answer your questions, but you'll have to drive out my way."

The chair hinges creaked as she leaned back. "Be glad to. What's your address?"

"There's no address. It's in the Mojave Desert, so you'll need a full tank of gas. Use a civilian car, nothing that calls attention to itself. I don't want the neighbors knowing my business." He gave her directions. "I'll leave the gate unlocked for you."

The conversation went dead.

She found Vaughn sitting at a circular table in the second-floor lunchroom, watching a morning news program and drinking coffee. She cleared the table of newspapers and food containers and threw them in the trash before sitting in the chair across from him. The door to the deck was open and a crisp breeze cooled the room. She filled him in on her chat with Cormack and told him she'd already signed out the keys to a car.

"You want to go *now?*" he said. "It'll take at least three hours to get there."

"Cormack may be the key to solving this case, Jason. And he's willing to talk. I don't want to wait for him to change his mind."

He picked up the remote and clicked off the TV. "I can't leave now. I've been subpoenaed for court this morning on an old Autos case from back in the day. Can't it wait until tomorrow?"

"I don't think that's a good idea. I'll just go alone."

"No way, Davie. You don't know shit about Cormack. He could have killed both Zeke and Juno."

"I doubt that. Brink said TidePool let him go because of a motorcycle accident. Cormack told me on the phone he was disabled and couldn't drive to L.A. The person who killed Zeke and Juno had to be mobile. If it makes you feel better, I'll run it by Giordano. Let him know the plan. He'll have to notify the Bureau anyway."

"Wait till tomorrow."

She grinned. "Are you worried I'll solve the case without you?"

Vaughn's fingers fussed with his silk pocket square. "Don't flatter yourself. I'm just worried you'll take the only decent ride in the lot and I'll get stuck with the germ-mobile."

"Don't worry," she said as she headed toward the door. "I'm taking the Jetta. Maybe the desert heat will kill some of the bacteria."

The Jetta had carried some questionable cargo, but she was confident it satisfied Cormack's request for a ride that didn't call attention to itself. Just to be safe, she slipped a bottle of hand sanitizer into her pocket. Before getting into the car, she squeezed some gel onto a tissue and swabbed the steering wheel and the gearshift. Then she filled the car with gas at the pump adjacent to Pacific's garage.

Gray smog shrouded the San Gabriel Mountains as Davie left Los Angeles. She reached Giordano on her cell just as he was due at a meeting with the captain. He peppered her with questions about Cormack but finally told her he'd notify the Detective Bureau downtown that she was leaving the county and cautioned her to keep in frequent contact with her partner. Her handheld radio wouldn't work that far away from the station, but she brought it along anyway. She had her cell, but didn't know how strong the reception would be. Adequate, she guessed, at least for a while.

She drove east on the 10 Freeway before transitioning onto the 15. She hadn't been out that way since she was eleven and her father took her to Las Vegas with a bunch of his cop friends and their kids. On the long drive, he'd given her a history lecture about Route 66. He called it "The Mother Road" because it had been the main thoroughfare between Chicago and Los Angeles and a major route for migrants escaping the dustbowl of the 1930s.

Bear had always been the fun parent. That trip was no exception. It had been a blast, even though her mother was furious with Bear and his friends when she found out they'd left the children unsupervised in the swimming pool while the adults drank in the bar. Neither Bear nor Davie understood the problem. It was daytime and she wasn't alone. Besides, she knew how to swim. It was much later when she realized her parents' marriage had been falling apart even then.

Harlan Cormack had told her he lived in a red trailer in the Mohave Desert, so she left the 15 for the I-40 near Barstow. Civilization disappeared as she drove farther into the low brush. The dry expanse of land seemed as wide as the ocean and reminded Davie how little of the West was inhabited or even habitable.

Just past Ludlow, a few derelict buildings broke the long expanse of nothing—the shell of a garage, a house, a gas station, and a series of small cottages that had once offered travelers a reprieve from the long straight road and the unrelenting heat.

Traffic was sparse. An eerie solitude surrounded her as she raced down the open road past those broken-down buildings. If she hadn't been monitoring the mileage, she would have missed the turnoff. It wasn't marked but it had to be the correct road, so she made a right turn.

The tires of the Jetta kicked up a rooster tail of dust and gravel that could be seen for miles in the flat terrain. She kept driving but didn't see Cormack's place. In the distance was a rusted-out trailer but it was silver, not red. As she got closer, she noticed a crude sign on what looked like a flap cut from a cardboard box that read TATTOO STUDIO. She felt a flicker of concern. Before she drove farther into the desert, she had to know if she was going in the right direction.

The hot wind burned her eyes as she pulled off the road. She got out of the car and made her way to a wizened old man sitting in a lawn chair under the shade of a tattered awning. He wore a black do-rag and a mask of suspicion. Nearby, a burro munched hay. Davie wondered why the man was living in a rusted-out trailer on some forgotten road. Maybe he'd lost his business to the Interstate and survived by selling tattoos to the occasional passerby.

"I'm looking for Harlan Cormack's place. He lives somewhere around here. Red trailer? Am I on the right road?"

The man's eyes narrowed in suspicion. "You must not have an invitation or you wouldn't be asking."

She pulled back her jacket so he could see the badge hanging from her belt and the gun in its holster. "You know Mr. Cormack?"

The dust cloud had reached the trailer and was hovering over them. Davie shielded her eyes from the gritty air and studied the man's guarded expression.

"Did I say I knew him?" he said.

"But you know where he lives, right?"

"I've seen his place."

"How far away is it?"

He wiped sweat from his brow with the back of his hand. "Couple of miles."

"Can you give me directions?"

The man squinted against the sun. "Maybe we can talk about it while I ink you a tattoo. It'll only cost you eighty-five an hour. You'd pay four hundred in Vegas. If you don't believe me, call and see for yourself." He held out a handheld device that looked like it came from a Smithsonian display of vintage telephones.

"What is that?"

"Satellite phone. Got it at a swap meet a couple of months ago. There's no cell towers out in the desert and sometimes a man needs to make a call."

She withdrew the twenty-dollar bill she always carried behind the plastic ID pocket hanging around her neck and held it up so he could see the denomination. "I'm not into tattoos. Will this cover the cost of a map?"

His eyes were intense as he grabbed the twenty from her hand. From under his chair he pulled out a walking stick. "I'll show you how to find the trailer, but the desert is unforgiving. Maybe you should give me the name of your next of kin in case you don't come back."

Davie smiled. He didn't.

The man leaned over and used the stick to draw a map in the dirt. She thanked him and returned to the car. For the second time that day, the Jetta created a dust trail that could be seen for miles.

19

HARLAN CORMACK'S RED TRAILER was located in a godforsaken area pimpled with brush, Joshua trees, and a cluster of boulders. A barbed wire fence surrounded the place. A sign hung from the metal gate that read: PRIVATE PROPERTY NO TRESPASSING.

There was no room to park along the narrow road so she put the car in reverse and backed up until she reached a turnout a short distance away. She turned on her cell to text her partner but as the old man had warned, there was no service. Her radio was also inoperable. She left the car and went by foot toward Cormack's trailer as the sun blazed overhead.

A padlock hung from the chain-link gate. Cormack had left it unlocked, as promised. There was a pickup truck parked near the trailer, so she assumed he was home. As she walked past the pickup, she peered inside. There were a few tools in the bed, but the cabin was empty. She made her way toward the trailer's front door.

A wooden platform with three steps led to the entrance. With her hand hovering near her .45, Davie climbed the risers and knocked, making sure she was positioned to the side of the door in case of trouble.

"Mr. Cormack, it's Detective Richards. We spoke on the phone earlier today."

In the distance Davie heard the howl of a coyote. No response came from inside the trailer. Maybe he'd just dozed off. She'd come all this way to ask him about Zeke Woodrow, and she wasn't leaving until she'd had that conversation. She knocked a couple more times.

"Mr. Cormack. Are you in there?"

No answer.

She leaned over the wood railing and peered into the window. The kitchen sink was full of dirty dishes. From inside the trailer she saw a flickering TV but heard no sound. An opened bottle of beer sat on a tray in front of the couch. But there was no sign of Cormack. Tension needled her neck as she turned the knob. The door swung open.

"Mr. Cormack."

She drew her Smith & Wesson and crept toward the back of the trailer, where she found a bathroom and a bedroom. Both were empty, so she returned to the porch and closed the door. The old man had warned her there were no cell towers out here, but she needed to call Cormack, so she holstered her gun and pulled out her phone again. Still no service.

She swept her gaze across the landscape in all directions until she came to a rusty oil barrel near an outcropping of rocks about a hundred feet away. There was likely no garbage pickup out here; maybe Cormack used it to burn his trash. There was something blue next to the barrel. It looked like clothing, a sweatshirt perhaps. She again drew her weapon from its holster, eyeing the surrounding terrain, looking for movement or a flicker of light reflected off a watch or eyeglasses. Spotting nothing out of order, she returned her focus to the swatch of blue.

As Davie inched closer to the barrel, she inhaled the odor of ash and decay. That's when she saw the body of a man sprawled on the ground, still holding a plastic bag full of garbage. She stared at the bullet wound in his head. Time, blood, and gore had made his features unrecognizable, but she knew without a doubt he was one of the young men in Lynda Morrow's old photograph.

She checked for a pulse but it was only a formality. His body was cool to the touch. The blood on his wound had already congealed and rigor mortis was beginning to set in. Harlan Cormack had likely been dead for at least a couple of hours, maybe since not long after they'd spoken on the phone.

Davie put her palm on her chest, hoping to contain the pounding of her heart. Waves of guilt pummeled her until she felt as if she were drowning. She should have saved Harlan Cormack's life but she had done the opposite.

She stumbled toward the gate, dropped to her knees, and vomited. She stayed slumped over the dirt for a long time. Finally, she wiped her mouth and ran toward the road. By the time she reached the Jetta, her lungs burned from the dust. She felt wasted and fragile as she slipped the key into the ignition and sped toward the tattoo artist's trailer and his satellite phone. When she got there, she called 911. Then she called her partner.

20

SLOWLY, METHODICALLY, SHE TOLD her partner the story, stripping away feelings from facts just as she had been taught to do, grateful that Vaughn wasn't around to see how the retelling of finding Cormack's body had pierced the protective shell she'd worked so hard to build.

When she ended the call with her partner she called Dag Lunds for a second time because there was a strong possibility he might be the next name on the killer's hit list. If so, she had to warn him. He didn't answer the call and once again she was forced to leave a message, this one more urgent than the last.

Davie stood stiff and mute as she watched the San Bernardino County Sheriff's Homicide team process the crime scene. Once the investigator had taken her statement and she was no longer needed, she somehow managed to fall into the Jetta and drive back to Los Angeles. It wasn't until the early morning hours of Thursday that she pulled into the station parking lot, too drained to venture into the squad room or check her desk for messages. She abandoned the department car, dragged her exhausted body into the Camaro, and drove home.

Once she arrived at her guesthouse, she looked for Hootch. He didn't come when she called him and she wasn't up for an all-out search. The furniture showed no evidence of damage. After his bowls were filled with food and water, she showered and tried to sleep, but her mind churned, replaying every move she'd made before finding Cormack's body, obsessing about every detail she had gotten wrong and every missed cue—analyzing, questioning, wondering what more she could have done to save Cormack's life. For hours she thrashed in her bed, tangled in the sheets, counting and recounting to one hundred. Nothing quieted her mind. For the first time, she regretted not accepting the shrink's offer of sleeping pills.

As a last resort she got out of bed, put on her swimsuit and a heavy sweater, and jogged to Alex Camden's swimming pool. The night air was cool and steam from the eighty-degree water rose like a mist in a creepy horror film. No one was home so the late-night splashing would go unnoticed. She dropped her sweater on a nearby chaise longue and slipped into the shallow end of the pool. It was rare to see stars in Los Angeles, but this night the marine layer had also obscured the moon. She shivered in the dark night, trying but failing to purge the feel of Harlan Cormack's cold skin on her fingers.

Lynda Morrow's old photo had caught all four men in the middle of a laugh, somebody telling one of their trademark corny jokes, she guessed. They all seemed so happy and carefree. Davie wondered what had happened to them in the years following that picture.

Three men, murdered. Who had wanted them dead? And what of the fourth man? Where was he? Was he dead or alive? Victim or murderer? She swam toward the deep end of the pool, back and forth until her arms and legs felt rubbery. The cold night air shocked her body as she crawled out of the pool. Throwing on her sweater didn't stop the trembling. Her bare feet slapped against the flagstone path as she made her way back to the warmth of her cottage. Hootch was perched on the countertop near the sink, no doubt waiting for the small brown bird that had been delivering twigs to a nest it was building in the eaves of the house. It was dark now and Davie suspected the bird had retired for the evening.

Her hair was still damp when her head hit the pillow, thinking about Dag Lunds and how she could never truly rest until she'd found him.

She didn't remember falling asleep, but sometime in the early morning hours of Thursday she was awaken by the jarring sound of a ringing telephone. It was her partner and he sounded stressed.

"You okay, Davie? Why didn't you call to let me know you got back from the desert okay?"

She untangled her legs from the sheets and sat on the edge of the bed. "Sorry."

Vaughn's tone was brittle. "I thought about the case for hours after you called. Three people connected to TidePool killed in the last few days. We're talking about related murders in multiple jurisdictions. The Captain is going to make us turn the case over to RHD."

Robbery Homicide was an elite unit housed at police headquarters in downtown L.A. and considered the crème de la crème of department assignments. It consisted of five sections, one of them being the Homicide Special, which investigated high-profile murders, serial killers, and cases in multiple jurisdictions, among others. When a case grew too complex for divisional detectives, it was usually reassigned to RHD.

Davie bolted to her feet. "Giordano won't let that happen."

"He'll let it happen because he has to. RHD has resources we don't have. They can coordinate with other law enforcement agencies, like the FBI, or the Army's Criminal Investigation Division, or Battlestar Galactica, if it floats their boat."

Davie wrapped the sheet around her body and went to the kitchen with the phone cradled against her shoulder. Hootch was sitting in his usual spot by the window near the sink, watching that squirrel performing a Flying Wallendas routine on the branches of the sycamore.

"I'm not ready to let it go yet, Jason. There are a few more—"

"Forget it, Davie. If the Captain says the case goes downtown, there's nothing we can do about it."

Davie let the sheet drop to the floor as she opened the cupboard in search of coffee. "Zeke Woodrow is the only homicide in our division. The rest aren't even in L.A. County. Karst was killed in Nevada, Cormack in San Bernardino County. I think they're linked, but we need to question Dag Lunds. He might be able to connect the dots for us. Once we interview him, I'll put all our notes in the Murder Book. Giordano can review what we have. If he thinks it's necessary, he can ask the Captain to send the case downtown. I just need another day or so. It'll be fine. Trust me."

"You can't keep Cormack's murder from Giordano."

"I'd never do that." Davie opened the bag of coffee, but there was only a half-teaspoon of grounds at the bottom. That wouldn't pack enough punch to bother with, so she threw it in the trash. "I'll talk to him as soon as I get to the station," she continued. "Then I'll follow up on a few more leads and put my notes in order."

"When are you coming in?"

She checked the clock on the microwave—6:10 a.m. "I'm out of coffee."

"Get your butt in here. I'll make a fresh pot."

"I'll be there in twenty minutes."

The squirrel was taunting the cat with its acrobatics. Hootch's tail slapped against the tile in annoyance. He wanted to be outside, doing what cats do, she supposed. It was time to find someone who could make those inside-cat/outside-cat decisions. One thing Davie knew for sure—allowing Hootch to settle into her house would only make his transition to a permanent home more difficult for both of them.

She didn't have time to make the bed, but she dragged the sheet back into the bedroom and threw it on the mattress. Only one of her black polyester pantsuits remained hanging in the closet. The other two were in the laundry basket because she hadn't had time to wash them. *Tonight*, she thought.

She corralled her hair into a knot, anchored by a stretchy band. From his perch near the window, Hootch stared at her with his hooded green eyes, as if he knew she was plotting against him. Her shoulders slumped at the thought of this new responsibility. It would have been better to place the cat with the shelter when she'd had the chance.

Davie had promised Shannon she'd find a good home for the cat but wasn't at all sure that would happen anytime soon. Before she left the house, she phoned Dr. Dimetri's clinic to ask if they could keep Hootch for a couple of days. They told her the facility wasn't set up for long-term boarding of healthy animals and explained that even if they were able to take him, he'd spend all his time alone in a cage with little human interaction. If Hootch had to be alone, he was better off at the cottage. To err on the side of caution, she would buy a scratch post as soon as she had a free moment.

The squirrel was gone. Hootch tracked her movements until she opened the front door to leave. Over her shoulder, she saw him open his mouth in a silent meow.

21

WHEN DAVIE DROVE INTO the station's parking lot, Jason Vaughn was waiting for her outside near the back door. He looked hyped-up with adrenaline as he handed her the cup of coffee he'd promised.

She drank and waited for the caffeine to stimulate her central nervous system. "Why are you out here?"

"An arrestee got sick in the hall outside the jail. Smells like hell in there. Let's go for a walk until somebody cleans it up."

Davie followed him toward the Centinela Avenue gate near the tree where several engraved rocks were placed on the ground, each bearing the name of a Pacific officer who had been killed in the line of duty.

The coffee made her feel more alert. "What's up?"

"I just heard from Christina Lunds. She couldn't find your number so she called the front desk. They transferred the call to me. She wanted you to know she contacted her ex about Zeke. He freaked out—her words, not mine. He wants to talk to us."

"Where is he?"

"At his cabin in Kern County. He stopped by a convenience store for supplies. They have Wi-Fi, so he got your messages and the one from his ex. He called her first because he thought she might be calling about his son."

"Did she give you directions to his cabin?"

"Yup." He held up a set of car keys. "I just filled the tank."

"What about RHD?"

"I told Giordano we were going to interview Lunds. Let's get his statement, file everything in the Murder Book like you said, and then if the Captain wants to send it downtown, I'm on board." He gave her the thumbs-up sign. "What do you say?"

She was disappointed at the thought of possibly abandoning Zeke's case but forced out a reply. "Sounds like a plan."

Three and a half hours later, Davie transitioned onto Highway 180 near Fresno and aimed the car toward the Sequoia & Kings Canyon National Park. The narrow mountain road hugged a meandering river through a steep, tree-lined canyon that looked like it had been carved during the last ice age. Brush struggled for purchase in the rocky terrain.

Vaughn hadn't said much during the trip. He seemed to be deep in thought and she didn't want to interrupt his meditation.

"It's pretty out here," he said, finally.

Out the window she saw clouds, puffy white and gray against a brilliant blue sky. In the distance was a snow-capped peak, one of the Sierra Nevada Mountains.

Davie glanced at her partner. "Maybe you should buy a place up here."

"Nah. Too far out for me. I'm a city boy."

She nodded and kept driving.

A couple of miles later, he said, "Davie, I've been meaning to ask you something."

The melancholy tenor of his tone made her feel apprehensive. "O-kay." She stretched out the two syllables like saltwater taffy.

"I'm thinking about putting in for a transfer."

She slowly turned her head and stared at him. "Out of Homicide?"

"Out of Pacific," he said. "To the Mounted Platoon."

She paused to process his words and then laughed because he had to be joking. The Mounted Unit was part of the elite Metro Division and included thirty-five officers and around forty horses that were assigned to crowd control and demonstrations. It sounded like a great gig for somebody, but she wasn't sure it was right for her partner.

"Jason, do you even know how to ride a horse?"

"I've been taking lessons," he said, his tone defensive. "This woman I know—"

"You mean this woman I'm *dating*—"

"You're wrong, Davie. She's my mom's age. I've known her since I was a kid. A couple of months ago, she invited my parents and me out to her ranch for lunch. She put me on a horse and it was so cool. Since then I've been riding with her every chance I get."

She tried to catch his eye but he was staring out the window, refusing to look at her. "Homicide to horses? Sounds like an odd career choice, Jason."

He whipped around and glared at her. "Look, I get you think it's weird but I like the idea."

Davie tensed. She thought about The Limit and wondered if her partner had reached it. In all the time she'd known him he'd always seemed calm, almost casual about life and work. Now she wondered if that had been a cover for how he felt when he was alone at night with his thoughts and memories of all the dead bodies he'd seen.

She softened her tone. "I'm sorry for laughing, Jason. It's just you've never mentioned horses before." Then she realized he might

136

have been trying to tell her about his plans that night at the Lucky Duck. "Maybe I wasn't picking up the right signals."

He shrugged and looked at the map. "Chill. It's no big deal."

That's exactly what she would have said to avoid talking about her feelings. She decided not to settle for that anymore. "Look, Jason. I didn't mean to shut you down. If the Mounted Unit sounds good, then apply for the transfer. I'll miss you, but you deserve to be happy."

He didn't speak for the next few miles until they rolled into the parking lot of a small convenience store.

"I'm not sure how much farther it is to Lunds's cabin," she said. "Let's fill the tank and buy some water."

Vaughn nodded and stepped out of the car. He stretched his back and tilted his face toward the sun, breathing in the fresh mountain air. "I'm going to find the can. Get me a Diet Coke and some Cheez-Its. I'll pay you back."

There were no other cars in the parking lot or at the pump. After filling the gas tank, Davie made her way inside the store. A card table held a sampling of potholders, pottery wind chimes, and casserole dishes with quilted covers. All looked homemade and all were for sale.

She grabbed a bottle of water from a cold case and a Diet Coke for her partner, then searched the junk food aisle for Cheez-Its. No luck finding them. If it was orange and chemically infused that her partner wanted, he'd have to settle for Cheetos.

As she walked toward the counter, she bumped her head on a wind chime similar to the one on the table. The tinkling conjured a woman in her sixties with a gray ponytail, round horn-rimmed glasses, and a steel-rod posture.

"Can I help you?"

Davie set the junk food on the counter. "How much for these?"

The woman looked at the items. "The Donner Party survived on more food than that. Did I mention this is the only store for fifty miles?"

Davie didn't object to contributing to the local economy, so she reached for two homemade oatmeal-raisin cookies wrapped in wax paper, sitting on the counter. "I'll take these, too." She hoped the cookies didn't end up being the best part of the day.

The woman pointed to the casserole dish, covered with a red quilted fabric and accented with tiny yellow flowers. "Sweet, isn't it? We're raising money for our volunteer fire department. Twenty bucks. Hard to find a bargain like that anymore. The cover's handmade."

Davie couldn't remember ever going to a potluck. Did people do that anymore? Helping firefighters was a good cause, though, *if* she wasn't being conned. Even if she was, it was only twenty bucks.

Davie reached into her purse for some cash and brushed against her Smith & Wesson nesting in the gun pocket. "Sold."

The woman totaled the items. "If you want a bag, it'll cost you twenty cents. That okay?" She didn't wait for Davie's reply. "It's none of my business but I hope you're with somebody, because it's not safe for a little thing like you to be out here by herself."

Davie bristled at the "little thing" reference. "You worried about four-legged or two-legged trouble?"

"You're out in the middle of nowhere, honey. You have to be ready for anything. I have some all-purpose knives on the shelf over there. They're expensive but people don't think about how much it costs when they're facing down an emergency."

Davie rolled her eyes. "How much?"

"Thirty-eight ninety-five," she said, picking one off the shelf. "I recommend the Leatherman. It has a couple of blades, a scissor, screwdriver, wire cutter, and whatnot. Comes with a genuine leather case."

Davie put the money back in her purse and rummaged around for her credit card. "You trying to make some kind of sales quota?"

She chuckled. "You'll thank me later."

Davie didn't need a knife. Maybe she'd give it to her partner as a goodbye gift. The tool folded into a slim profile and would easily fit into a pocket of a designer suit—or a saddle. The clerk packed everything in a paper bag and gave Davie directions to the forest service road that led to Dag Lunds's cabin.

When Vaughn saw what was in the bag, he chuckled. "A casserole dish? Do you even know how to cook?"

"I got you Cheetos and cookies. Stop complaining."

He continued rummaging inside the bag. "What's with the Leatherman?"

"It's for you—protection in case we run into bears."

"Not funny, Davie. They're dangerous animals, you know."

He unwrapped one of the cookies as she pulled the car onto the highway under low billowy clouds.

22

DAVIE MANEUVERED THE CAR over a series of access roads until she came to a narrow unpaved driveway. About a quarter mile farther was a modest log cabin surrounded by pine, sycamore, willow, and oak trees. Four teak rocking chairs graced the wraparound deck. A Harley-Davidson Lowrider leaned on its kickstand in the clearing in front of the house.

Davie rolled the car to a stop and looked at her partner. "You think this is it?"

"Looks like how his ex described the place. She didn't mention the Harley but he doesn't have to tell her everything." As Davie reached to open the door, he grabbed her arm. "Just a reminder, we have to be careful about Lunds. He might be our killer."

"Agreed," she said. "He's a suspect until he's not."

A brisk breeze chilled her face as she slid out of the car, grabbed her purse, and slung it over her shoulder. Her boots crunched over the uneven ground as they walked toward the cabin past a cardboard box that had been shoved under the deck. It held numerous liquor bottles.

All empty. She remembered Christina telling her Lunds didn't go to bars because he liked to drink at home. Davie wondered how long it had taken him to consume all that booze.

Vaughn tipped an imaginary glass to his lips. "Looks like old Dag has an intimate relationship with John Barleycorn."

"Or he uses the alcohol to clean bear wounds."

Vaughn humored her with a chuckle but scanned the terrain nonetheless.

Before Davie reached the front door, she heard a man's voice: "I'm over here."

The sound startled her. Her heart pounded as she turned to see a square-jawed man with rugged features standing in the shadows at the side of the cabin.

He was Zeke Woodrow's contemporary, so he had to be in his sixties, but he looked as fit as a twenty-year-old. His hair was gray and cut short. The thermal long-sleeved shirt he wore was tight enough to define the taut muscles of his arms and chest. She guessed his worn denim jeans didn't look that way because of some manufacturing process. A day's growth of beard was the only thing that kept him from looking like a model on an AARP recruitment poster.

Vaughn squinted against the sun. "You must have heard us drive up."

Dag Lunds walked toward Davie and extended his hand. Close up, she saw that his face was weathered from the sun, his expression somber. "I've got a motion detector. Knew you were here as soon as you turned off the main road."

His handshake was warm but firm. Since neither of them knew much about his state of mind, Vaughn hung back, watching. Lunds noticed and didn't repeat the hand-shaking courtesy with her partner. Instead, he gestured for them to follow him toward the back of the house. They passed two Adirondack chairs sitting on a weedy, rock-strewn clearing and continued down a small slope to the edge of the river. Lunds stopped next to an upside-down wood canoe that was resting on two sawhorses. An array of tools and paint supplies were laid out on a nearby rock.

He pointed toward several large boulders littering the bank. "Have a seat."

Davie picked a flat spot on one of the rocks and set her purse on the ground. Vaughn remained standing a few feet away.

The river was swollen with fast-moving white water from an early spring runoff. The roar threatened to drown out their conversation, though it didn't appear there was anyone within miles who could hear them even if they shouted. On the opposite bank was a dense area of trees and brush growing in the shadow of a steep rock outcropping. To Davie, the scene formed a picturesque tableau—a perfect place to go when the real world became too real.

Lunds picked up a square of sandpaper, folded it onto a block, and ran it along the underside of the boat. "Can I get you anything to drink? Coffee? Water?"

"We've come a long way to talk to you," Vaughn said in a tone that was crisp and professional.

Davie noted her partner's guarded expression and changed direction. "We know Christina told you about Zeke Woodrow's murder, but she didn't know that Juno Karst and Harlan Cormack are also dead."

Lunds flinched at the sound of their names. His eyes squinted into slits and something dark and dangerous past over his face, like a steel door closing off any vestige of emotion or compassion. She'd seen that sort of look hundreds of times on the faces of fellow cops. She felt a chill because she had a similar steel door that closed every time she put on her badge. The shrink had told her there was a price to pay for stoicism. Maybe he was right.

"How?" Lunds said.

"They were all killed within the last week," she said. "Each shot in the head with a single bullet. We think their deaths are related and we're worried you may be in danger, too. We need to know about any common enemies you had or anything you did together that might have given somebody a reason to target you."

He resumed sanding, but his jaw twitched with tension. "What do you want to know?"

"Everything," Vaughn said.

Lunds glanced at her partner and then returned his gaze to her. "The four of us have been together since Vietnam. That covers a lot of time."

"Just start from the beginning," she said.

He laid his hand reverently on the canoe and closed his eyes, like he was summoning memories he'd prefer to forget. "I met Zeke and the others not long after I got to basic training in Fort Benning. We were all in the same infantry unit. After basic, the four of us signed up for Ranger school. Training was intense. When we finished, about a hundred of us left for Alaska and then on to Vietnam. When we landed, they loaded our flak jackets, M-16s, and M50 machine guns onto school buses with bars on the windows and drove us through small villages to our base. We were there for about six weeks."

He pulled a chip brush from his back pocket and swept the sanding dust from the canoe's hull. A ray of sun had muscled through the cloud cover. The light illuminated particles from the wood that floated around his head like a halo. Davie didn't speak because she didn't want to interrupt his story with formal interview questions. Not just yet.

Lunds left the silence hanging in the air before he went on. "The local women would sleep with you for a pack of cigarettes. People listened to Jimi Hendrix and smoked opium joints—OJs—that kept you stoned all night. They cut holes in cardboard boxes and blew smoke inside to bump up the effect. There were other narcotics. Some guys took them all, and why not? They made you feel invincible."

"Did you use drugs?" Vaughn said.

Lunds met her partner's stare. "I came from a family of straight-laced Swedes. All four of us had similar backgrounds. We smoked some weed, but once we went into the jungle, the war got real. We quit smoking dope because once you got outside the wire, you had to stay alert if you wanted to stay alive."

Davie leaned forward and rested her elbows on her knees. "Outside the wire?"

"Once we left the safety of base camp."

His story was interesting but Davie wasn't sure what all this had to do with Zeke Woodrow's murder. Still, she wanted to keep him talking. "So all four of you stayed together?"

Lunds's brow furrowed with tension as he worked the sanding block. The sound reminded Davie of a brush sweeping across a snare drum. "We saw things we couldn't unsee, knew things we could never talk about. We thought and worked with one mind. That made us closer to each other than you can imagine. The Army liked that bond and the secrecy, so they kept us together."

"How long were you in Vietnam?" she said.

"Until the war ended. Back then you could only extend your deployment for six months. After that, they forced you to see a shrink before you went back. Some guys never wanted to go home. They loved the drugs and the women and the killing. *We* did our jobs because we loved our country, the Army, and each other—and not particularly in that order."

Davie's leg was tingling from sitting on the rock. She shifted her position to relieve the stress. "Zeke's ex-wife told us he was addicted to Dexadrine when he got home."

144

Lunds picked up a rag, doused it with alcohol, and proceeded to wipe down the hull of the canoe. "We were all addicted to some degree. The Army passed it out like candy—enough to keep you awake until you came home upright or in a body bag. I preferred the French version—Maxitone Forte. I bought it on the street. My pockets were full of it, one hundred milligrams of dextroamphetamine liquid. It came in a glass vial about half the size of your finger. I'd snap off the top and inject it. It kept me awake for twenty-four hours at a time. The right dose made me paranoid and that's exactly what I needed to stay alive. I stopped using when I found out guys were getting hepatitis C from the needles. Withdrawal was intense."

"What exactly did you do in Vietnam?" Vaughn said.

Lunds glanced at her partner. "You ever hear the term LRRPs?" He pronounced it *lurps*, which sounded like a dog drinking water. "It stands for long-range reconnaissance patrols. Early in the war, the enemy got good at ambushing our guys, so the Army dropped teams—four to six men—into the jungle and left them there to search for Viet Cong and destroy them. They stopped calling it that before we were in country, but they didn't stop sending men into the jungle. We were out there alone for months at a time without rules, support, or accountability. All we had was each other. Our training turned us into killing machines, but that mission turned us into animals. We learned to do whatever we had to do to stay alive."

The thought of being trapped in the jungle triggered feelings of unease. Davie made a mental list of the people she would trust on a mission like that and came up with Bear, Vaughn, Detective Giordano, Grammy, and maybe one or two others. It was ridiculous to think of an elderly woman crawling through the jungle with an M-16 slung over her back, but her grandmother had the heart of a warrior and Davie knew Grammy would sacrifice her life for her. Davie's breath caught, remembering the murder suspect she'd killed to save her grandmother's life.

She forced out the next question. "I know it was a long time ago, but did anything happen back then that might explain the murder of your friends?"

He appeared reflective, taking a few moments to catalog his memories. "A lot of bad things happened back then. Murder was common and casual. Some guys were afraid to go home. Afraid of what they might do to the people they loved."

Vaughn pushed rocks aside with his feet. "How did you all end up working for TidePool?"

Lunds popped the lid on a jar of varnish, poured some into a tuna can, and dipped the brush into the thick liquid. "A former Ranger started the company. He recruited me after I retired from the Army, and I brought in the others. We all still work there except for Harlan. They pushed him out after he got hurt. Claimed he was too broken to bother with."

Vaughn crossed his arms. "What did you do for TidePool?"

"At first we worked security details," he said, "for oil companies, embassies, corporate interests, anybody who needed protecting. Later, we trained younger people to do the physical work."

"Zeke came back from an assignment in Hong Kong a few days before he was killed," Davie said. "Something may have happened on that trip that upset him. Did he give you any hint what that might have been?"

"Zeke called me Sunday night, but I wasn't home. I tried to reach him but we never connected. His message wasn't specific. I'm not sure what he wanted."

Zeke had called his daughter Sunday as well, but he never showed up at her condo as promised. Davie was certain he had something important to tell the people he trusted but he was killed before he got the chance.

"How often did the four of you work together on TidePool assignments?" Vaughn said.

"Almost never. I can only remember two jobs—one was guarding the Turkish ambassador on a trip to L.A. The other was in Istanbul but the details are classified."

"Did anything happen on one of those assignments that might have made you a target?" Davie said.

Lunds loaded the brush again and swept more varnish across the hull of the boat. "Not that I recall."

"Zeke was wearing his Army dog tags when he died. Can you tell me why?"

Lunds hesitated before responding. "He always wore them before a mission."

"You mean during the war?" she said.

"Then, but after, too, including when he traveled for TidePool. He said feeling them on his chest helped him focus."

The hard rock pressing against her tailbone had now made her leg numb. She rose to her feet to get the kinks out and teetered on unsure footing.

Lunds noticed. "There are a couple of folding chairs by the back door. You'll probably be more comfortable sitting on one of them."

"I'll go look." Vaughn walked toward the cabin.

Davie watched him go and then turned toward the heavy brush lining the opposite bank. Just beyond the river's edge were jagged rock formations and a pebbly beach. A tree stump, splintered and dead, leaned out toward the river.

The rock had not only cut off her circulation but had also chilled her bones. She hobbled toward Lunds to banish the prickles shooting through her leg. She bent over the canoe, admiring his handiwork. "Looks like it has a history."

He met her gaze and held it. "Everything has a history."

True, she thought. Given enough time, she hoped to forget some of hers. "What kind of wood is it?"

"The gunwales are cherry but the planking is western red cedar."

The canoe's two cane seats resembled the material in the kitchen chairs from her grandparent's old house. "It looks vintage."

He scrutinized her, deciding if her interest was real or fake. "The canoe belonged to my father. It's been in storage since he died. Seemed like the right time to get it back in the water."

His expression softened. It made her wonder how long his father had been gone and if their relationship had been close. She was about to ask him another question when she glanced toward the opposite bank and saw a deer emerge from the trees and wander down to the water to drink. Lunds looked, too.

Questions about his father would have to wait. "You shouldn't stay here, Mr. Lunds. It may not be safe. The department has something called Emergency Witness Relocation Funds. We can put you up at a safe house."

He kept his focus on the deer. "I can handle myself."

"You mean like Zeke Woodrow handled himself?"

"Zeke didn't know he was a target. He let his guard down. Thanks to you, I don't have that problem."

She swept her hand over the smooth surface of the hull. "Just be careful."

Lunds was still staring at the opposite bank. She turned in time to see the deer prick its ears and bolt between the trees. She felt the hard jolt of Lunds's hand against her shoulder. Then she was airborne. Icy water slammed her body. Bullets pinged off the rock next to her head. They had to be coming from the opposite bank. Something splashed in the water next to her, dragging her under the surface toward the middle of the roiling rapids. Her hip hit a boulder. Pain radiated up her spine.

She opened her eyes to see Dag Lunds clenching her jacket in his right hand, towing her into deeper water. She thrashed in the turbulence, shouting a warning to Vaughn. But the effort sent water flooding into her mouth and down her throat. A moment later, she surfaced, choking. Lunds was next to her, pulling her onto her back. The faint smell of burnt gunpowder swept past her on the breeze and disappeared. All she could see in front of her was raging white foam. The sound was deafening.

"Don't try to swim," he shouted. "Keep your head and feet out of the water. Point your legs downstream."

She was a good swimmer but that skill was of no use to her now. The rapids swept her along. Her heavy clothes weighed her down like an anchor. She tried to pry off her boots but the move threatened her fragile position in the water. She had to stay afloat, keep her head and feet out of the water as Lunds had instructed. Her neck muscles felt weak. She sensed the water getting warmer but realized her body was growing numb from the cold.

Her partner must have heard the shots. He would run to investigate. If the shooter had a scope on his rifle, as she suspected, Vaughn would make an easy target. She imagined him lying on the ground, bleeding out on the dirt while she was powerless to help him.

23

DAVIE HAD LOST TRACK of how long she'd been struggling in the river. All she saw was thunderous white water crashing through the narrow canyon, waves peaking at least three to four feet high. A giant boulder loomed ahead, threatening to smash her to bits. Even if the water pushed her toward the bank, the steep rock outcroppings allowed no way to climb to shore. Farther downstream, the water tumbled forward and then disappeared—a waterfall.

A few yards ahead of her, she spotted Dag Lunds clinging to the roots of a tree where the river had worn away the soil. As she tumbled past him, he extended his arm. It took all the strength she could dredge to grab onto his wrist, while the force of the water tugged at her and weakened her grip. Her hand slipped. If she couldn't hold on, she was going to die.

As her fingers slowly slipped away, Davie felt Lunds's legs scissor around her torso. He grabbed her jacket with his free hand and pulled her toward him. When she got closer to the roots, she wrapped her arms around the nearest one, hoping the tree wouldn't break away from the shore and sweep them both away. Water trickled from her nose down her throat. She gagged. Coughed up water. Gasping for air, she held onto the roots because her life depended on it.

She didn't know how far downstream the rapids had taken her, but she heard no more gunshots. It was unlikely the sniper had been able to follow them through the dense brush and trees—at least not yet.

"I'm going to lift you up," Lunds shouted over the noise. "When I do, put your foot on my shoulder and grab on to anything on shore that's stable. Then pull yourself onto the bank."

"What about you?"

"One thing at a time."

Lunds reached under the water with his free hand as she raised her foot. She pushed against his hand as he boosted her out of the water far enough to latch onto another branch higher up on the tree. He supported her on his shoulders until she was able to crawl onto the bank.

Then she extended her hand to him, leveraging every ounce of her 104-pound body to anchor him as he groped his way to safety. If he hadn't been so fit, he'd still be in the water. Once he made it to shore, Davie collapsed on the ground, panting from exertion, too weary to move.

She saw Lunds scanning the far side of the riverbank. "We can't stay here. We have to find cover."

With his help, she struggled to her feet. Together, they stumbled toward a stand of trees and collapsed on the ground.

Lunds's voice sounded raw and raspy as he lay next to her. "Are you all right, Detective?"

Instinctively, she reached for her badge. It was gone. Swept away by the current. She felt gutted. That badge meant everything to her, not only because it bore her father's old detective number but also because she'd suffered and sacrificed to earn it. Her body trembled as she searched the inner pocket of her jacket and found her cell, wet and probably damaged beyond repair. Polyester might be water-resistant in the rain but not when submerged in a river.

She felt wasted and closed her eyes. "My phone's wet."

Lunds continued scanning the terrain. "It doesn't matter. There's no coverage out here anyway."

A moment later, he rolled over, grabbed her hand, and started rubbing it between his. She felt warm air blowing on her face.

She opened one eye and saw him looming over her. "What the hell are you doing?"

"We've got to find dry clothes. You have zero body fat and you're quaking ten on the Richter scale."

Her body *was* shivering from cold and stress. Davie tried to respond but she was so exhausted she could only muster a nod.

"I'm guessing my cabin's about a mile away," he continued, "but that's a long hike in wet clothes, especially since the air is getting colder. There's a convenience store just up the road. Let's go that way."

"I have to find my partner. See if he's okay."

"The store has a landline and Wi-Fi," he said. "You can call from there."

She struggled to her feet, glancing toward the river. Dry grass sloped to a bank lined with boulders and trees. Dead branches littered the stream. Foothills rose in the distance. *Such a beautiful scene*, she thought. But as she knew, things weren't always what they seemed.

Davie's hair had escaped its knot and now hung in red clumps around her shoulders. She peeled off her jacket in hopes the sun would dry her cotton shirt but it clung to her skin like plastic wrap. Lunds's shirt was made for river canoeing but it wasn't waterproof.

Her department ID was still in the plastic lanyard around her neck, along with the twenty-dollar bill she'd replenished after her encounter with the tattoo artist the day before. Her Smith & Wesson was in its gun pouch in her handbag at the cabin.

Davie's hip hurt. She wouldn't be running with Joss for a while. She hobbled behind Lunds on the trail for about ten minutes before the convenience store appeared. The bell over the door rang as she walked inside and saw the same pony-tailed clerk standing behind the counter. At first, the woman looked startled by Davie's appearance. Then she grinned.

"Can't say you're the first people I've seen in here who took a dip in the water, but most of them put on a swimming suit first."

"I need to use your phone." Davie fumbled for the water-soaked twenty-dollar bill behind her ID, wondering why her words sounded slurred. Her fingers were so stiff that the money slipped out of her grip and dropped to the floor.

The woman frowned as she surveyed Davie's condition. "Honey, you look like you need more than a chat on the telephone. You're shivering." She eyeballed Lunds. "Looks like hypothermia. I have an Ascotherm IMO 86 in the back room. That'll warm her up."

Davie bent down and tried two times before she snatched the bill. "I have to call my partner."

"Let's start with some dry clothes," Lunds said. "Do you sell anything besides T-shirts?"

The clerk motioned for them to follow her. "Come with me. Both of you. There's a lost-and-found box in the back room. Nothing fancy but at least you'll be dry."

"I'm fine," Lunds said.

"Yes, you are," she said with a wink, "but you're also wet. You need to change out of those clothes. Trust me on this. The river is running fast and cold this time of year. You have to be careful."

"I *need* to use the phone," Davie shouted. "My partner—"

"Dry clothes and then the phone," Lunds said to her. "Detective Vaughn wasn't in the line of fire. I'm guessing he's fine."

"Guessing?"

"You can't help him if you end up in the ER."

The clerk hustled them to a storage room and a cardboard box filled with an array of mismatched shoes, single socks, and ratty castoffs. Davie grabbed a wool sweater with a hole in the elbow and a pair of XL orange sweatpants that would be clownish on her small frame. There were no shoes in her size, not that she would wear somebody else's footwear in any event. She cringed as she thought of all those foot fungus pictures she saw on the Internet. Her boots were wearable, even if they were saturated with water.

Davie changed in the restroom at the back of the store. As she stripped off her soggy clothes, she gaped at her image in the mirror. Along with the cat scratches on her shoulder, there were now ugly new bruises blossoming on her back and thigh. That's when she realized how weak and achy she felt. Her wet clothes went into a plastic garbage bag the clerk had provided. She hung her head and dried her hair under the wall-mounted hand blower, standing there for longer than she needed until her body felt somewhat warmer.

She hurried back into the store and found Lunds looking over a rack of protein bars. He had changed into a pair of surfer shorts with a loud geometric design and a long-sleeved T-shirt with a logo for some heavy metal band.

"Phone," she said.

Lunds pointed toward the wall behind the counter. "The clerk is making coffee. She said cell coverage is bad in the canyon but you can use the landline. If your partner is looking for us along the river, he may not get the call."

Cell reception was the least of her worries. At this point, she didn't even know if her partner was alive to answer the call. Since her cell was waterlogged, Lunds told her to give his number to Vaughn in case she had to leave a message.

"Tell him we're going back to the cabin. We should be there soon."

Davie hurried to the telephone and pressed in her partner's cell number. Her heart sank when he didn't answer. "We've got to get back to the cabin. I have to make sure he's okay."

A moment later, the clerk appeared from the back room with two steaming cups of coffee in Styrofoam containers. Davie limped toward the door.

Lunds grabbed both cups. "Is there anybody who could give us a ride back to my place?."

"Sorry, honey. My husband drove the truck into Fresno. He won't be back for a couple of hours. I might be able to raise somebody from the volunteer fire department, but it would take them a while to get here."

Lunds met Davie at the door and handed her one of the coffees. "It'll be quicker to walk if you can make it. If your partner isn't there, it means he's probably safe and out looking for us. We can take the Harley and go looking for him, but it's better to wait until he contacts us. Regardless, we'll be more comfortable at my place."

Lunds was right. There was no benefit in staying at the store. "I can make it."

24

WITH HER COFFEE IN hand, Davie followed Lunds toward the cabin. They stayed off the main road in case the shooter was driving the route, looking for them. The caffeine and dry clothes, not to mention the exertion of walking, soon brought warmth back to her body, except for her feet, which squished inside her wet shoes. But her hip hurt and her limp grew worse.

"You think it's safe to go back to your place?" she said.

"I'd guess the shooter is gone, at least for now."

Lunds knew the woods, so she didn't worry when she became disoriented and hopelessly lost. He was a least a foot taller than she was but he kept measuring his stride so she wouldn't fall behind. Twenty minutes later, they reached the cabin. As soon as she saw the structure ahead of her, she limped toward the clearing where the detective car had been parked. It was gone. Despite Lunds's assurance that Vaughn was safe, she wasn't convinced the missing car was a good sign. She imagined Vaughn wounded, hanging on to life, struggling to drive himself to the nearest hospital.

She made her way toward the side of the house where her partner had gone in search of folding chairs. Her pulse throbbed as she canvassed a wide swathe of the grounds surrounding the cabin but found no trace of him or any blood trails that indicated he'd been wounded.

Lunds appeared behind her, offering his cell phone with an outstretched hand. "Call him again. Tell him where we are and to meet us here. And give me your phone. I'll see if I can make it work again."

Her fingers fumbled as she passed him her cell and then entered Vaughn's number on his keypad. She waited for an answer but was forced to leave another message.

Her purse was still sitting by the rock near the water's edge. Her Smith & Wesson was undisturbed in the gun pouch. Lunds had already cleared the cabin. There was nothing to do now but wait. She entered the cabin, pried off her boots, and collapsed on a couch in the living room. She thought about calling her boss, but the lack of cell reception wouldn't allow her to tell him the whole story without interruption, so she decided to wait until she located Vaughn.

Under the weight of stress and exhaustion, she drifted off to sleep. Sometime later, a ringing phone awakened her. She sat up, groggy, and looked around for the source of the noise. Lunds wasn't in the living room, but the call wasn't coming from his cell, because it was sitting silently on the table next to her.

She padded barefooted toward the kitchen, following the noise and found that the ringing was coming from a phone submerged in a bowl of rice on the counter. Her phone. The rice must have wicked enough water from the internal mechanism to make it function again. Davie was surprised that trick actually worked.

She answered in a voice that was hoarse with emotion.

"Where the hell are you?" Vaughn shouted. "I've been going crazy out here looking for you."

Her words spilled out in an uninterrupted volley. "I left a bunch of messages. Didn't you get them? Are you okay? We're fine. Never mind. We're at the cabin. Can you come and get us?"

He huffed air before answering. "I'll be right there."

As Davie ended the call, she heard footsteps. She looked up to see Lunds moving toward her. While she'd been sleeping, he'd changed out of the lost-and-found clothes and into a pair of jeans and a plaid lumberjack shirt. In his hand were a fleece jacket and a pair of thick socks.

"I assume that was your partner. Is he okay?"

She nodded. "He's on his way here."

His brow furrowed as he handed her the jacket and socks. "We can wait for him on the porch if you'd like, but you'll need these. And by the way, I put your clothes in the dryer. No guarantee what they'll look like when they come out."

Davie put on the jacket and socks and followed him to the porch, where the four teak rocking chairs waited. She again asked him who might have wanted all four former Rangers dead, but he didn't have a clue. After that they barely spoke—just sat and rocked—until fifteen minutes later when she saw the Crown Vic's tires throwing gravel and dust as it screeched into the clearing. Vaughn bolted out of the car and sprinted to the porch.

"You okay, Davie?" His expression changed from concern to disbelief as he paused to study her orange sweatpants. "What the hell are you wearing? You look like a traffic cone."

She leaned back in the rocker and looked at the breeze ruffling the treetops. "I was worried about you, too, Jason."

For the next fifteen minutes the three of them sat on the porch and debriefed. Vaughn told them he was at the side of the cabin when he heard the shots—at least a half dozen of them. He took cover and inched his way toward the river, but by the time he got there, she and Lunds were already in the water and the shooting had stopped.

"We need to go across the river," Davie said, "see if we can find any spent shell casings."

"You're joking, right?" Vaughn said, pointing to the distant hills. "That's a forest out there. Haven't you heard the expression 'finding a needle in a haystack'?"

"Nobody said it would be easy," she said, "but we have to try."

Lunds rose from the chair and walked around the side of the cabin toward the river. Davie and Vaughn followed and found him at the river's edge, staring across to the opposite bank.

"You shouldn't be standing in the open," she said. "The shooter might still be out there, watching."

Lunds pointed to a place midway up the mountain. "That's where I'd stand to take the shot. The rocks are jagged, but there's a narrow path that leads up to a ledge that's wide enough to lay prone. He could spread his arms to aim and get a clear shot at us. There's plenty of cover so nobody would spot him."

"Can you tell us how to get over there?" she said.

He turned to study her expression and then nodded. "I'll take you. I've hiked up that way dozens of times. It's not far from the road. Your partner said he heard at least six shots. If the shooter was a pro, he picked up any spent shell casings, but if he was in a hurry, he may have missed one or two."

Davie and Vaughn followed Lunds to the cabin. He disappeared down a hallway toward the back of the house and emerged minutes later carrying Davie's clothes.

"At least they're dry." He pointed toward the hallway. "You can change in the spare bedroom. It's the last door on the left. I tried to dry your boots with a pair of shoe warmers but they're still damp."

Davie found the bedroom and put on her black pantsuit. The boots were still oozing water, which made walking annoying but not difficult. She put the sweater and orange sweatpants into the plastic bag. Vaughn was waiting for her in the driver's seat of the detective car. She transferred the bag of borrowed clothes into the trunk. Lunds fired up the Harley and sped out of the clearing. Vaughn floored the Crown Vic and followed.

"Why are you keeping those ratty clothes?"

"I thought we could return them to the convenience store on the way out of town. Somebody else might need them."

"Who? A CalTrans flagger?"

Lunds led them across a bridge to the other side of the river. After about a mile or so, he stopped the motorcycle along a wide section of the shoulder and removed his helmet. Vaughn parked the car behind the Harley.

Lunds pointed up hill. "We'll go the rest of the way on foot."

Vaughn removed several evidence envelopes, a camera, and three sets of gloves from the Murder Kit in the trunk and brought up the rear as the three of them hiked into the woods.

They'd been climbing for about fifteen minutes when Lunds stopped abruptly. He pointed to the trail ahead. "The brush is trampled down. Somebody was here recently."

Vaughn scanned the area. "Could have been a hiker."

Davie turned and whispered, "Or a bear."

"Joke all you want," he whispered back. "I hear they pick off the little ones first. I figure you'd make a tasty hors d'oeurve."

Vaughn snapped photos of the broken twigs before continuing up the trail. When they reached the ledge, Davie turned and swept her gaze across the terrain. Lunds was right. From this vantage point the shooter had a clear shot across the river toward the cabin. The type of rifle he'd used was unknown, but the shells would likely be large enough to see. She glanced over her right shoulder and began to search.

After twenty minutes of beating through the dry brush, the arms of her jacket were filthy and snagged. Nettles had torn the skin on her hands and face. Added to the bruises on her thigh and back, her body felt broken along with her spirits.

She had found nothing and began to worry that the shooter had picked up the spent shells and taken them out of the area just as Lunds had speculated. Her energy was fading, so she lay on a fallen tree to rest, letting a ray of sun warm her face. She heard Vaughn in the distance, calling her name.

As she turned her head toward the sound of his voice, the sun bounced off a shiny object in the underbrush. She bolted to a sitting position and fixed her gaze on the spot of light near a hollowed-out log. Lying on the ground was a metal object, a large-caliber spent shell casing.

"Jason," she shouted. "Over here."

Branches snapped and the brush parted. "Find something?"

She pointed to the object.

Vaughn stared in disbelief. "Looks like the guy got careless." He pulled out an evidence envelope he'd brought from the car, slipped on latex gloves, and slid the casing inside. "When we get back to L.A., the firearms geeks can tell us what kind of gun he used."

"Where's Lunds?"

"I lost track of him. I guess he went up the trail to see if the shooter left anything up there."

Davie glanced uphill. "Let's go find him. Then we have to call Detective Giordano. Let him know what's happened."

25

DAVIE FOUND LUNDS HIGHER up on the trail, staring at the river below. She didn't want to startle him so she cleared her voice before speaking. "We found a shell casing."

He nodded as if he'd known she was there all along. "Some sort of military rifle, I'd guess."

"Probably, but we won't know for sure until we have the casing analyzed at the lab."

His body was rigid and his muscles taut. She reminded herself somebody had just tried to kill him. That had to be stressful, even for a former Army Ranger and especially for somebody who had once suffered from PTSD and recently lost his three best friends.

"If you show me the casing, I can probably tell you what caliber it is and maybe what kind of weapon it came from."

"Thanks," she said, "but it's already sealed in an evidence envelope. I'll have it analyzed as soon as we get back to L.A."

He didn't pursue the offer any further. In fact, he didn't speak at all during the hike down the hill. She and Vaughn followed the Harley back to the cabin and waited on the porch while Lunds went inside. A few minutes later, he returned, carrying a small black bag.

"You travel light," she said.

He locked the front door. "It's the only way."

"Where will you go?"

He strolled down the steps to the Harley and stowed his travel bag on the back. "I'll let you know when I get there. You have my cell. You can call if you need me."

Davie hovered near him as he put on his helmet. "Look, I live in a guesthouse behind a security gate and a seven-foot brick wall. You could camp out there for a night or two until we can arrange for a safe house. I'll bunk with my dad."

He threw his leg over the seat. Then he smiled, the first she'd seen from him. "Thanks, but I'm better off alone."

She understood his point of view. It's probably what she would have said under the same circumstances. Except, sometimes it was better to accept help and not play the hero. *Something to remember*, she thought. She stepped away from the bike. "Your call."

"Promise you'll let me be there for the takedown."

Under similar circumstances, she'd want to watch the arrest of a man who'd killed her three closest friends, but civilians weren't invited to the show, not even when they were former military. "I can't promise that."

Without responding, he fired up the motor and roared out of the clearing toward the main road. Once he was out of sight, Vaughn made a U-turn to drop off the clothes at the convenience store, and then headed toward L.A.

As soon as Davie got a cell signal, she put Giordano on speakerphone. Her boss must have sensed the emotion in her voice because he said, "You okay, kid?"

"Yeah," she said. "It's just cold up here, that's all. There are some new developments in the case you need to know about."

"Shoot," he said.

The word made her cringe. As they drove back to the station, she told Giordano everything that had happened in the past twenty-four hours, including the attempt on Dag Lunds's life.

"Jeez. I let you out of my sight for a few hours and—"

"We're fine," she said. "But we have two open homicide cases in different jurisdictions—Woodrow's in Pacific, Cormack's in San Bernardino County, and I believe a third, Juno Karst's in Nevada. Now there's a fourth felony, an attempted murder in Kern County. We didn't notify local law enforcement; it would have taken forever for them to respond to the scene."

"Don't worry," Giordano said. "I'll call them."

"The point is," Davie said, "all four of those men worked together for decades. I don't know if all their deaths are related to TidePool, but I believe all of them *are* related. When will Homicide Special want the case?"

"When you're ready to make an arrest," he grumbled.

Vaughn chuckled.

"You think I'm joking?" he said. "I'll run it by the Captain. Don't take it personally, but I'm guessing he'll be happy to send it downtown. It'll lower his homicide numbers at COMPSTAT."

Giordano was talking about the meetings held by the department's top brass to discuss crime statistics in each division. From what she'd heard, the recriminations for upticks were brutal.

"I hope you can talk him into keeping the investigation at Pacific," she said, "at least for a while. Jason and I have put this case together without any help. We've collected forensic evidence and interviewed witnesses. We can write all the search warrants we need and coordinate the service. If we want a surveillance team, we can request help from downtown."

"You two did a great job, kid, but RHD has fifteen dicks sitting on their asses doing freakin' nothing. Let them coordinate with the other cop shops and bring in the experts."

"But there are still leads we can—"

Giordano interrupted her midsentence. "Look, I know how you feel. It's tough when you've given your all on a case and then have to give it up. Like I said, you two have done a great job, but believe me, it's best for everybody that we do this right. I'll clear it with Maciver and the Captain and then call the other law enforcement agencies to let them know we're sending the case downtown. As soon as you get back to the station, write your three-fourteen and make sure all the information is in the Murder Book."

"Roger that," she said without enthusiasm and then ended the call.

Vaughn turned to look at her, assessing her mood. "Well, that sucks but I did warn you."

Davie's cheeks burned. Not only would Dag Lunds not be there when detectives made an arrest, she wouldn't be there, either. She felt a bond with Zeke Woodrow, as she did with all of the victims, but now somebody else would follow the case through to the end. Letting go was tough to accept.

It would take a while to write her final report. Maybe she'd find some overlooked evidence that would break the investigation wide open. If not, she hoped the anger she felt would eventually turn into the final stage of grief—acceptance.

———

By the time she and Vaughn got back to the squad room it was after five o'clock. Detective Giordano had already notified San Bernardino's

Homicide detectives and the Goldfield County Sheriff's office that the Woodrow case was being kicked downtown and that somebody from RHD would contact them. Based on information she and Vaughn had uncovered, Nevada told her boss they were reopening the Juno Karst investigation as a possible homicide.

Davie spent the next hour at her desk computer, reviewing the forensic evidence and witness statements, writing a summary of the crime and the follow-up investigation, and typing an official request that the case be transferred. The only thing left was for Detective Giordano to sign the report and get the Captain's approval.

Giordano wasn't at his desk when she printed the report, so she left the pages stacked in his in-basket and wandered outside to a median in the parking lot to get some fresh air. She sat at the picnic table and laid her head on her arms. She thought about the uncertainty of the coming days. Her boss might ask her to work a cold case or let her take a couple days off to nurse her physical and emotional wounds.

She still had on the same clothes that had survived the river, a hot dryer, and a trek though the underbrush in the mountains above Lunds's cabin. No one had commented on her appearance, but the snags on her jacket and pants and streaks of dirt imbedded in the polyester made her look like a hostage held by some third-world rebel army. Her body ached and the bruises were already turning vivid shades of purple and yellow.

She wasn't sure how long she'd been sitting there contemplating her next move—ten minutes, she guessed—before she saw her partner jogging across the pavement toward her.

He stopped at the table, only slightly out of breath. "Giordano wants to see us in Maciver's office."

Davie didn't want to go. "You can answer any questions they have."

"He wants to talk to both of us. Maybe he's going to give us a commendation."

Davie braced her hands on the picnic table and rose to her feet. "Lead the way."

When she and Vaughn got to Lt. Rich Maciver's glass office, Giordano was already there, sitting with his fingers laced together on the tabletop. Maciver looked thin-faced and earnest in his neat Class A uniform. Most detectives wore business attire in the squad room—what the department called soft clothes—but lieutenants like Maciver came from patrol and most had never worked as detectives. He looked younger than his actual years, which made him seem more college dormitory proctor than a cop clawing his way up the LAPD's chain of command.

Davie's 3.14 report lay on the table in front of the lieutenant, signed and stamped with RHD HANDLING. She had updated Zeke Woodrow's Murder Book in preparation for the transfer. It was also on the table.

"Everything is in order," she said. "I've also prepared a things-to-do list with possible interviews to conduct and search warrants to write—"

Maciver's brown eyes conveyed sympathy. "I hear the passion in your voice, Detective. This case means a lot you, doesn't it?"

In truth, all her cases meant a lot to her. Despite the grueling hours and the raw emotions, that sacred bond with the victims and their families was what drove all Homicide detectives to seek justice for the dead.

"Jason and I could have solved the case," she said, "given a little more time."

"We all agree." As Maciver spoke those words, he swept his gaze around the table to encompass everyone, an inclusive gesture that surprised her. "That's why you and your partner are going downtown. You'll be on loan to RHD for the rest of this DP, or as long as they need you."

Davie was stunned. She turned toward Vaughn to judge his reaction. He was grinning. He looked elated.

Giordano pushed back his chair. His face was flushed. "What the hell? You didn't tell me that."

Maciver's expression was impassive. "I didn't know until a few minutes ago, Frank. The Captain just got the request from RHD. They need Richards and Vaughn to help them run the case. Their detectives don't have time to play catch-up."

Giordano's hands balled into fists. "What about *my* time? They're taking half of my workforce."

"We have a serial killer on our hands. Your detectives know everything about the investigation. RHD needs that knowledge. I'm sorry, Frank. The case has to go downtown. Richards and Vaughn are going with it."

"And what happens if they don't arrest a suspect within this DP? Who's going to investigate homicides here?"

"You'll just have to manage with two detectives. You can step in and help if necessary."

"Fifteen effing detectives aren't enough for them?" Giordano said. "I'm trying to run my squad. I can't afford to lose these two. Maybe one of them but not both."

Davie thought of her partner's excitement when Maciver announced the news. At first that surprised her, until she remembered his comment about transferring to the Mounted Unit. Vaughn was restless and ready for a change now. Homicide Special wasn't horses, but maybe this was what he needed. Most detectives would die for an opportunity like this, but she liked working at Pacific and she liked working for Frank Giordano.

"Send my partner," she said to Maciver. "RHD doesn't need me. Jason knows as much about the case as I do. I'll stay here."

Maciver pushed the Murder Book toward Davie. "I don't think you understand, Detective. You're both going downtown. RHD made the request. There's nothing any of us can do to change that."

Giordano raked his hand through his thinning hair. "Wait and see. They'll use my peeps for grunt work and then take all the credit. Bunch of lazy prima donnas."

She understood Giordano's frustration. She felt it, too, but was powerless to change anything. If the LAPD brass ordered you to go, you went. With the Murder Book tucked under her arm, she followed Giordano toward the door.

Over his shoulder he said, "Make us proud, kid."

"Will do, boss."

At least she and Vaughn would stay partners for now. She thought of Dag Lunds and his band of brothers. He'd said they moved with one mind. That didn't describe her relationship with Jason Vaughn. They approached police work in different ways, but their commitment to each other and to solving murders was in perfect harmony. Maybe Vaughn would have the opportunity to stay at RHD. If so, she would be happy for him.

26

"I HAVE THIS CAT ..."

The shrink nodded in approval. "I'm encouraged by that news. Research shows comfort pets are instrumental to recovery for PTSD sufferers."

Comfort pet? Davie stared at the shrink's thin smile and thought about Hootch. She didn't know much about cats, but this one was standoffish and wary. That might be feline nature or maybe he was still adjusting to the loss of someone he trusted.

"He won't play with any of his toys," she said.

"Did you buy the toys so you could play with him or so he could entertain himself while you were gone?"

She thought about that before answering. "Somebody else bought them. Mostly, he prefers to bat a paperclip across the floor."

"Give him time. I imagine he'll come around." The shrink rested his elbows on the desk and studied her face. "You look more rested. Has your sleep improved?"

Davie wanted to laugh. She had counted for nearly an hour before falling into a black pit of sleep. She'd barely managed to drag herself to this seven a.m. appointment. "I never sleep all that much when I'm working a case." She considered leaving it at that but at the last minute added, "The counting helps quiet my mind ... sometimes, at least, enough to fall asleep."

He nodded and wrote something on his tablet. "I'm glad you tried the meditation exercises. They seem to have helped, wouldn't you say?"

"Why do you always make me restate the obvious?" she said. "I just told you they helped."

"I want to make sure I'm not misinterpreting your experience." He waited for a moment before adding, "What else is happening in your life?"

Her gaze swept the room and noted a cartoony-looking greeting card displayed next to a pile of books. It was past Valentine's Day and not yet Easter. April Fools? If so, she wondered who would send a card like that to his office. Maybe it was a thank-you from one of his patients.

Davie heard the shrink clear his throat and remembered he'd asked her a question. "I almost drowned." She told him about the attempt on Lunds's life, falling in the river, and how she'd felt those moments in the water would be her last.

"But you survived."

Davie thought about that for a moment. "The man who saved my life was a soldier. He told me things. Horrible things he saw and did to protect his friends and survive the war. At night when I'm alone in bed I sometimes close my eyes and think about how I killed two men to protect people I love, and I wonder why I'm still alive."

"People are sometimes called upon to make life-or-death decisions. You wouldn't be human if you didn't mourn the loss of life, even if it was a necessary part of the oath you took—to protect and to serve. Isn't that it? Your job now is to forgive yourself."

Davie squeezed her eyes shut. "It's hard."

"Sometimes it is." He looked at the wall clock. "Our time is up."

Davie collected her purse from the floor and prepared to leave. "See you next week?"

The shrink slipped his notes into a file folder and scribbled something on a piece of paper. "Actually, I'll be away for a couple of weeks. If you need to talk about anything, here's a number you can call. We'll set up another appointment when I get back."

She studied his expression for hints to his thoughts. "Why do I get the feeling you're brushing me off?"

He smiled. "*Feeling?* I'll take that as progress."

27

AN HOUR LATER DAVIE sat in an RHD conference room on the sixth floor of the Police Administration Building in downtown Los Angeles, wearing a clean suit she'd laundered the night before. The building's sharp angles and massive glass windows were a stark departure from the boxy shabbiness of the old Parker Center.

Before reporting for duty, she stopped by the personnel office to order a new detective badge to replace the one she'd lost in the river. They gave her a temporary and told her a badge with Bear's old number would have to be ordered from an outside vendor and it might take a couple of months to come in.

The setup at the Homicide Special Section, where she and Vaughn were temporarily on loan, was similar to Pacific's squad room with its workstations and desk computers, except everything was newer and shinier here. Plus there was a view from an actual window.

Sitting across from her at the table was Det. Reuben Quintero. She'd crossed paths with him on a previous homicide case when he was in

Commercial Crimes Division. Davie was surprised to find him here and even more surprised to learn he had been promoted to a D-3 supervisor and assigned as the lead Investigative Officer for the Woodrow case.

Quintero was all sinew and attitude, with short black hair, a wiry build, and nicotine-stained fingers from a chain-smoking habit. He encouraged everyone to call him Q, like he was some one-name celebrity—Adele, Bono, Cher, Prince, and Q. She refused to indulge his grandiosity and had always called him by his full name because she knew it annoyed him.

He leaned toward her and lowered his voice. His breath smelled of mint. "Look, Richards, let's make sure we're on the same page. My lieutenant expects you to tell me everything you know about this investigation the minute you know it. Understood?"

He was referring to a situation that happened a few months back, when he'd accused her of withholding evidence during a brief encounter as their two cases intersected. He'd blown the incident out of proportion and she'd told him so. That had annoyed him, too. She wasn't convinced Quintero had gotten over it, so a dose of caution was in order.

Davie placed Zeke Woodrow's Murder Book on the table in front of her. "If you don't trust me, you could have just taken my partner on loan. My boss would be happy to keep me at the division."

Quintero had an intense personality, but today he seemed more jittery than usual. "I know Giordano is pissed, but we're friends. I'll make it up to him. As for you, you're a cat-five hurricane, but you know your stuff and you know this case. You and your partner uncovered a shit storm here. I give you credit for that. Not everybody would have linked all these murders the way you did."

She leaned back in the chair and assessed his backhanded compliment. It seemed sincere. "Thanks. How'd you get back into RHD?"

Quintero grabbed the Murder Book and pulled it to his side of the table. "None of your damn business. Where's your partner?"

"Parking the car."

"Text him and tell him to get his ass up here. We have work to do."

Texting wasn't necessary because a moment later Vaughn sauntered into the room with a paper cup in his hand. Walking behind him was a man wearing a tie but no suit jacket. The sleeves of his white shirt were rolled up past his wrists. He was in his mid- to late thirties with broad shoulders and high cheekbones. His dark hair was streaked with gray at the temples and cut in a short spiky style. He acknowledged Quintero with a nod and slid his athletic body into a chair at the table. Davie waited for Quintero to introduce him, but that didn't happen.

Vaughn removed the lid on the cup, releasing steam and the scent of hot milk into the air—a latte, his drink of choice. Then he flashed a cocky grin. "Sorry I'm late. I had trouble finding a parking spot. I thought RHD big shots had valet."

"*We* do, smartass," Quintero said. "You hinterland dicks have to park on the street." He gave Vaughn a good-natured slap on the back and pointed to a chair. "Sit down. Tell me everything you know about this case and everything you don't know. Start with the easy stuff first."

The man turned toward Vaughn and extended his hand. "I'm Jon Striker. Q's D-2."

As he reached out to shake Vaughn's hand, Davie noticed a tattoo inked on the inside of his right forearm in blue cursive script, but all she could read was the letter *e* at the end of the word. Davie sensed the energy in the room shift as he turned his focus toward her with an intensity that made her uncomfortable.

"Davie Richards," she said. "Pacific Homicide."

He outranked her, so she studied his expression to determine if he was irritated that she hadn't walked over to shake his hand. His face

175

was impassive, but the wrinkles around his sapphire eyes hinted at mild amusement.

Vaughn settled into a chair at the table with his coffee. Davie shifted her focus to Quintero as he walked toward a nearby whiteboard and picked up a green marker. The day before, Davie had faxed him a case report, but she and Vaughn went over the details again as Quintero wrote each victim's name on the board, along with the date they died.

Quintero poised the marker over the whiteboard. "What about forensic evidence?"

Davie flipped to a report in the Murder Book but it wasn't necessary. She could almost quote it from memory. She told Quintero about the theft of Zeke's computer from his house in Santa Barbara and the blood sample collected by the local PD.

"We're still waiting for the results," she said.

Quintero studied the names on the whiteboard. "Karst was killed first in Nevada. As I recall, the report said a Glock 19 was left at the scene. What about the other murders?"

Vaughn leaned in. "We don't know what kind of gun killed Woodrow. There were no spent shell casings found at the scene and no weapon has been recovered. The bullet might be lodged in the victim's head, but there's a backlog at the morgue, so the autopsy hasn't been scheduled yet."

Davie felt Striker's attention drilling into her. "Did you find out what kind of gun was used in the Cormack murder?"

Davie was used to working with men, but at the moment there was an excess of testosterone in the room and the fumes were getting to her. She got up and walked toward the window, wishing she could open it to breathe the fresh air.

"The techs are still processing evidence," she said. "They'll call as soon as they know anything concrete."

Quintero drew an arrow from each victim's name to the type of weapon. The arrows leading to Woodrow and Cormack ended in a question mark. "What about the shell casings from Kern County?"

Vaughn pulled a rolled up piece of paper from his jacket pocket and spread it out on the table. "We stopped at the crime lab this morning before coming here. The casing is a 7.62x51mm NATO. They think it's from an M110 semi-automatic sniper rifle. The Army used them in Afghanistan until recently."

Quintero nodded and wrote *M110* next to Lunds's name. "How would the killer get access to an arsenal like that?"

Vaughn laid the report on top of the Murder Book, but before he could answer, Striker spoke in a low, steady voice. "Glocks are easy to find and you can buy M110s on the Internet, but they're expensive—over twenty grand. The shooter could have gotten all the firearms from a dealer or a private owner."

Davie stared at his full lips. They barely moved as he spoke, like he was some badass ventriloquist. She wondered how he knew that information. He'd likely read the report she'd faxed and perhaps done some checking on his own. If so, she was impressed.

Quintero held the marker between his index and middle finger like a cigarette. "What's next?"

Davie peered out the window at the downtown cityscape. There were tall buildings out there, but you couldn't prove that today. The tops were obscured by gray smog as opaque as Jon Striker's inner thoughts.

She reviewed Zeke's military service and his work for TidePool Security Consultants. Striker seemed to hang on her every word, but his expression still gave no clue what he was thinking. She had the feeling he was trying to figure out what made her tick. *Good luck with that*, she thought.

Davie shifted her gaze from Quintero to Vaughn, avoiding Striker. "Like my report says, about two weeks before the murder, TidePool sent Zeke Woodrow and Juno Karst to Hong Kong on a business trip. We think something may have happened there that triggered the killing spree."

There was a slight tremor in Quintero's hand as he poised the marker on the whiteboard, ready to write. "So, who was this client the victim went to see?"

"Guardian Advanced Technologies," Vaughn said. "They're a multinational defense contractor with offices all over the world, including a small office in Irvine."

Quintero set the marker in the whiteboard tray and turned to face Vaughn. "Irvine? Like in Orange County?"

Davie nodded. "It's a long shot but we could drive down to see if Guardian knew of any confrontation that occurred during that trip. If so, maybe they can tell us who was involved and what happened."

Quintero unwrapped a piece of gum he'd pulled from his pocket and shoved it into his mouth. "How could a shooter kill three former US Army Rangers all by himself and attempt to kill a fourth—unless he was a cop or military himself?"

"It's none of my business," Davie said, "but you seem jumpy—"

"You're right," he said, pointing a nicotine-stained finger at her. "It's none of your business. I stopped smoking. Two weeks ago. Can't you tell? That's why I'm in such a good mood. What else do you know? You think the shooter had help?"

Davie had never smoked but she'd heard plenty of people talk about the challenges of quitting cold turkey.

She walked back to the table but didn't sit. Standing gave her leverage. "Hard to say. If he acted alone, he covered a lot of territory in a short amount of time. He missed killing Lunds, but he may try again."

Striker had been quiet for a while but reentered the conversation at the mention of Lunds's name. "Where is he now?"

"I'm not sure," she said. "I offered him protection but he felt safer on his own. He gave me his cell number if we need to reach him."

Quintero rolled the marker between his palms as he paced. "Okay, so here's the plan. I'll send Striker and one of our other detectives to Irvine, see what Guardian has to say."

Davie leaned over the table and pulled the Murder Book toward her. "Jason and I know the case. It makes more sense to send us. We have only one shot at this interview. We can't afford to screw it up."

Quintero worked the gum until his jaw clicked. "You always have to drive, don't you, Richards?"

"It's better that way, especially if you want to get to where you're going."

Davie glanced at Striker to get his reaction. His hand was balled into a fist that covered his mouth. She could tell by the wrinkles around his eyes that he was hiding a smile. This assignment had just gotten a whole lot more interesting.

28

ORANGE COUNTY WAS KNOWN for conservative Republicans, pricy master-planned communities, and the happiest place on earth—Disneyland. If OC had a superstar, it was Newport Beach and that's where Davie and Vaughn were going.

Before they left headquarters, Davie had called Guardian and spoken to the company's Director of Human Resources. The woman agreed to contact her counterpart in Hong Kong to find out if the company had received any complaints about Zeke's Asia trip. She wasn't keen on speaking with LAPD detectives in person but finally agreed to meet them following a business lunch she'd scheduled at a yacht club.

Davie drove south on the 405 in heavy traffic. Vaughn was in the passenger seat checking emails on his cell. Angelenos calculated travel time in minutes rather than miles, but these days it was impossible to judge how the traffic would be flowing at any given time. If this jam didn't clear in the next few miles, she calculated it would take them an extra hour to get to their meeting.

Vaughn was stretched out in the passenger's seat with his head tilted back and his eyes fixed on the screen of his phone. The air conditioner wasn't working and the heat had coaxed out the odor of the menthol vapor rub he carried in his pocket.

Vaughn pressed buttons on his phone. "I'm bored. Let's turn on the siren."

"Not a good idea if we ever want to make D-2. What were you looking at?"

"Just checking to see if San Bernardino identified the gun in the Cormack murder," he said. "Nothing yet. We still have a lot of territory to cover. Those four guys worked together for over forty years. They could have made all sorts of enemies in that time. If we can't uncover a motive, how can we narrow our search?"

"Like we always do, by eliminating suspects until there's only one left."

Vaughn turned off the phone and slid it into his pocket. "What did you make of Striker?"

"Too early to say."

"He's not very talkative."

Davie cracked the window to let in some air. "He doesn't need to be Mr. Congeniality to help us clear this case."

Vaughn paused and then changed the subject. "If you subtract travel time, Zeke was only in Hong Kong for a week. What could have happened in seven days that triggered him to retire?"

"He was nearing that age. Shannon told us he'd been thinking about it for some time."

Vaughn's handheld radio blasted out a 602 call—Criminal Trespass. He lowered the volume. "Maybe Zeke uncovered some kind of illegal activity at Guardian. If so, he must have told Juno Karst. They were both there. Maybe that's why he was killed, too."

"That doesn't explain Harlan Cormack's death. He wasn't on that trip. He didn't even work for TidePool anymore. Dag Lunds wasn't in Hong Kong, either. In fact, he refused to travel in Asia."

Davie moved into the carpool lane and stepped on the gas. The car shot forward at a steady clip. "It's possible the killer knew or suspected that Zeke had told something to all three of his friends. Karst was killed shortly after he returned to the States. That tells me the shooter was under some sort of time pressure to kill them all before they passed along whatever they knew."

"The killer needed money and guns, and he had to locate all four men. That takes time to plan."

"TidePool may know more than they're telling us. After we hear what Guardian has to say, we'll talk to them again."

The Guardian HR director greeted them at the front door of the yacht club with a perfunctory smile that was pleasant but bland and noncommittal. She guided them to a conference room off the hallway that had a view of small sailboats stacked on racks. The woman already knew they were investigating a homicide, so Davie didn't waste time with small talk.

Davie opened her notebook and prepared to write. "Can you tell us who from your company was at that meeting with TidePool?"

"I didn't know so after you called, I sent an email to our Hong Kong Chief Financial Officer. Here's the response I got." She handed Davie the printed copy of an email that contained a list of names. The Guardian negotiating team included the CEO, two senior vice presidents, the CFO, and a couple of account executives.

None of the names were familiar to her, but they might be familiar to Dag Lunds. She handed the email to Vaughn to read. "Did your CFO mention anything about a conflict between Mr. Woodrow and any of your employees?"

"I wouldn't know about that, but I alerted him you might have questions. Hong Kong is a fifteen-hour time difference, so it's tomorrow afternoon there. He's standing by to speak with you."

The woman opened a teleconferencing program on her laptop. A moment later, a man's face appeared on the screen. He was Asian, early thirties, wore glasses, and spoke with a British accent. He told them TidePool's presentation had been routine. There were many details that still had to be hammered out before any contract was signed, but the meeting had been a positive step forward. He also stressed that TidePool was not the only company they were considering for their security needs.

"Did you speak with Mr. Woodrow during the time he was in Hong Kong?" Davie asked.

"Yes, of course, and Mr. Karst as well. We had several dinners together. I was born in London, but I have family here. The two men particularly enjoyed the ferry ride to Kowloon to a restaurant owned by my uncle."

"What was your impression of them?"

He pushed the glasses higher on his nose with his middle finger. "Their credentials were impeccable—former soldiers and honorable men. I was terribly sorry to learn they were dead."

Davie leaned toward the screen to better read his expression. "Was there anything that caused you concern?"

He hesitated. His frown indicated there *was* something but he seemed uncomfortable talking about it.

"Anything," she added, "even the smallest incident, could be important to our investigation."

He removed his glasses and wiped the lenses with a cloth. "I don't want to cause a fuss, but there *was* something that happened on the last day. I saw Mr. Woodrow and Mr. Karst standing by the limo waiting to leave for the airport. Mr. Woodrow was staring at me in a most aggressive way. It seemed so odd because I thought we'd built a rapport during our time together. I tried to think of anything I'd said that might have offended him, but there was nothing. His demeanor made me uncomfortable and perhaps a little frightened. I've never seen such hostility coming from a man's eyes. He looked like he would have killed me if given the chance."

Davie remembered Dag Lunds telling her the Army had turned them into killing machines and that murder during the Vietnam War had been frequent and casual. She wondered if Zeke had experienced some kind of flashback. "Had Mr. Woodrow ever confronted you before?"

"No. Never. That's why it was so alarming. It made my skin crawl."

"What happened next?"

The CFO put his glasses on. "I moved away, out of his line of sight. As I was leaving, I glanced over my shoulder. That's when I realized he hadn't been looking at me at all. He'd been glaring at another man who was standing behind me at the time."

"Was the man glaring back?" Vaughn asked.

"Yes, it appeared he was. He looked shocked."

Davie glanced at her partner, halfway expecting to hear a bolt of thunder from the revelation. "Did you know the man Mr. Woodrow was focused on?"

"It was Van Kuris. Our Director of Security."

Davie felt a tingling sensation in her neck. They had a name. Van Kuris. She just had to find out what had happened between those two men that had triggered Zeke's rage and possibly set the killings in motion.

"Did you see the two men speak to each other?"

"I went back to my office shortly after that, so if anything happened, I didn't see it."

"What can you tell me about Mr. Kuris?"

"I'm fairly new to the company, so I don't know much about his background, except I heard he's Canadian and I know he speaks fluent Mandarin."

"Can you describe him for me?"

"I'm not sure of his age, but older, I think. Someone told me he's about to retire. He looks fit. I've always assumed he had some sort of cosmetic surgery because his face and neck are quite taut for a man his age, and his skin looks a bit too smooth, if you know what I mean. I wondered if he was just vain, or if he was covering scars, possibly from some sort of accident."

"Did he ever talk about his past, like any military experience? Could be anything from Vietnam to the Middle East."

"Certainly he never discussed that with me. Did the Canadians even fight in the Vietnam War?"

"I'd like to speak with Mr. Kuris," she said. "Do you have his contact information?"

"Yes, of course, but he's out of the country at the moment—on emergency leave. I believe he went to visit a sick family member in Ottawa or some such place."

Vaughn had been quiet throughout the interview, but he perked up when he heard that. "When did he leave?"

"I don't know exactly but I'd guess a few days ago."

Everything was apparently going well until Zeke saw Van Kuris in the lobby of a Hong Kong hotel. What she didn't know was if Kuris was a phantom from Zeke's past, someone he wasn't expecting to see there, or if the beef was specific to that trip.

Dag had told her Zeke wore his dog tags whenever he went on assignment. Somebody removed one of those tags from his body as they did on the battlefield, which is why she thought the murders might be related to his military service. Canada didn't fight in Vietnam, but all four men had served in hotspots all over the world. Kuris may have encountered Zeke and his friends in other wars.

"Does Kuris have a Canadian passport?" Vaughn said.

The CFO shrugged. "He may have dual citizenship, but he definitely has a Hong Kong pass. He's a permanent resident here."

"Do you have a photo of him?"

"We don't publish photos of our executives for security reasons," he said, "but I can probably access one from our personnel files. If you give me your email address, I can send it to you."

"That would be helpful. For now I need a description."

The CFO rattled off Kuris's stats: height (5'9"), weight (175), nicknames (unknown), scars (unknown), other distinguishing marks (unknown). He also told them Kuris had a company credit card and gave them the number, but cautioned that his trip was personal and therefore he was not authorized to use it.

Davie looked at her partner. He shook his head. They had no further questions at the moment so they ended the interview and the HR Director closed the lid of her laptop.

Out in front of the yacht club, a woman leaned over the bow of a powerboat trying to catch the loop of a mooring line with a boat hook. She missed. The skipper powered the boat backward and then forward as the woman tried again. And failed again. The skipper was screaming at her from the fly bridge. The woman screamed back. She tried one more time and finally snagged the line. The incident reminded Davie how fast even small disagreements could escalate. Had some minor argument triggered the murder of three men, or was the motive due to ancient history?

29

DAVIE AND VAUGHN LEFT the yacht club but instead of walking to the car, Vaughn turned toward the beach. She welcomed the detour because they faced a tedious drive back to L.A. in a car without air conditioning, and they'd already been sitting inside for way too long.

Davie put on her sunglasses to shelter her eyes from the glare. "What do you think of the Van Kuris lead?"

Vaughn flipped his hand in a dismissive gesture. "We're supposed to believe Zeke gives this Kuris guy the stink eye and he kills three people as payback? Nobody saw them arguing. They didn't even speak to each other that we know of." Vaughn tapped his finger on Davie's glasses. "Maybe the sun was in Zeke's eyes and he was just squinting."

Walking had made Davie warm, so she stripped off her jacket and slung it across her arm. "Kuris was the director of security. You can't get a job like that without a background in law enforcement or the military. If he was in the military, he might have crossed paths with Zeke."

"The guy is from Canada. I know they're one of our allies, but it still seems farfetched."

"I know it does, but the day after his encounter with Zeke, Kuris requested an emergency leave to visit a sick relative in Ottawa. A few days after that, Juno Karst was killed in Nevada, Zeke in Los Angeles, and Harlan Cormack in San Bernardino County. Then a sniper tried to kill Dag Lunds."

"At the moment, there's no link between Kuris and the victims," he said. "Lunds wasn't in Hong Kong, and Cormack didn't even work for the company anymore. Zeke retired from the military three years ago. If that's what motivated the killings, somebody waited a long time for revenge. It makes more sense to focus on the two TidePool assignments the four of them worked together. You think RHD has the budget to send us to Istanbul? I love their rugs."

"I wouldn't bother renewing your passport just yet."

They turned right when they hit the sand, strolling along the sidewalk past upscale beach houses set on narrow lots. Newport's tony real estate stood in stark contrast to the quirky shops along the boardwalk of Pacific Division's Venice Beach. For all its warts, she preferred Venice.

"Maybe we're overanalyzing this," Vaughn said. "What if they picked a fight in a bar with a bunch of skinheads and the murders were payback."

"If it was something that recent, Lunds would have told us about it."

"Maybe he's not who we think he is. His ex-wife said he had PTSD. Something could have happened that made him snap. Maybe he killed Zeke and the others."

Davie grabbed her partner's arm and pulled him to a stop. "What are you saying? Somebody tried to kill him, too."

Vaughn turned toward her, his face a stone mask. "But they missed, didn't they? What's the likelihood of a guy with a sniper rifle not hitting his target? Lunds could have had an accomplice up on that ridge, somebody who also helped him pull off the other murders."

Davie flashed back to the image of Lunds sanding his father's canoe and calmly relating his war experiences. His affect had been flat as he talked about all that violence. She supposed he could have known the sniper was on that hillside. But the more plausible explanation was that he sensed trouble because of his Ranger training or his days as a LRRP in Vietnam. The deer bolted because he sensed the shooter and Lunds pushed Davie into the river to save both of them. If it had been a setup, he could have let her drown, but he didn't. He saved her life.

"You don't actually believe Lunds killed his friends, do you?"

"Probably not. I'm just reminding you not to lose your edge until we know all the facts." Vaughn checked his watch. "Let's go back to the car. The freeway is going to be jammed if we wait any longer."

Davie had spent the last ten years on the job judging people's characters. She'd gotten it wrong on occasion, but she couldn't imagine Dag Lunds killing three of his closest friends. Even so, Vaughn's theory was plausible and a good detective never closed her mind to possibilities.

"You drive," she said. "I'll call Lunds and ask him to meet us at Pacific. Ninety minutes should give us enough time to get back to L.A. and for Guardian to email the photo of Van Kuris. We'll show it to Lunds, see if he remembers the guy. Then we'll ask for his alibi for the time of all three murders."

30

DAVIE HAD ONLY BEEN gone from the Pacific squad room for a day, but it felt as if it had been forever. It was good to sit at her desk again. Giordano wasn't there and when she checked the log sheet, she saw that he and Detective Montes had been called out on a drive-by shooting, which meant they wouldn't be back for hours.

While Vaughn called Quintero to update him on what had happened in Newport Beach, Davie printed a color copy of Van Kuris's employee photo she'd received from Guardian's CFO. She was typing up her notes on the Newport interview when her phone rang. It was the front-desk officer letting her know Dag Lunds was in the lobby. She grabbed her notebook and found him leaning against the wall by the front door, staring at the ATM machine on the walkway outside. He must have sensed her approach because he turned to face her.

She was shocked by his appearance. His eyes looked red-rimmed and hollow, as if he hadn't slept for days. His skin was pale and gaunt. She recognized the signs of stress and lack of sleep.

Lunds flashed a rare smile. "You look dryer than the last time I saw you."

She smiled back and motioned for him to follow her into the squad room. "No more white water rafting for a while. How's the canoe coming along?"

"I haven't been back to the cabin. I'll probably head that way in the next day or so to put it back in storage."

She wondered if giving up on the restoration of his father's canoe was a sign of depression. "Maybe on the weekends—"

He cut her off. "It's a retirement project. I'm not there yet."

She wondered how he could continue his employment with Tide-Pool after what had happened to Zeke and the others, but maybe he loved the work or needed the money. Davie led Lunds into the detective's inner sanctum, where she found an empty interview room and gestured for him to sit. Vaughn lurked just outside the door but made no attempt to question Lunds.

The room was small. The table and chairs were mismatched and scarred. It was a good place to interrogate suspects because you didn't want them to be comfortable. Witnesses like Lunds just had to suffer through the indignities of the city's budget shortfalls. She reached out to close the door but he held up his hand to stop her.

"Don't ... please."

She noticed a film of sweat on his forehead and remembered how trapped she'd felt driving up the garage ramp at LAX. "Claustrophobia?"

He didn't answer, just looked away.

Christina had told them that Lunds came back from the Gulf War with PTSD. Davie wondered if he still had issues and if he was getting help for the symptoms. A wave of compassion washed over her as she thought about what he must have gone through. She'd met a lot of good people in her day, and she had a feeling Dag Lunds would be added to that list when this investigation was over.

She slid into a chair, opened her notebook, and placed the color photo of Van Kuris on the table in front of him. "Have you ever seen this man before? Maybe on one of those assignments you all worked together for TidePool?"

Lunds picked up the photo and studied it for a long time before returning it to the table. "I'm not sure. Who is he?"

"His name is Van Kuris. He's Guardian's Director of Security. As I mentioned before, when Zeke was in Hong Kong, a witness saw a nonverbal confrontation with Kuris in the lobby of the hotel. It might not mean anything, but we're following every possible lead."

"As I told you before, Zeke and I never worked together in Asia. He could have run into Kuris anywhere and at anytime. They might have had a history with each other, but it didn't involve me."

"Except somebody targeted all four of you. If it wasn't Kuris, who could it be?"

He paused a moment and then shook his head. "I don't know."

"Look again. Forget about his hair and clothes. He may have changed since you saw him last. Concentrate on his facial features."

Lunds picked up the photo again, studying it carefully. A moment later, he looked up at her. His facial muscles were taut with tension. "Do you have a computer I can use?"

"Why? Do you know him?"

"I'm not sure."

Davie got up. "Follow me."

She led him to her desk and pulled up a second chair for Lunds. Vaughn followed. Once she'd logged on to her computer and opened the Internet browser, she slid the keyboard toward him and watched as he accessed a website dedicated to Vietnam-era MIAs. He typed the name John Latham and waited. A photograph of a young soldier appeared on the screen. A caption identified him as a man who'd gone missing toward the end of the war.

Lunds looked gaunt and haunted as he rolled his chair back to give Davie a better look. She held the photo of Kuris next to the screen and allowed her focus to dart from one image to the other. There was no doubt the young soldier bore a strong resemblance to Kuris. They couldn't be father and son because the two men would be around the same age.

"Are you saying Van Kuris is really an MIA named John Latham?"

"No wonder Zeke was upset," Lunds said. "He was staring at a ghost."

Kuris wasn't part of the talks, but when Zeke saw him standing in the lobby of the hotel, he must have realized the guy looked familiar. The Guardian CFO believed Kuris had had cosmetic surgery. If so, his attempt to look younger might have made him easier for Zeke to recognize.

Davie's mind churned with all the unlikely scenarios that included several farfetched assumptions: that Zeke had known Latham in the US Army, that he knew he was MIA, that he ran into him in Hong Kong after almost fifty years, and that he recognized him despite all that time and the cosmetic surgeries.

"All of you knew Latham from the war?"

Lunds bolted to his feet, his breathing shallow. "I've got to get some air."

Davie wanted answers but knew they would come to her faster if she gave Lunds some space, so she led him outside to the picnic table on the parking lot median. Vaughn followed but hung back in the shade of a tree, watching.

Lunds didn't sit at first, just paced, obviously under duress. She waited patiently as he worked out whatever was troubling him. A moment later, he sat on the bench and rested his head in his hands.

She reached out to him but pulled back at the last second. It was unlike her to touch a witness, because she never knew how they might react. "Are you okay?"

"Not really."

"Tell me what happened."

When he finally spoke his voice was low and stripped of emotion. "The four of us were on patrol in the jungle, looking for the Viet Cong unit that was ambushing our troops. We heard small arms fire in the distance—a lot of it. We thought it was the enemy, so we ran toward the sound until we came to a village. The gunfire had stopped by then. We saw bodies. Everywhere. A US soldier was bent over a dead girl who looked about five years old. His eyes were bloodshot like he hadn't slept for days and he was laughing like a psycho. I could tell he was juiced up on some serious shit."

"John Latham?"

Lunds nodded. "He was a second lieutenant. He wasn't wearing his bars, but a lot of officers stripped them off their uniforms in case they got captured by the enemy."

"Did you find out what happened?"

"They'd just moved into the village. The little girl ran toward them with something in her hand. Everybody had seen things like that before. You couldn't tell who the enemy was. During our first week in Nam a young kid walked into a bar where some of the guys hung out. He pulled the pin on a grenade and blew up everybody in the place. So, when Latham saw that child, he started shooting. His men started firing, too. They didn't stop until they'd wiped out the whole village. The body count wasn't as bad as My Lai but it was bad—fifty people, mostly old men, women, and children."

Lunds pinched the bridge of his nose and closed his eyes. Davie held her breath and waited for him to continue. "I was looking for survivors when I heard someone screaming like a wounded animal. I ran toward the sound and saw Zeke kneeling next to that dead girl. That's when I noticed what was in her hand—a mango. All those people dead—because of a piece of fruit. Of all the horror we saw in all those wars, Zeke never stopped thinking about that little girl. I think that's why he was so protective of his own daughter."

A wave of anger and revulsion washed over Davie as she realized Van Kuris/John Latham was a war criminal. "So, what did you do?"

Lunds broke off a splinter of wood from the table and inspected its sharp point. "Zeke and Juno wrestled Latham to the ground and grabbed his weapon. He was pissed, to say the least. He threatened to shoot us for dereliction of duty, assaulting an officer, and just about anything else he could think to throw at us. He knew when we reported the massacre his life was over."

Vaughn stepped out of the shadows. "So, what *did* happen when you reported it? The Army must have investigated."

"There wasn't time to report it. We knew the gunfire would draw the enemy, so we left the dead where they lay and led the rest of the unit toward the nearest LZ. About two clicks outside the village, we ran into an ambush. The Viet Cong had us surrounded. We radioed for a gunship but in the chaos, we lost track of Latham. The unit was evacuated. Zeke made the sergeant promise to report the incident to the commanding officer. We assumed he did, but we never followed up. Once everyone was safe, we went back into the jungle to complete our mission. It wasn't until later that we learned Latham was MIA."

Vaughn walked over to Lunds and hovered over him. "You expect us to believe Latham sees Zeke in Hong Kong and decides to kill the four of you? What about the sergeant and the other members of his unit? He'd have to wipe out every single witness to be safe."

The same question was floating through Davie's mind.

Lunds leaned back as if distancing himself from Vaughn's aggressive posturing. "You're assuming they all survived the war. Let's say they did. I can't speak for them, but they weren't innocent. They participated."

Davie rose to her feet, because she was unsure about Lunds's emotional state and she wanted to be ready for whatever happened next. "How did he get out of the country?"

"After he disappeared, we assumed he was either captured or killed by the Viet Cong. Now I suspect he used the chaos of the mortar attack to make his way out of the area to safety."

Vaughn glared at him. "Who is Van Kuris?"

Lunds glared back. "I don't know. Latham could have pulled a dog tag off a dead soldier and used his identity to avoid capture or he could have just made up the name like he made up his Canadian citizenship. You're the detective. That's for you to find out."

"So," Vaughn said, "after Latham killed Zeke he cut off one of his dog tags because he considered him a battlefield casualty?"

"All I know is Zeke wore his tags to Hong Kong. I imagine lots of people saw them."

Davie asked a question to cut the tension. "When Zeke flew back to L.A. he went from the airport to Alden Brink's office. You think he told Brink that one of Guardian's employees was an Army deserter and a war criminal?"

"Brink is a lawyer not a decision maker. Zeke was a loyal guy. He'd warn the CEO first, because there'd be fallout from the Army's investigation. Juno might have seen Latham also, and I believe Zeke tried to tell me when he called the night before he was killed. I just wasn't there to hear his story."

"Did Zeke tell you he was planning to retire?"

"No. I brought him into TidePool. He wouldn't retire without letting me know."

Again, Davie wondered about the logistics of killing four men but she knew everything was doable if the killer was motivated. Latham/Kuris worked for an international defense contractor and must have had access to weapons and contacts all over the world. He could have killed Zeke and Juno before they left Hong Kong, but the death of two Americans would draw unwanted attention. Better to make the hits in remote parts of the US and hope law enforcement didn't put two and two together.

"If Guardian had contracts with the US government," Davie said, "wouldn't Latham need a security clearance? How could he get one if he was an Army deserter living under an assumed name?"

Lunds bent his head and stared at the ground. "Documents can be forged for a price. They must have accepted whatever he gave them."

"Can you account for your whereabouts in the past two weeks?" Vaughn said.

The question was so abrupt Davie was thrown off balance. Lunds jerked his head upright. His fists balled. A vein in his forehead pulsed as he shot out of his seat. "You mean do I have an alibi for the time my three closest friends were murdered?"

His angry outburst was so sudden and unexpected that by reflex Davie's hand covered her weapon. She was still, barely breathing, anticipating what might happen next. "We had to ask."

"No," he shouted, pointing to Vaughn. "*He* had to ask." Lunds must have sensed the situation was spiraling out of control, because he inhaled deeply to regain his composure. "For the record, Detective, I was in Kabul on assignment for TidePool. Check with the CEO if you want to verify my *alibi*."

Vaughn's hand hovered over his weapon. "Don't worry. We will."

31

LUNDS STORMED TO HIS car. Vaughn watched him drive away, his body still juiced with adrenalin. "Didn't I warn you?" he muttered. "That guy is trouble."

After her partner went back inside the station, Davie remained at the picnic table to process what had just happened. She was no shrink so she couldn't make a diagnosis, but she knew the symptoms of PTSD included sudden outbursts of anger. Given Lunds's past history with the condition, coupled with the murder of his friends and the attempt on his life, she wondered if all those events had triggered a relapse.

Back at her desk in the squad room, she searched the Internet for every scrap of information she could find on the Vietnam War. Over 58,000 soldiers had died, another 150,000 wounded. She found her uncle's name on one website. Davie could still visualize his face in the photograph on the fireplace mantel of her parent's house where the family had lived before her parents divorced and everybody went their separate ways. Her mother still had the photo but over time it had been relegated to a dresser in the spare bedroom.

She returned to the MIA website that Lunds had shown her and was shocked by the number of military personnel still unaccounted for. She pulled up John Latham's photo again and noted that his hometown was listed as Seattle, Washington. Latham's parents might not still be living, but he could have other relatives waiting for his remains to be found and one day returned to them. Davie had to find them.

The first order of business was to confirm if Van Kuris had entered the US in the last ten days. It seemed farfetched that he had orchestrated these murders in such a short time, but she had to start somewhere. Eliminating possible suspects was part of the job, as well. She called Quintero and filled him in on the new lead Dag Lunds had provided, and the Seattle angle.

"I'll ask Striker to follow up with Immigration."

She ended the call and told her partner what Quintero had said.

Vaughn threw up his hands. "Why Striker? It's our lead. Quintero is making the Mounted Unit sound better and better."

"Giddy up." She grabbed her notebook and walked toward the parking lot.

When they arrived at PAB twenty minutes later, Davie checked in with Quintero and then hunkered down at her desk, searching for information on Latham's Seattle relatives. Vaughn wandered off to take a phone call just as Detective Striker walked through the door. His jacket was off, his tie was loosened, and he was carrying a stack of papers.

He stopped at her desk and handed them to her. "You may be interested in this. It's a credit report for Latham's father, Robert. He's still living in Seattle with a younger woman. Could be a second wife, but I think it's his daughter."

Davie thumbed through the pages of the report. "That was fast. It's only been thirty minutes since I called Quintero."

"No reason to sit on the information."

Davie flipped through the paperwork. "Robert Latham has a lot of credit cards."

Striker rolled a chair over to her desk and sat. "And a lot of debt. But the balance on each card is paid in full every month. Mr. Latham is in his eighties, and I can't find any other sources of income except social security and a small pension from a former employer."

"You think John Latham is sending money to help support his old man?"

He leaned forward and rested his forearms on his thighs. His head was bent, his eyes on the page, giving her a perfect view of his long dark eyelashes. "I ran a title search on Robert Latham's house. He and his wife borrowed money for a second mortgage shortly after their son went missing. I'm guessing if we get a search warrant for bank records, we'll find they wired that money to a bank somewhere in Asia right after they got it."

"Wired it to their son?"

He sat up and crossed his arms over his chest. "Latham was on the run and didn't speak the language. He needed money to survive, at least until he established his new identity and melted into the population. I'd guess the parents supported him until he got settled."

Davie kept reading. "This says they paid off both mortgages in the Nineties. Where did they get the cash?"

"Latham was probably established by then. I'm guessing he gave them the money as payback for helping him and maybe continued supplementing their income over the years, especially when they got older."

Quintero hustled into the room and stopped at Davie's desk. "What's going on?"

Striker leaned back in the chair and let Davie tell Quintero about the credit report. It was a generous thing to do.

Quintero turned to Striker. "Did you contact Immigration to see if Kuris entered the country?"

"They're checking. I'm still waiting to hear back."

Quintero ran his hand through his hair and paced. "If Latham, or Van Kuris, is back in Hong Kong, he's out of our reach. Even if we ask local law enforcement to arrest him, they won't and for sure they won't extradite him to L.A., especially if they know the death penalty is on the table."

"If he's our suspect," Davie said, "I don't think he'd leave the US while Lunds is still alive. We need to go to Seattle and interview Latham's dad. If he supported his son until he got established and is receiving money from him now, the two are still close. If Latham is in the US, it makes sense he'd stop in Seattle for a visit. Even if he didn't, the dad might know where his son is now."

"Okay, Richards," Quintero said. "You and Striker fly up there and see what you can find out."

Davie didn't have to look at Jon Striker to know he was staring at her with that unreadable expression of his. "It's more efficient if I go with my partner."

Quintero pointed his finger at her. "In case you hadn't noticed, you're not in charge here."

Striker stood, towering over both of them. "I agree with Detective Richards. She and her partner are used to working together. You should send them to Seattle. I'll stay here and serve a search warrant for records at a local branch of Robert Latham's bank."

"You think you're going to find records from that long ago?" Quintero said.

"A lot of organizations are digitizing old records," Davie said. "Latham's bank might be one of them." Davie's temple pounded with tension as she waited for Quintero's decision.

He gave Striker a hard stare and then shook his head. "I don't blame you. I wouldn't want to travel with her, either."

She wondered if Striker's intervention was another magnanimous gesture to a colleague or if Quintero's assessment was closer to how he felt. It didn't matter whether Striker wanted to travel with her or not, because knowing she'd be going with Vaughn eased the pressure in her head.

"I'll call the travel desk and get permission forms," she said. "Then I'll book the tickets."

32

DAVIE STARED OUT THE window as the plane approached the Seattle-Tacoma International Airport. All she saw under the gray cloud cover were green trees and water. The scene was a pleasant change from the dead lawns and dusty streets of Los Angeles.

Before she left L.A., she'd called the Seattle Police Department as a courtesy to let them know she and her partner would be in town on police business. The detective told her to call if he could be of assistance. She and Vaughn had no luggage so after the flight landed, they went directly to the rental agency and picked up their Toyota Corolla, the cheapest car they could find.

Davie entered Robert Latham's address into a navigation app on her cell phone and followed the directions to the freeway. Traffic was heavy on the 5, as bad as any day in L.A., maybe worse. It was 9:30 a.m. when they arrived at the destination and parked on the narrow street.

"It's raining," Vaughn said.

Davie opened the car door and pulled her jacket over her head to protect her hair from the downpour. "It's Seattle. Let's go door knock the place."

The house was a small one-story in the Ballard district, not far from Shilshole Bay. It was set high above the street with a driveway that led up the hill to a detached one-car garage behind the property.

The rain came down in sheets as they ran up the steps to the porch. Neither had brought a raincoat. Davie was born in L.A., and she wasn't even sure she owned one. They ducked under an overhang above a porch that was supported by two round wood pillars, both in need of paint. The wood landing sagged and creaked under their weight.

A woman answered her knock. She was in her late fifties and rail thin with strawberry blonde hair streaked with gray and gathered into a ponytail by a fluorescent pink stretchy band. A black sweater was paired with a gauzy black dress that seemed flimsy for the cool weather. She looked vaguely familiar but Davie wasn't sure why.

Davie flashed her ID. "Ms. Latham?" She was guessing. She hadn't been able to confirm who the woman was.

"Yes," she said, glancing at the badge with a wary expression. "What do you want?"

"We're from the Los Angeles Police Department, here to speak to Mr. or Mrs. Robert Latham."

The woman's expression soured. "Why?"

"It's about a homicide investigation."

"My mother died two years ago. My father isn't well. Neither one of them have ever been to Los Angeles. So, why are you on the doorstep, asking about a murder they know nothing about?"

"The victim is a man named Zeke Woodrow."

"Never heard of him." The door began to close.

Davie stopped its momentum with her hand. "Your brother John Latham served in Vietnam with him." The door swung open again.

The mention of her brother's name escalated her surliness. "My brother is dead. He never came back from that war."

"We have reason to believe he's still alive and living in Hong Kong," Vaughn said. "Would you know anything about that?"

She shook her head in disbelief. "How dare you intrude on our grief after all these years? Have you no decency?" She slammed the door shut. A dead bolt clicked into place.

Vaughn threw up his hands in frustration. His suit was wet and he hadn't had any caffeine since leaving the airplane. He raised his voice loud enough to be heard inside the house. "We know your parents took out a second mortgage on this house a few weeks after your brother went missing. What happened to the money?"

There was silence and then she shouted, "Go away or I'll call the police."

"We *are* the police," Vaughn yelled back. "Now you know and so do all of your neighbors."

"I don't have to listen to this."

Davie pulled her jacket around her neck to ward off the cold air. She considered the possibility that the woman was telling the truth and truly believed her brother was dead. Now she was unhappy stuck in this house caring for an ill father. Davie couldn't force her to tell what she didn't know, but three men were dead and she was their current suspect's sister. They'd come a long way to talk to her. Davie couldn't just leave without breaking through her hostility.

"We believe your brother is a deserter from the United States Army," Davie said. "If you're protecting him, you could face charges. You need to talk to us."

More silence and then the door opened. "Stop yelling at me. I don't know what you're talking about, but if it means you'll go away and leave me alone, I'll listen to your *story*." She punched that last word to let them know she suspected it was going to be fiction.

Davie and Vaughn stepped into a small living room full of tired furniture and old carpet that had absorbed the musty smell of mildew and urine. The woman pointed to one of two couches that faced each other with only a narrow walking path between them.

"Make yourself comfortable."

"Ruthie, who's at the door?" The sound came from somewhere in the back of the house. It was a man's voice, gravelly and ancient.

Ruthie's face sagged. "It's nobody, Daddy. Drink your tea."

"My cup is empty."

She squeezed her palms against her temples. "There's more in the pot. Just pour it in your cup."

Vaughn remained standing by the door. Davie sat on one of the couches. "How long have you been taking care of your dad, Ruthie?"

She sank onto the opposite couch next to a pile of laundry. "My name is Angela. Ruthie was my mother's name. I stopped correcting him a long time ago. It doesn't do any good to remind him. It just makes him upset."

Vaughn looked up from sifting through a pile of mail on a table near the door. "Alzheimer's?"

"His doctor calls it dementia. What's the difference? He can remember the license plate number on his first car but not a teapot I brought him fifteen minutes ago."

Davie's damp clothes were sticking to her skin, sending a chill up her spine. "I'm sorry about your dad. That's got to be tough."

Angela glared at her. "Why did you say that? You don't know me. They're just empty words, and I'm sick of hearing them from people like you."

Vaughn's hair was plastered down with rainwater. He ran his hand over his scalp and shook the excess water onto the floor mat. "When was the last time you saw your brother?"

Angela pulled half a dozen boxer shorts from the laundry pile and began to fold them. "I told you. He died in Vietnam."

Vaughn's expression hardened. "Let me lay it out for you. A witness saw your brother in Hong Kong, recognized him, and told other people he was alive. The witness got killed because of it."

Davie heard a squeaking sound. She turned to see an elderly man pushing a walker into the room, wearing a two-day beard, a pair of rumpled boxer shorts, and a dingy gray T-shirt embossed with the silhouette of an airplane and the words PEREGRINE AVIATION. His eyes were rheumy. Static electricity had frothed his wispy white hair into peaks.

When he saw Vaughn, he smiled and turned the walker toward him. "Johnny! You're here. You said you weren't coming till tomorrow. Give your old man a hug."

As Robert Latham got closer, Davie inhaled the odor of sweat and urine, which caused her to question the daughter's commitment to care-giving. Vaughn grimaced and reached for his tube of menthol.

Angela put her head in her hands and sighed. Then she struggled to her feet and walked toward her father. "Daddy, that's not Johnny. This man is collecting money for the policeman's ball. I told him we didn't have any to spare. Go back to your room and have some tea."

Mr. Latham frowned. "I have to wait for Johnny. When is he coming home?"

"Soon. I'll let you know when he gets here."

"He promised to give me a ride in his new car."

Davie wasn't sure if Mr. Latham was remembering back to when his son was young or if his memory was more current.

"It's got tinted windows like the movie stars have."

Davie glanced at Vaughn. The witness at LAX had seen a BMW with tinted windows leaving the scene of Zeke Woodrow's murder. The garage video confirmed that information. Robert Latham's recall may have been cloudy, but maybe he could remember a recent conversation with his son.

"That sounds like fun," Davie said. "What kind of car is it?"

Mr. Latham frowned. "I can't remember. Does it matter?"

"No, sir," she said. "Not a bit."

"Nice shirt," Vaughn said, dabbing a thin layer of menthol under his nose.

Latham looked at his chest as if he'd forgotten he was wearing a shirt. "That's Johnny's airplane."

Angela's body stiffened as she moved toward her father. "No, Daddy. That's not Johnny's plane. I got that shirt at the Goodwill, remember?"

"Johnny didn't give it to me?"

"No," she said, helping her father turn the walker around and steer it toward the hallway. She returned to the couch a moment later and collapsed in a heap.

"Your father's short-term memory isn't completely gone, right? He remembers your brother telling him about his car. Is it by chance a BMW 740i?"

The color drained from Angela's face. "How would I know what kind of car he drives?"

"*Drives?*" Vaughn said. "I thought you told us he was dead. Look, I know you want to tell us the truth. Now's the time."

She stared at her hands for several moments. When she spoke, her tone was flat. "I was just a kid when John disappeared. I didn't understand what happened at first. All I knew was my parents told me they couldn't afford to send me to summer camp or couldn't pay for new school clothes. They were always short on money. But when they said they couldn't help me with college tuition, I began to question why. My dad had a good job and my mom worked part-time as a church secretary. She wasn't paid much, but pleading poverty just didn't make sense to me. When they finally confessed, I was angry they'd mortgaged my future to protect my brother. They warned me not to tell anyone or we'd all be sent to prison."

"When was the last time your brother was here?" Vaughn said.

She tucked a loose strand of hair behind her ear. "Maybe six months ago. At first, he never came home. He was afraid. But in the past several years when he traveled to British Columbia on business, he'd drive across the border to visit Daddy. He'd stay at the house because he didn't want to risk checking into a hotel. He could have afforded to move Daddy into a skilled nursing facility, but he'd rather protect himself and have me work like a dog to take care of him. I'm worn out from the responsibility. I just can't take it anymore."

"Then why do you do it?" Davie asked.

Angela shot her a hostile glare. "Because he supports us, that's why. Without him, my father and I would be living in a shelter or out on the street."

"Ruthie, I still hear you talking. Who's out there?"

Angela picked up a white shirt from the clothes pile and inspected a dark stain that hadn't come out in the wash. "It's just the neighbor, Daddy. She wants to borrow a cup of sugar."

"I'm out of tea. Can you bring me some?"

She threw the shirt on the floor. "It's in the teapot, Daddy. Just pour yourself another cup."

"It's not hot."

Angela turned her face toward the hallway and shouted. "It's a thermal pot. It's hot enough."

"I hear talking out there. Who's with you?"

She threw her head back and stared at the ceiling. "Nobody, Daddy. It's just the radio."

"I thought so."

Vaughn crossed his arms and scrutinized her. "It didn't bother any of you that he was a deserter?"

She covered her face with her hands. "He was my brother. My parents convinced themselves they weren't doing anything wrong."

"What did you do when they told you?"

Angela laid an undershirt on the couch and smoothed the wrinkles out with her hands. "I moved to Arizona. Got a job, went to school, married and divorced. In other words, I made a life for myself—until my mother died and I had to come back to take care of *him*." She gestured toward the hallway.

Davie peppered Angela Latham with questions until she admitted that after her brother deserted, he made his way to Bangkok and later to Hong Kong, where he became Van Kuris, worked at odd jobs, and learned the language. She denied he had other aliases. He eventually got a job at Guardian and worked his way up to Director of Security. She said her brother was secretive about his life, so she couldn't even confirm if he was married or had children.

"Where is he now?"

Angela culled a dozen white socks from the pile and began sorting them into pairs. "Is there a reward if I tell you?"

Angela had given up her life to take care of her father and now she faced losing the income her brother provided. Davie wondered how she'd feel if Bear got sick and she was left to care for him. Not as bitter as Angela Latham, of that she was sure.

"What I can tell you is that charges could be filed against you for harboring a fugitive or even as an accessory to murder."

Her face twitched, like she was swilling mouthwash. "Maybe I should talk to my lawyer."

She hadn't specifically asked for a lawyer, so Davie moved on to the next question. "Where's your brother now?"

She had matched all the socks and began rolling them into balls. "I'm not sure, but he called two nights ago. He wanted to talk to Daddy. All I could hear was this side of the conversation. Dad kept asking when he was coming home. He said things like 'that's a nasty business' and 'Nixon should bring our boys home.' It sounded like my brother was close by and that he might be dropping by to visit, but you can't count on that. My father's memory can't be trusted. He said some things I didn't understand, which isn't unusual for him."

"Like what?"

"Just gibberish. I asked him later what he meant but by that time he didn't even remember my brother had called."

Davie asked Angela for any family photos of her brother, but she had thrown them all out after her mother died. At least John Latham's employee headshot was in the Murder Book, along with the picture from the MIA website.

Davie passed the interview to Vaughn, who asked all the standard questions: Who were Latham's known associates living in the US? Did she know his address, phone, and credit card numbers? Angela gave them her brother's cell number but claimed she had no other information.

"I'd like to get a swab of your mouth," Davie said. "Your dad's, too. Would that be okay?"

Vaughn's raised eyebrows said *That wasn't part of the plan.*

"I don't like the idea." Angela said. "Why do you need that?"

Davie thought of the blood sample they'd collected in the Santa Barbara cottage. If she had samples from known relatives, she could at least compare the two to see if there was a familial connection.

That would give weight to their theory that John Latham had been in Zeke's house and strengthen the case against him.

"It's just routine," Davie said. "We want to make sure the man we're looking for is actually your brother."

"I don't want you putting anything in my mouth. If Daddy doesn't mind, that's up to him."

Robert Latham didn't protest or even ask why she was collecting the samples. He just signed the consent form and waited for instructions. Maybe he'd become so accustomed to people doing things to him he no longer questioned them. Davie got the swabs from the portable Murder Kit in the car and swiped them over the inside of Robert's cheek. She put the swab in a tube, as she had done with the blood samples. When she was done, she handed Angela her business card. "If you hear from your brother, call me. Please don't mention that we spoke."

"Yeah, sure. Whatever."

She and Vaughn left the Latham house and settled in the car.

"What do you make of that?" he said.

Davie caught his eye and held it. "She gave up her brother without much of a fight."

Vaughn nodded. "You think she's throwing him under the bus to protect somebody else?"

"Maybe." Davie pressed a series of numbers on the keypad of her cell. "She might also know where her brother is, but I don't trust her to tell us. I'm going to ask Seattle PD to keep an eye on the house for a few days. See if Latham shows up."

While Davie was on the phone, she asked the detective to run Angela Latham's name through the criminal records database, but she had no rap sheet. Davie tried the number she'd given them for her brother's cell phone but found it was no longer in service.

The reservation back to L.A. wasn't for a couple more hours but Davie hoped they could get an earlier flight. If Latham were still in Southern California, he most likely wouldn't be there for long. As she headed back to the airport, Vaughn called Quintero to let him know what they'd discovered.

33

As soon as Davie and Vaughn got off the plane from Seattle, they drove downtown to PAB. It was Saturday, but murder investigations don't recognize weekends. When she entered the squad room she found Jon Striker huddled in conversation with a female detective she didn't recognize. He sensed her presence and studied her with a mixture of curiosity and anticipation. She was used to scrutiny, but his made her feel uncomfortable because she had to admit, she found him intriguing. Davie purged those thoughts from her head and beelined to her cubicle to transcribe her notes from the Angela Latham interview.

Twenty minutes later she heard footsteps. She looked up and saw Detective Quintero charging toward her with a piece of paper gripped in his hand. He looked juiced up on something, probably nicotine gum.

He stabbed the paper with his right index finger. "Striker just heard from Immigration and Customs. Van Kuris flew into British Columbia the day after Woodrow landed at LAX. From there it would have been easy for him to rent a car and slip across the US border."

Davie accepted the email from him and studied the text. "How soon will we know for sure?"

"We're working on it. The sister told you he didn't have other aliases, but she could be lying. Striker notified airports, border crossings, and everybody else to be on the lookout for Latham traveling as Van Kuris. Like I told you before, if he flies back to Hong Kong, we probably won't get him back."

"I still think he may try to kill Lunds before he leaves," Davie said.

"Too risky. His sister probably told him we're looking for him. Latham needs to leave the country, the quicker the better. I've set up a meeting with the lieutenant to discuss our options. Once we put everything together, we present the case to the DA's office and ask for a warrant. We'll request extradition just in case we don't scoop him up before he disappears. Is the Murder Book up to date?"

Davie didn't believe the case was strong enough to file with the DA's office. There were still loose ends and unknowns. Educated guesses alone wouldn't convince anybody of Latham's guilt. She'd learned that the hard way during the first Grand Theft investigation she worked at Southeast Burglary. The case had been kicked back for lack of evidence and accompanied by a stern lecture from the Deputy DA, warning her to get her shit together before annoying him again. It was embarrassing but instructive. She didn't want this case to fall apart because of guesswork or overconfidence, but she understood Quintero and the lieutenant would make the final decision, not her.

"We can pick up Latham and question him without a warrant," she said. "Right now we don't even know where he is. I think we should wait until we get the DNA comparisons back before going to the DA. If Robert Latham's saliva is connected to the blood found in Santa Barbara then we'll know Latham stole Zeke's laptop. At least that would connect him to the burglary if not the murder."

"We have to keep the lieutenant in the loop. She can go over the evidence and say yea or nay."

Davie spent the next half hour writing her follow-up report while Vaughn organized the forensic information, including an analysis of the shell casing found in Kern County and the surveillance video showing the man with the ball cap speeding out of the airport garage. When everything was stacked in a tidy pile, she set it on Quintero's desk.

While she waited for him to read and sign the new report, she mulled over Latham's motive for killing Zeke. The guy was in his sixties. Not old, but not in his prime. She wondered why he'd risk coming back to the US to kill four men because of something that happened decades ago. If extradition from Hong Kong was as hard as Quintero claimed, it seemed more reasonable to stay in Asia and fight whatever charges came his way. What was the worst that could happen? Guardian might fire him, but Latham was near retirement age anyway. He must have set aside money to live out his so-called golden years, maybe even enough to support his father and pay lawyers to fight extradition.

Fifteen minutes later, Quintero dropped the reports on her desk. "Good work, Richards. The lieutenant is waiting for you in her office."

"Me? Aren't you coming?"

"Hell no. That woman hates me. I'm going to let you and your partner take the heat."

Davie picked up the reports. "Thanks for your support."

Quintero chuckled. "I'm sure you'll return the favor."

"You can count on it."

Lieutenant Betty Repetto's office was at the end of a long hallway. Davie only knew her by reputation but figured somebody had put her as far away from other people as possible because she was a hard-core cop who didn't care about political correctness or who she offended. She'd also heard the woman was smart, tough, and fair as long as you did the work and built your case from facts and didn't ignore exculpatory evidence. If you screwed up, she'd kick you to the curb. Even those who had felt the lash of her sharp tongue respected her.

Vaughn walked behind Davie as they approached Repetto's office. Her door was open, but out of caution Davie knocked to announce their presence. Repetto was bent over a stack of papers wearing her signature work uniform—a dark skirt and an American flag pin attached to the lapel of her matching jacket. Davie heard she had a Beretta strapped to her thigh under that skirt.

The lieutenant gestured for them to enter the room. "Come in. Sit."

Vaughn eased into one of the two guest chairs. Without speaking Davie set the case files on her desk within easy reach. Repetto adjusted her glasses and slid the file in front of her. Davie sat back and waited, looking for clues to Repetto's personality through the items she kept in her office. There were framed commendations and certificates and a coffee cup printed with an LAPD lieutenant's badge and a number she assumed was Repetto's. There were no family photos or other personal items.

Her partner leaned forward and opened his mouth to speak. Davie grabbed his arm to stop him. He swung his torso toward her, confused. She put her finger to her lips warning him not to interrupt.

Some supervisors welcomed verbal explanations, but she'd heard Repetto thought pitching was for Hollywood movie scripts. She insisted on reading the report in silence to make sure it held up, because if you had to explain the case or gin up enthusiasm, you'd failed Homicide Detective 101. If the lieutenant had any questions after reading the report, she would grill the detectives, especially if she found any weaknesses in the evidence or the logic, which she frequently did.

Vaughn shrugged off Davie's hand and turned to Repetto. "The suspect is a flight risk, so—"

The lieutenant lifted her attention from the page and gave Vaughn a death stare. "Did I give you permission to speak?" She paused for a moment to let the question sink in—but not long enough to entertain an answer. "No, I don't believe I did. Until I do, keep quiet so I can concentrate."

Vaughn's jaw muscles twitched while Repetto resumed reading, making a few notes on the pages. When she finished, she turned to Davie. "Your name's on this report so I guess you wrote it." Davie nodded. "It's good—a little obsessive-compulsive, but good. Your partner over there may be no slouch himself, but I don't know either of you, so I can't say for sure."

While she appreciated the compliment about her report, she held her breath and waited for the lieutenant to notice what wasn't included. It didn't take long.

Repetto glared at Davie. "You collected blood and saliva evidence. Where are the results?"

"We just got the saliva this morning. The samples haven't been analyzed or compared yet."

Repetto's chair squeaked as she leaned back. "This investigation started in Pacific, right?"

Vaughn still looked shell-shocked by her rebuke, so Davie assumed the lead. "My partner and I worked the case until it got complicated."

"So your captain sent it to us."

Davie nodded. "RHD has more resources—"

Repetto scribbled a note on the page. "Spare me the bullshit, Richards. I've been in this job long enough to know how it works. You division detectives think you do all the work and RHD takes all the credit, right?"

If Davie didn't know better, she'd have sworn it was her boss Frank Giordano sitting in that chair. She didn't answer Repetto's question because they both knew it was rhetorical and commenting further would be counterproductive.

Vaughn leaned forward, apparently hoping to redeem himself in the lieutenant's eyes. "I just wanted to say what an honor it is to finally meet you."

It was Vaughn's well-meaning attempt to be charming, but all Davie could think was, *Oh crap.*

Repetto removed her glasses and laid them on the desk. There was a deadly silence in the room as her stare burned a scarlet tattoo onto her partner's forehead—a *B* for *brownnose*. Davie could tell by Vaughn's wary expression that he realized his mistake but was at a loss on how to correct course.

"Someday I hope I can say the same about you, Detective," Repetto said, "but I have my doubts. Just so you know, I like false praise about as much as I like sloppy writing. You'd be wise to remember that. No self-respecting Deputy DA would file this case because all you've got is an interesting theory." She pushed the paperwork across the desk toward Davie. "If you're harboring any notions of staying at RHD, keep working until you have something to show me."

Davie filed away Repetto's bias against sloppy writing for future use. She nodded and followed Vaughn out of the office. She caught up with her partner at the elevator as he stabbed the down arrow.

"Sorry, Jason. I would have warned you but I didn't know until the last minute we'd be presenting the case to her. But it's good news she even mentioned a permanent position for you in RHD."

"No thanks," he said. "Look, Davie—my suit is still soggy from the Seattle rain. I'm tired, and I've had enough abuse for one day. I'm going home."

She waited for a moment as the elevator doors closed, assessing the level of her partner's unhappiness and what she could do to snap him out of his funk.

"Surviving Repetto is a right of passage. He'll get over it."

Davie whipped around to see Jon Striker standing behind her. His jacket was off and slung over his shoulder. The dark shadows on his cheeks indicated he was in need of a shave.

"Did you set us up just to amuse yourself?"

Striker's face was a stony mask. "I would never set up another cop. Q didn't tell me about the meeting or I would have been there."

"How did you find out?"

"It doesn't matter." He swept his gaze over her black pantsuit, crumpled from rain, travel, and hours of hunching over a desk. "You just need to know that Repetto and Q are good people. We all care about closing this case. You and your partner did a damn fine job on this investigation to date. Just think of us as force multipliers." Without waiting for her to reply, he walked past her down the hall.

Davie returned to her temporary desk and worked alone until the early evening, when she decided to go home, too. Maybe a hot shower, cool sheets, and some mac-and-cheese baked in her new casserole dish would provide clarity on what to do next. She'd been chasing leads for six days straight with little time off. There were other detectives working on the case now, so she decided to take Sunday off and regroup.

On Monday morning, Davie left her house with her temporary badge clipped to her belt and her gun secured in a holster. Before reporting to RHD, she stopped by Pacific Station to check her desk for any subpoenas or department bulletins that might have been dumped there.

When she got to her desk in the detective squad room, she saw a bouquet of red roses in a plastic vase, along with a pink Mylar balloon that read CONGRATULATIONS! An envelope attached to a wood dowel was tucked between the foliage with a note that read *RHD! Kick ass and take names! SH.*

Spencer Hall.

She grabbed the vase and rushed out of the squad room, shouldering open the door to the women's restroom. The vase thudded as it hit the bottom of the trash can. She planted her feet wide apart on the tile floor and fumed, refusing to acknowledge that she might be overreacting. At least Vaughn hadn't seen the flowers. There would have been no end to his lecturing.

She caught her breath and went looking for Detective Giordano. As she exited the restroom, she nearly collided with flower man himself.

"What were you thinking?" she said in a low voice. "Flowers? In the squad room? Where everybody could see them?"

He seemed taken aback. "I heard you went to RHD. That's a big deal. I just wanted to let you know I was happy for you. Why are you so upset?"

She noticed that his tie was crooked and wondered who straightened it now. Not her. Those days were over. "You're giving people the wrong idea. We're not a couple."

He sighed and ran a hand through his blond hair. "I know, Davie. You've made that clear. But I thought we were friends."

Davie was a week into the Woodrow murder investigation and she hadn't made an arrest. Her nerves were on edge. She considered the possibility that she was taking out her frustration on Hall. Maybe she'd ask the shrink to sort it out at their next appointment.

"I'm sorry. We *are* friends. Thanks for the flowers."

"You're welcome." He walked past her without meeting her gaze and proceeded toward the watch commander's office.

Davie glanced up and saw Joss Page standing by the door of the squad room, wearing a sympathetic expression.

"Don't worry," she said. "I think Taylor Swift has already written a song about him."

"Which one? 'I Knew You Were Trouble'?"

Joss walked toward her. "I'd guess more like 'We Are Never Ever Getting Back Together.'" She laughed. "So … the flowers. Do you mind if I take them home to my mom? I'll sneak them out to my car. Spencer will never know."

"Works for me."

"And by the way, running is a great stress reliever." Without waiting for a reply, Joss strolled into the restroom to rescue the flowers.

Davie found Giordano upstairs in the roll-call room bent over some paperwork. The room was set up in typical classroom style with rows of tables and chairs facing toward audio / visual equipment on either side of a head table. The space was used for a variety of meetings, including sharing intelligence with patrol officers at the beginning of each watch. It was appropriate to find her boss there, since intelligence sharing was exactly what she wanted to do.

Davie walked down the center aisle and stopped in front of Giordano. "You got a minute?"

He turned the papers over so she couldn't see what was on them. "Sure. How's it going, kid?"

"Jason and I met with Lieutenant Repetto on Saturday. She said there wasn't enough evidence to file with the DA's office and told us to keep working on the case."

He chuckled. "That must have been ugly."

"Brutal. But she's right."

Giordano sat for a moment, thoughtful. "Your partner probably thought he could finesse her with his charm but I'm surprised at you. Why didn't you just wait before involving her?"

"Because I'm not in charge of the case."

Davie straddled a chair across the table from Giordano and updated him on the evidence she'd collected on John Latham/Van Kuris but also her concerns about what it meant.

Giordano frowned. "You think Latham is the wrong guy?"

She leaned back, gathering her thoughts. "It's the logistics. Zeke bumped into him unexpectedly in Hong Kong. It must have been a shock to both of them. But what happened next seems so farfetched."

"In what way?"

She leaned forward with her elbows on the table. "We're supposed to believe that Latham told Guardian he had a family emergency and requested leave. He got it and flew to British Columbia. He crossed the border into the US without anybody knowing, collected an arsenal of heavy-duty weapons, and located all four men, not even knowing for sure if they were all still alive. Then he traveled hundreds of miles to take out three people. He didn't kill Lunds, but it wasn't because he didn't really try. Seems like a lot to accomplish with little information in a short amount of time."

Giordano tapped his pen on the table. "But not impossible, especially if he's motivated. You said he worked for an international defense contractor. He must have had contacts in the US who could supply him with weapons and information."

"So, why did Zeke decide to fly back to Hong Kong? What was he planning to do? Kill Latham? Bring him back to face justice? None of that makes sense. He was responsible for a disabled daughter. The risk of injury or death on a mission like that seems excessive. Why not just contact the Army's law enforcement division and report Latham? Let them handle it."

Giordano set his pen on the table. "Who would profit from Woodrow's death?"

"Not his daughter. She idolized him. Even if she inherited his assets, she'd lose his love and support. Not TidePool. The Guardian contact was worth a lot of money, and they were eager to win the bid. They certainly had a huge stake in making sure nothing went wrong. From what Alden Brink told me, they're privacy fanatics. Clients might be upset if Zeke destroyed a potential client's reputation over something that happened fifty years ago, but TidePool could claim it was their patriotic duty to report him. Plus, Guardian was interviewing other security contractors and TidePool knew that."

Giordano continued his litany of thought-provoking questions, getting her to think of all the angles. "Who stands to lose the most if Latham is exposed?"

Her cell chimed with an incoming text. She focused on the screen and saw her partner's name. She pushed a button to silence the phone. "Latham, of course, but also his father and sister. His sister told me without her brother's money, she and the father would be in financial trouble."

"What does Guardian have to lose?"

"Not much. It might be embarrassing for them, but I doubt it would damage the company in any real way. They'd claim Latham, aka Van Kuris, lied to them about his past. They might feel pressured to fire him but that's about it."

Giordano leaned forward to meet her gaze. "Like I've always told you, murderers lie for a lot of reasons—because they have to, because they think they're smarter than you are, and sometimes they lie for the pure joy of it. But they always lie. Figure out who's lying and you'll have your killer."

"That's easier said than done. First, I have to have a plausible suspect."

"No one ever told you it would be easy."

She nodded toward the stack of pages. "Your retirement paperwork?"

He leaned back in the chair and laced his hands behind his head. "Yeah. Pain in the ass trying to figure it all out."

"Save yourself the aggravation and stick around for a while."

He looked up and smiled. "Thanks, kid. Appreciate that."

As soon as Davie left the roll-call room she called her partner and told him she was at Pacific. He sounded stressed. "What's wrong?"

"I just got a call from the serology lab. The DNA comparison came back. They can't prove it was John Latham's blood we found in Santa Barbara. Our entire case just came unglued."

34

VAUGHN ARRIVED AT PACIFIC station fifteen minutes later. Davie sat across from him at a table in the employee break room, reading the serology report he'd brought with him. His jacket was off and slung over the back of a chair.

"How did you get the results so fast?" she said. "I didn't expect them until next week."

"You underestimate me, Davie. All I had to do was flash one of my movie-star smiles and *boom*."

"In other words, our case was next in line."

He smiled. "Something like that."

She continued reading. According to the report, the serology lab had first analyzed the blood she'd collected from the door of Zeke Woodrow's house and developed a profile, which they ran through the FBI's national database—Combined DNA Index System, or CODIS. They required two conditions be met before the profile was uploaded into the system—the sample had to be from a Forensic Unknown and the profile had to meet minimum quality standards that involved loci and alleles, a complicated process that made Davie's head spin. She was lucky her sample met the criteria, but was disappointed to read they'd found no exact match in the database. Next they did a familial DNA comparison between the blood sample and the buccal swab she'd taken from Robert Latham's mouth.

"Wait a minute," she said pointing to the last page of the report. "This says the two samples do share a number of alleles, so it's possible whoever left the sample in Santa Barbara could be a relative of Robert Latham. They also share an identical Y chromosome, which is passed down from the father to his sons and grandsons, so the blood sample could be John Latham's or another relative from the same line, like a brother or a son. They just can't say that for sure."

Vaughn walked to the counter and poured himself a cup of coffee. "John Latham doesn't have a brother. I suppose it's possible he fathered a son who acted as his accomplice, but Angela couldn't even confirm her brother has any children. The bottom line is we can't prove anything." He added powdered dairy creamer and held up the cup. "You want some?"

Davie found an empty pot and filled it with bottled water. "Immigration still hasn't confirmed Latham entered the country, right?"

"Right. And we don't know where he is."

She grabbed a teabag from the counter. "If he's using another alias he could have returned to Asia from anywhere, even from Canada or Mexico. Lunds told us his boss is a former Ranger who recruited him into the company. Maybe Lunds can persuade the CEO to pressure Guardian into helping us locate John Latham."

"Don't you think we should check with Quintero first?"

She poured the hot water into the cup with the teabag and watched the water turn murky brown. "Like Bear always says, it's easier to beg forgiveness than ask permission."

35

WHEN DAVIE REACHED DAG Lunds by phone, he agreed to speak with her but not if Vaughn came along, so she had to call Quintero after all.

When her partner heard she'd agreed to Lunds's terms, he wasn't happy. "Look, Lunds is a hothead. It's risky for you to interview him alone."

"You're right, but he has information we need. This isn't the time to bargain about who's in the room when he gives it up. I'll ask Quintero to go with me."

Vaughn pulled car keys from his pocket and headed toward the door. "I still don't like the idea, but call me if you need anything."

When she reached Quintero, he told her he was busy but agreed to send Striker to pick her up at Pacific. Davie hadn't worked closely with Striker and was hesitant about doing the interview with him, but there was nothing to do about that now. They could talk strategy in the car.

Striker arrived at the station a short time later. Davie slid into the passenger seat, inhaling the faint aroma of leather from his shoulder holster. As he turned toward her, the sunlight beamed through the window like a camera flash—bright and fast—illuminating the contours of his high forehead, sharp cheekbones, and blue eyes.

"Where are we going?" he asked.

"Not far."

A faint smile appeared on his lips, leaving her to wonder if he thought she was referring to something more than distance on a map.

Dag Lunds was staying on a friend's sailboat in a slip in Marina del Rey, an area in Los Angeles County where boatyards, high-rise apartment buildings, and restaurants shared a zip code with one of the largest small-boat marinas in the world.

Once they arrived at the marina, they found the gate leading to the slips locked. Striker was tall, so he leaned over the chain-link fence to unhook the clasp, but his arm wasn't long enough to reach it.

He nodded toward the fence. "You want to climb over or shall I?"

Davie considered her still-aching hip and bruised back. She held up her cell phone. "Let's just text Lunds and save ourselves a trip to the ER."

His mouth twitched in a wry smile. A few minutes later, Lunds ambled up the ramp and opened the gate. He hesitated when he saw that Davie wasn't alone.

Striker preempted any challenge by extending a hand and introducing himself. "I'm sorry for the loss of your friends."

Lunds accepted his handshake and led them along a walkway to a boat that had a mast, two sails, and a confusing tangle of ropes. The vessel looked old but well cared for. It was just shy of forty feet, she guessed. Davie followed him up a two-step footstool to the deck of the boat. Striker climbed aboard behind her.

Before they went below, Lunds pointed out several handholds and cautioned them to hang on at all times. "One hand for you, one hand for the boat."

Lunds scrambled down the companionway steps to a salon made of wood and fiberglass with Davie close behind. She noted the brass clock and matching barometer hanging on the wall, a gimbled oil lamp, and the faint smell of diesel.

Lunds gestured toward a bench amidships. "Have a seat. I was just making Turkish coffee." He scrutinized Striker. "Or do you want something stronger?"

Both declined coffee. Striker's broad shoulders forced him to turn sideways to descend the companionway steps. He hovered by the entrance, blocking any sunlight that filtered through the marine layer.

Davie leaned against the mast in the center of the boat. "We've been trying to reach TidePool's CEO. We were told he's in the Middle East on assignment but would call when he had a chance. So far, he hasn't responded. You work for him, so I assume he'd take your call. I'd like you to make that happen."

Lunds looked at his watch and then turned a knob on the stove. Flaming gas whooshed out of the burner under a pan of water. "If he's still there, we're dealing with a significant time change. He may be in the middle of something."

Striker's tone was pleasant but firm. "We're asking you to interrupt him, Mr. Lunds."

The two men exchanged a look that Davie recognized as alpha males battling for space at the fire hydrant. After a moment of tense silence, Lunds picked up his phone and punched in a number. Davie held her breath and waited.

"Bro," Lunds said as he dropped two heaping spoonfuls of coffee into the water. "It's me. I'm with somebody who needs to talk to you." He handed Davie his cell.

Striker trained his eyes on Lunds while Davie spoke with Tide-Pool's CEO. She talked and listened while Lunds added sugar to the pan and stirred the mixture until it began to foam. By the time she ended the call, the coffee had built to a thick froth, filling the boat with a fragrant aroma.

Lunds gently stirred the mixture. "Did he confirm my alibi?"

"He told me you were in Kabul, just like you said."

"So, you believe me now, that I didn't kill Zeke and the others."

Davie paused for a moment feeling the sway of the boat. She understood that Lunds had been bruised when her partner questioned his alibi, but asking the details was his duty, something Lunds should understand.

"For the record, Mr. Lunds," she said, "I never believed you killed Zeke or the others, but we can't assume somebody is innocent just because he's a nice guy or because he's had a hard life. We had to eliminate you as a suspect. It's nothing personal." She moved toward the exit. "Thanks for your help. We'll be in touch if we need anything else."

Striker shot her a puzzled look. She'd been impressed about how thoroughly and quickly he'd familiarized himself with the facts of the case. He knew as much about Zeke's murder as she did, so if he wanted to ask additional questions she assumed he would do so. Instead, he followed her off the boat and up the ramp. Just past the gate, Davie felt Striker's hand on her arm, pulling her to a stop.

His tone seemed casual, but she knew his mood was anything but. "Mind telling me what's going on?"

She pulled away from his grip and held out her hands, palms up. "You want to talk *here*?"

"It's as good a place as any."

"Suit yourself," she said, "but let's walk."

They moved side by side past rows of slips before stopping. Davie leaned against a fence and waited for the roar of a jet taking off from LAX to fade. "The CEO claimed he didn't know anything about John Latham

231

or Van Kuris, but he had lots to say about Alden Brink. Brink started having problems not long after he was hired. He was manipulative and obsessed with being right. Coworkers mostly tolerated his behavior until he got into a spitting contest with a former SEAL who didn't appreciate Brink telling him how politicians had corrupted the military."

"He sounds like a borderline sociopath," Striker said.

"The CEO was ready to fire him—until the Guardian contract was dangled in front of his nose."

Striker stopped and crossed his arms over his chest. "What does Guardian have to do with anything?"

The sun made the water shimmer as Davie delivered the news. "Guess who brought Guardian to the table in the first place."

Striker raised his eyebrows. "Brink?"

"Brink told the CEO that Guardian was ready to do a major deal for security in areas not already covered by their own team, but only if he was involved. Brink was known for exaggerating his accomplishments but, turns out, this time he was telling the truth. He had an in with Guardian. The CEO wanted the business because it was worth a ton of money, so he decided to give Brink one last chance to redeem himself by sending him to L.A."

"Which begs the next question—is there a link between Latham and Brink?"

"I'm not sure, but HR is emailing Brink's personnel file. I think we should go back to headquarters and see what it has to say … that is, unless you have something better to do."

Striker's tone was matter-of-fact. "The car is closer than headquarters."

He didn't have to remind her there was a computer in the city ride, but she preferred to review the files at her desk, not reading over his shoulder in a stuffy car. But she had to admit he was right. When

Davie settled into the passenger seat, she logged into her email and opened the attachment that contained Brink's personnel file. His employment application alone was thirty-four pages long.

"This is going to take a while," she said.

Striker leaned closer until their shoulders touched. "Then we'd better get started."

The car seemed hot, so Davie reached over and pressed the lever to open the window. When she returned her focus to the screen, she made sure there was distance between her shoulder and Striker's. Her only hint that he noticed was in the smile wrinkles around his eyes.

Davie began scrolling through the pages of Alden Brink's personnel file. He'd been at the company for three years. His work product was mostly good, although not stellar, but he had a volatile temper and an aversion to admitting he'd made a mistake. The company disciplined him several times, mostly counseling, but also restricting his assignments to the in-house legal office at TidePool's Virginia headquarters, supervised by a more seasoned attorney. There was nothing about a promotion to director of the real estate division as he'd claimed. Davie wondered if he'd fabricated the title or if it was a new development that hadn't yet made it into his records.

Davie and Striker continued scrolling through the pages, each of them pausing for the other to catch up. Near the end of the documents, Davie found a life insurance policy that had been offered by the company as an employee perk.

"The payout amount seems high," she said. "A hundred thousand dollars."

"Look at that," he said pointing to a sidebar. "Brink is paying a monthly premium above the amount paid by the company. Looks like he picked up the tab to boost the amount."

Davie advanced to the next page. Her pulse quickened as she stared in disbelief. She pointed to a line on the bottom of the form. "Look at the name of his beneficiary."

Striker studied the page and turned slowly to meet her gaze. "Angela Latham."

Davie leaned against the headrest, breathing deeply to slow her racing pulse. "Alden Brink is John Latham's nephew."

The puzzle pieces were falling into place. The Seattle PD had run Angela's name through their databases. The search hadn't turned up anything, but it had been limited to criminal records. She remembered meeting Angela Latham and thinking she looked familiar. Angela admitted she'd lived in Arizona for a time. Brink had graduated from an Arizona law school, according to the diploma hanging on the wall in his office. The DNA evidence also made sense. Latham's father shared a Y chromosome with the person who left the blood in Zeke Woodrow's house. She'd thought John Latham was that person, but now she believed it had been Alden Brink who stole Zeke's computer and left blood on the door in his haste to get away. Brink knew his mother and grandfather would suffer if anything happened to his uncle or to him, so he upped the amount on the insurance policy death benefit.

The door hinges groaned as Davie escaped the stuffy car and began to walk. Motion and fresh air helped organize her thoughts. Out in the main channel, a cluster of small sailboats raced around a buoy and a group of twenty-somethings partied on the upper deck of a houseboat, drinking beer and playing loud music.

She waited until Striker caught up to her. "How long do you suppose Brink knew his uncle was working for Guardian?"

As usual, he appeared calm. She wondered if anything ever rattled him. "Hard to say, but if he knew from the beginning, he had a vested interest in hiding his uncle's war background from TidePool."

Davie jammed her hands in her pockets to ward off a chill as she continued walking and brainstorming possible scenarios. Brink's job was secure until Zeke saw Van Kuris in Hong Kong and recognized him as John Latham, a deserter and a war criminal. Zeke went straight to Brink's office when he got home. He must have told Brink that not only was he was about to blow up a lucrative contract with a major client, but he was also going to out Latham to the Army. Brink must have panicked. He couldn't let the news get out. It would destroy his uncle, his career, and maybe send his mother to prison. That's when he decided to eliminate the witnesses to his uncle's crime. Getting their addresses wouldn't have been a problem—he had access to Tide-Pool's employee files. He could easily plan the hits because he knew where they'd be.

The sidewalk ended at a concrete wall. Davie turned around, not sure how long they'd been walking or how far they'd come. Striker's lips barely moved when he stated what she already knew. "It's a great theory. It might even be the way it happened. Now we need to prove it. Let's do a follow-up interview with Brink. Press him for details."

"Good idea," Davie said, "but there's somebody we should talk to first."

36

FERN POTTS LIVED IN a ground-floor apartment in an aging building just off Santa Monica Boulevard in West Hollywood, a hip and vibrant city carved into the middle of Los Angeles between Hollywood and Beverly Hills. In the early eighties, the LGBT community's search for a homeland led to the area's secession from L.A. and WeHo was incorporated as its own city.

A wreath of dried flowers hung on the entrance to Fern's unit. The temp answered the door in a pink terrycloth bathrobe and a matching towel twisted around her hair. Except for two white circles that exposed watery blue eyes, her face was plastered with cosmetic mud in a color Davie labeled sea turtle green.

Davie willed herself not to comment on the ghoulish mask. "Remember me? Detective Richards? I stopped by your office a few days ago."

Fern pulled the robe tight across her chest when she saw Striker standing on the walkway. "I'm not senile. Of course I remember."

"This is Detective Striker," Davie said with a nod of her head. "Do you mind if we come inside and ask you a few questions?"

"About what?"

"About TidePool and Mr. Brink."

"I told you, I've only worked there a few days."

"That's okay. You might have seen something you didn't think was important at the time but could help our investigation."

Fern conjured up an exaggerated shudder. "I heard you tell Mr. Brink that somebody died."

Davie stepped closer to the threshold. "Two TidePool employees were murdered in the past several days." She didn't mention that another man, a former employee, had been added to that list, making it three, and that a fourth had nearly been killed. No sense burdening her with the enormity of the loss.

"Am I in danger?"

"We don't think so, but we're being cautious. That's why we're here."

Fern checked her watch. "I'm not due at work until two, but I have to wash this goop off my face in fifteen minutes."

"This won't take long."

"Wipe your feet on the mat first," Fern said and then waved them inside with a broad sweep of her arm.

The apartment was about six hundred square feet and packed with oversized furniture that gave new meaning to the term shabby chic. There were several dust-coated silk plants dotting the room and a collection of owl figurines watching them with wide-eyed stares.

Fern lowered herself onto an overstuffed chair covered in chintz that must have come from a much grander house. She pulled the bathrobe neatly over her legs. "So, what do you want to know?"

"Were you working a week ago Monday when Mr. Woodrow came to the office?"

She picked up an emery board and began filing her fingernails. "That was my first day. There wasn't much to do. The phone wasn't even hooked up. It's still not hooked up, because Mr. Brink has been gone a lot. He gave me his mobile and told me to answer it if it rang."

Davie spent a moment jotting down the dates Fern claimed Brink had been absent from the office.

"Did Mr. Woodrow have an appointment the day he came in?" she asked.

Fern flicked her hand like she was batting away an irritating gnat. "He came barging in just like you did. I don't know what his problem was but he almost knocked me over. Everybody is in such a hurry these days."

"Did you hear any of the conversation he had with Mr. Brink?"

She straightened her spine and set down the nail file. "Don't insult me. I'm not an eavesdropper."

"I saw you standing outside Mr. Brink's door the day I was there. You weren't listening?"

"I was just walking by. And by the way, when he said I hung up on you? He made that up. I know how to use a cell phone. He was the one who cut you off."

Before Davie could remind Fern that listening to that conversation qualified as eavesdropping, Striker shot her a glance and crouched in front of Fern's chair.

"We're not accusing you of anything, Ms. Potts, but you *do* look like an intelligent woman who knows human nature. I'm guessing you could tell what was going on in that room just by the expressions on their faces."

Fern patted the towel and sniffed. "Well, that's true." She paused for a moment and then asked if he wanted a fresh-baked macaroon.

"No, thank you," he said. "I'm sure they're delicious. Did Mr. Woodrow say why he came to the office?"

She leaned forward and lowered her voice in a conspiratorial tone. "He didn't tell *me*, but he was very angry."

Striker leaned in and matched her tone. "Angry at Mr. Brink?"

"Not at first. But later I heard shouting, so I put my ear to the door ... you know, in case I had to call for help."

"Of course. Very smart of you. What were they arguing about?"

Fern batted her eyes at Striker, oblivious to her reptilian-colored mask. "Something bad happened on his trip to Hong Kong, so bad Mr. Woodrow didn't want TidePool to work with that client anymore. Mr. Brink tried to reason with him at first. He said the contract was too important to trash over a personality conflict. He offered to put another employee on the account but Mr. Woodrow was having none of that."

"Did he say what the conflict was about?"

"I'm not sure, but Mr. Brink accused this Woodrow guy of having a wild hair up his—well, you know the rest. He warned Mr. Woodrow to let it go. They argued like that for a while. Mr. Brink told him he was going to assign the account to another employee and that was final. That's when Mr. Woodrow told him he was quitting."

Davie looked up from her notes. "Quit, not retire?"

"You got a hearing problem? I said he quit."

Davie exchanged a knowing look with Striker. If Fern was telling the truth, then everything Alden Brink had told her was a lie. Davie didn't know the whole story and couldn't prove Brink killed those three men, but he *was* involved in some way.

"Please don't tell Mr. Brink you spoke with us," Davie said.

"Why not? You said I wasn't in danger."

Striker reached out and patted her hand. "You're part of an official homicide investigation now, Ms. Potts. Can I depend on you to keep this meeting confidential?"

Fern made a cross over her heart with her index finger and whispered, "Of course, Detective."

On the way back to the car, Davie said, "That was impressive."

He flashed a male version of Mona Lisa's smile. "I have a few moves."

Yes, she thought, *I bet you do.*

————

When Davie and Striker returned to RHD, she sat down to finalize her interview notes. He went in search of Quintero to update him on what they'd learned. Davie sensed movement and turned to see Jason Vaughn approaching her desk. He pulled up a chair and listened as she updated him on the case.

"We need to bring Brink in for questioning," he said.

"I'm down with that, but we don't know where he is. He's probably armed, so we need a plan before we go. Striker is strategizing with Quintero."

"How long will that take? If we were in charge, we'd scoop him up before he even knew he was a suspect. I think we should stake out his office, see if he's there. Once we have eyes on him, we can call for backup."

Davie doubted Brink knew he was under investigation, but once he figured it out, she wasn't sure how he'd react. "It's not just you and me anymore, Jason. We're part of a team. I don't think we should do anything without telling Striker and Quintero."

"You're talking like we're not partners anymore, Davie. I don't get it. You don't even like Striker."

His comment surprised her. She wasn't sure how she felt about Jon Striker. She didn't dislike him, but she must be sending a contrary vibe if her partner thought so.

"My objection to a stake out has nothing to do with Striker. Going it alone is a bad idea. Quintero wants to control everything and if we ask him, he'll say no."

"You're the one who always says it's better to beg forgiveness than to ask permission," he said, turning toward the exit. "I'm going to the Westside."

Vaughn was at the elevator when she caught up with him. "Okay, I'll go with you, but we're just there to watch, right?"

He winked and punched the elevator button. "Right."

———

She and Vaughn had been parked across the street from Brink's office for about an hour when they saw his Mercedes exit the garage and drive toward the San Fernando Valley.

Vaughn reached for his cell. "I'll call Quintero."

It was against her better judgment, but she put her hand on this arm. "He might just be going to lunch. Let's follow him for a while."

Davie trailed Brink's Mercedes along Sepulveda Boulevard until he got to Sherman Oaks where he turned onto a side street and entered the garage of a modest three-story apartment building.

"You think he's in for the day?" Vaughn said.

"Let's wait a little longer. If he doesn't come out, we'll call for re-inforcements."

Davie pulled to the curb a block away. She watched and Vaughn checked his incoming emails. "You going to the Margaritaville party at Garcia's on Sunday?"

"Is she that new MAC detective?"

"Yeah. Her."

"I didn't get the memo."

"Everybody's invited. I don't know her very well but she seems normal. A bunch of guys from the squad room will be there. It could be fun—"

Davie reached over and grabbed Vaughn's arm. She pointed toward the apartment building. "Brink's on the move."

Alden Brink's Mercedes pulled out of the garage and onto the street. As the car drove by, Davie could see that the backseat was filled with cardboard boxes. She followed the vehicle onto the 405 North and tailed him as he transitioned onto the 101 toward Ventura and then exited at Topanga. It wasn't until he turned onto the dead-end road that she knew where he was going—to the house where Zeke Woodrow had once lived.

She couldn't follow him up the hill without being seen, so she eased the car to the shoulder of Topanga Canyon Boulevard behind an oleander bush and waited. Vaughn played solitaire on his cell while Davie stared at the road, willing Brink to reappear. Fifteen minutes later, the Mercedes bumped down the dirt road and continued toward Pacific Coast Highway. The boxes were no longer in the backseat.

Vaughn eased the cell into his jacket pocket. "Aren't you going to follow him?"

"Call Quintero and let him know we spotted Brink heading toward PCH. Ask him to have the nearest black-and-white follow him until a surveillance team can get there. I want to find out why Brink was at the house."

37

DAVIE STOPPED THE CAR at the top of the hill and saw that the gate had been fitted with a new lock. She couldn't risk tampering with it. There was no choice but to leave the car parked on the road and hike the rest of the way on foot.

When they reached the top of the hill, she noticed that curtains now covered the front windows. The place looked dark and hermetically sealed. She had no intention of entering but she turned the front doorknob anyway and found it locked.

She pointed toward the side yard. "Let's have a look."

Vaughn followed as she crept along the path until she reached the garage window. She rose onto her toes and peeked inside.

"See any BMWs parked in there?" Vaughn said.

"That would be convenient, but it's empty."

"Even if the Beemer is his, he's probably not stupid enough to keep it here."

There were three trash and recycling bins lined up against the garage like police cadets in formation. The lid of the blue recycling bin was overflowing with empty boxes that had once contained a set of frying pans, a microwave, and a cell phone.

"Looks like somebody's moving in," Vaughn said.

When they reached the patio, Davie saw that new curtains also covered the French doors, except for a small opening where the seams didn't meet. She peered through the crack and saw a dining room table, several small appliances on the kitchen counter, and a half dozen cardboard boxes stacked on the floor.

"You think Brink is the new tenant?" Vaughn said.

"TidePool sent him to L.A. to open a satellite office, so he's probably going to be here for a while. The company owns the house. Now that Zeke doesn't live here anymore, it makes sense Brink would move in."

Davie walked to the edge of the patio and scanned the horizon. All she saw was hazy-blue sky, eucalyptus trees rippling in the wind, and gray-green brush clinging to the dry hillside. Three birds wove in and out of the airspace like aerial acrobats. Davie watched, mesmerized as they caught an updraft and soared high above the terrain in search of prey.

A rustling sound made her jump. A rabbit darted through the brush midway down the hill where she had first seen Hootch crouching inside the drainpipe. She squinted against the sun and noticed that a cluster of tumbleweeds now clogged the opening. They looked unnatural sitting there, like they'd been herded together by some force other than the wind. As she swept her gaze along the terrain, she noticed some of the ground cover had been torn away, carving a narrow path into the hillside leading from the patio. It looked like somebody or something had skidded down the slope.

"Jason." Her partner joined her at the edge of the flagstones. She pointed toward the damage. "What do you make of that?"

He studied the fresh trail. "Definitely looks like somebody's been down there recently. Could have been kids."

"I'm going to take a look."

Vaughn pulled a pair of sunglasses from his jacket pocket. "I'll stay here in case you fall and break something. Somebody has to call Med Evac to haul you out of there."

"Good idea," she said. "I wouldn't want you to get your suit dirty."

He gave her a jovial slap on the back. "That's what makes you the perfect partner."

Davie planted her boots sideways, stepping and skidding down the hill in the loose dirt, careful not to lose her balance. The last thing she needed was to twist an ankle, adding insult to the cat scratches, sore muscles, and all those bruises.

By the time she got to the drainpipe, her clothes were covered with dust and her hands were scratched from grabbing rocks and dry chaparral to steady her descent. She pulled away the tumbleweeds and stared into the dark opening of the pipe where Hootch had been sheltered from the elements. There was nothing in there.

She walked the area looking for a safer path up the hill, her boots sinking into the soft dirt. Several moments later something underfoot jarred her spine. It wasn't a rock because the ground under her boot seemed smooth and even. She squatted, rapped the spot with her knuckles, and heard a dull thud. Something was buried just beneath the topsoil.

Curiosity and dread set her heart racing as she brushed away the dirt until her efforts exposed the top of a metal box at least three and a half feet long. Her fingers dug deeper into the earth, scooping away soil until she saw what looked like a locked gun case.

"Jason," she shouted.

Vaughn looked down the hill toward her. "What do you need? A rescue helicopter?"

"A search warrant. Call Quintero. Tell him to get here as soon as he can and tell him to bring a shovel and some rope."

———————

Davie clawed her way up the hill, grabbing onto any bush or rock that gave her leverage against the steep incline. Vaughn was waiting for her at the top with a blank search warrant form he'd pulled from the Murder Kit in the trunk of the car.

She brushed dust off her suit and sat down on the edge of the patio to write the statement of probable cause and the parameters of the search. When she was finished, she bypassed the DA's Command Post, which was generally used for telephone warrants in the field. Instead, she called the direct line of a deputy DA she knew and trusted. Davie filled her in on the case and her reason for being at the house.

Law enforcement wasn't allowed to go inside a residence to search even if they'd seen potential evidence through a window or open door, but Davie had found the box outside. She wasn't even sure it had been buried inside the property lines. Brink might have hidden it on state-owned Topanga Canyon parkland. If it was ever found, he could claim it wasn't his, though a jury wasn't likely to buy that excuse.

After determining that the case was suitable for a telephonic search warrant, the DDA added a judge to the conversation and activated the tape recorder. Under oath, Davie read the warrant and the judge gave her a verbal authorization to proceed with the search.

She was required to have a supervisor at the scene, so while Davie had been on the telephone with the judge, Vaughn confirmed that backup was on its way. Detective Quintero was annoyed they'd gone off without telling him, but her partner caught the brunt of his lecture. Vaughn also called the real estate manager to drive over to see if her keys still opened the door. Brink hadn't yet changed the locks, because Amber Johnson was able to access both the gate and the front door. The woman seemed shaken. As soon as the detectives went inside the house, she hurried back to her car and drove away. Davie guessed this would be her last official duty for TidePool.

Thirty minutes later, two vehicles raced up the drive, kicking up clouds of dust. Quintero spilled out of the passenger side of the lead car and jogged to the front porch where Davie and Vaughn waited. Jon Striker lingered just outside the driver's side door scanning the area. *Look around, don't walk around*, the LAPD's crime scene mantra. Two RHD detectives Davie didn't recognize rolled out of the second car.

Quintero's breathing was labored from the jog. He worked a piece of gum—peppermint from the smell of it. "A couple of our guys are following Brink, so we'll know if he comes back this way. What did you find?"

Davie filled him in on the details. Striker remained on the porch, watching as Quintero conducted a briefing before the search began, outlining what they were looking for: weapons, keys and anything they opened, receipts, Zeke's stolen computer, and other evidence related to the murders. He also reminded the detectives where they were allowed to search: the residence, the garage, any vehicles, and the exterior of the property.

Once they were inside the house, Quintero told the two RHD detectives to recover the box from the hillside and assigned Vaughn to look around outside while Davie searched the ground floor.

Striker walked toward the stairs to check out the second floor but stopped in front of Davie, invading her comfort zone. He reached out and pulled a twig from her hair, presenting it to her like a prom corsage. "I thought we were a team, Detective."

It was a subtle rebuke but she got the message. She should have called to let him know they were following Brink.

After Striker disappeared up the stairs, Vaughn strolled toward her, frowning. "You have a weird look on your face. What did Striker say to you?"

"He said 'good job.' Let's look around. We need to find the key, so we can connect Brink to whatever's inside that box."

Vaughn left to search the exterior of the property. Davie remained on the first floor, where she found several cases of cola stacked in the dining room. It appeared Brink had an addiction to caffeine in a can, which might explain why he'd taken a soda from Zeke's refrigerator in Santa Barbara.

It wasn't until she walked past a mirror hanging on the dining room wall that she noticed her clothes were still dusty and more twigs were caught in her hair. The scratches on her hands stung as she brushed soil from her pants before moving toward the kitchen. She hoped to locate a sample of Brink's handwriting for comparison with the so-called suicide note found with Juno Karst's body, but all she found was an instruction booklet for the microwave and an extra set of keys to the house, but none for a car or a gun case.

In the bathroom she found a new set of beige towels. She shook them out but nothing was hidden inside. People sometimes concealed contraband behind pictures on the walls, but there was no artwork. Bed mattresses were favorite hiding places, but there were no beds on the first floor.

Davie's gaze swept the living room. Propped against a wall in the living room was another shadow box, similar to the three she'd seen at his office. This is one was filled with military medals, including several Purple Hearts. Brink obviously liked to collect things, maybe even dog tags. Then she noticed the drapes hanging from metal rods. Brink was only partially settled into the house but he'd taken the time to install curtains on all the windows. She assumed he didn't want anyone invading his privacy, but it still seemed odd.

She dragged a chair from the dining room to the window coverings and unhooked the rod from its cradle. She unscrewed the cap of the curtain hardware and tapped the rod on the floor. Nothing fell out. She threaded the rod back through the curtain and hung it up again. Then she ran her fingers along the bottom seam of the curtain. Nothing. She was searching the second curtain when her fingers felt something hard.

She pulled out her cell and texted her partner: COME INSIDE. BRING YOUR LEATHERMAN.

Vaughn entered the house through the French doors. He handed her the knife tool she'd bought at the convenience store in Kern County. Davie pulled out the scissor attachment and picked at the seam until it opened. A key fell to the floor.

38

DAVIE PUT ON GLOVES and picked up the key by the edges. "What do you suppose this opens?"

Vaughn smiled. "Only one way to find out."

The two RHD detectives had horsed the box up the hillside with ropes and positioned it on the flagstone patio. They were sweating and covered in dust and didn't look happy. From the box's dimensions, she guessed it must weigh at least twenty pounds, a lot of weight to pull up a steep and unstable slope.

Quintero loomed over them, supervising the recovery. As Davie got near, he turned to her. "I called the squad room. One of our guys checked the property lines. Your guess was right—the box was buried in Topanga State Park. Brink'll say it wasn't on his property and therefore, it's not his."

"It might not matter," Davie said, holding up the key, "if his fingerprints are on this or whatever is inside that box."

Quintero dusted the key for prints but they were smudged and of no use, so he slipped the key into the padlock. It popped open. Inside was a disassembled semi-automatic sniper rifle—an M110—the weapon likely used to target Dag Lunds. Also inside were Zeke Woodrow's missing dog tag and a letter to the Army Zeke had written, outlining John Latham's crimes.

Vaughn whistled softly. "Brink must have figured the original file was on Zeke's computer. That's why he stole it. Risky keeping all this evidence so close to his house."

"No more so than storing it in a rented storage locker," Davie said. "I'm guessing he wanted it to be accessible. He knows we've been here once and saw the house was empty. He also told us TidePool would probably leave it empty. This place is isolated, so he assumed it was safe to leave the weapon buried on the hillside."

"He may have thought he was safe until he bought these."

Davie turned and saw Striker holding a towel, the same beige color as the ones she'd found in the downstairs bathroom.

"A guy's got to take a shower," Vaughn said.

Striker held up a slip of paper. "The price tags were in a wastebasket upstairs, along with a receipt from a department store. Guess where he bought them."

Davie accepted the paper from his outstretched hand. She studied the sales slip, saw the name of the store, the list of each purchase—two bath, two hand, two wash, two kitchen. Next she read the date and time of the sale. Her jaw tingled as she lifted her head and stared at Striker. "He bought these towels at a store in Las Vegas on the same day Juno Karst was found dead a few miles away."

Vaughn let out a soft whistle. "That's cold. He kills a man and then goes shopping for bathroom accessories."

Quintero wandered into the room from the patio. "What's going on? Find something interesting?"

Striker briefed him and then added, "The store will probably have surveillance video. If we're lucky, we can confirm it was Brink who made the purchase. The sales slip indicates he used a credit card. He might have charged other services, like at a hotel or rental car."

"Let's go hook him up," Vaughn said.

Quintero extracted the gum from his mouth, wrapped it in a piece of paper, and slid it into his jacket pocket. "I get that you want to prove you're a badass with a DIA, but it's too dangerous. We'll present it to the DA's office. Once we get a warrant, the team will scoop him up."

Quintero was talking about a Detective Initiated Arrest and he was right. It *was* dangerous, but the detectives who put the case together always wanted to make the arrest.

Davie leaned in to get Quintero's attention. "We still don't know if Brink acted alone or if Latham was involved."

"Latham is back in Hong Kong."

Davie frowned. "How do you know that?"

"We heard from Immigration this morning. Latham flew out of the Vancouver airport yesterday. Border agents have no record he ever crossed into the US and no indication that Brink flew to Canada to meet him."

Everything was moving quickly now. Brink would be picked up soon. After the search team finished taking photos and collecting evidence, they returned everything else to its original location and locked the front door.

The two RHD detectives drove the rifle and case to the crime lab to have it compared to the shell casings they'd found in Kern County. Davie and Vaughn returned to headquarters, where Davie updated her reports and all the supporting evidence to present to the DA's office. Then she turned the file over to Quintero.

Vaughn sat with his feet on his desk. "You want to take bets on how long it will take for the warrant to get into the system?"

Davie sat on a nearby chair. "Sometimes it takes a while, but I'm sure Quintero will hover over them until it's done. The surveillance team is following Brink, so at least we know where he is."

While Davie waited for Quintero and Striker to return from the DA's office, her partner asked the department store to send a copy of their surveillance video. With all the evidence piling up against him, she hoped Brink would make it easy on himself and surrender.

The case was out of her hands now. Detective Quintero was the I/O. It was his show. She felt deflated. Dag Lunds wouldn't be there when they made the arrest. Quintero would never have agreed to that because having a civilian present would only complicate the operation and possibly endanger lives. She might not be there, either, and that disappointed her.

Vaughn was meeting a new love interest for drinks later that night, so Davie decided to go home and check on Hootch. On her way, she stopped by the pet store and bought him some new toys, including a feather attached to a pole, a cloth mouse filled with catnip, and a scratch post the same shade of wisteria as the walls in her cottage. She hoped it compensated for her failure as a caregiver.

Davie drove her Camaro past the gates of Alexander Camden's mansion to her guesthouse at the back of the property. As she got out of the car, she noticed the sun had coaxed the scent of rosemary from the bushes in Alex's herb garden. She grabbed the cat toys and scratch post from the trunk and went inside the cottage, where she found Hootch curled up in his usual spot on the kitchen counter. Those impossibly long whiskers sprouting from the white fur around his mouth and his silky coat made him seem beatific. The way he stared out the window sometimes made her wonder if he was looking for Zeke to come and rescue him.

She set the sack of toys on the couch and the scratch post on the floor. "What do you see out there?"

Hootch turned toward her, his eyes narrowed into slits.

"Sorry," she said. "Just asking."

She filled his dish with kibble and added fresh water to his bowl. "You should really cut me some slack. I've never had a cat before, so I'm not sure what to do."

Hootch continued watching her. She found the brush from Dr. Dimetri and swept it through his coat. "I'm not doing a great job of taking care of you, but I'm trying."

The cat didn't seem to mind being brushed, so she kept it up until clumps of hair accumulated between the bristles. She ran her hand over Hootch's coat from his charcoal and beige head to his long silky tail until he began to purr. She picked him up for the first time since that day he'd crawled up the Topanga hillside. He was heavy. Again, she estimated twelve or thirteen pounds. She carried him to the couch and set him down near the sack from the pet store.

"I bought you some cool stuff." She pulled out the catnip mouse and laid it in front of Hootch. He sniffed at it but didn't seem interested. He also rejected the feather on the pole. Even when she dangled it in front of his nose, he just glared at her with a look that said, *Really? That's the best you can do?*

She couldn't even pick out a decent cat toy. Worse yet, she was now talking to Hootch and pretending to read his mind, which made her wonder if she had gone off the rails. Bringing him here had been a mistake. He should be in a permanent home right now with good cat toys instead of with her and a lame feather on a stick.

Engaging the cat seemed futile. Instead of wasting her time trying to be charming, she showered and went to bed. Sometime in the night, she woke up and found Hootch again curled up in the crook of her arm. The next morning he was gone from her side. All the proof left of his midnight visitation was a clump of charcoal cat hair stuck to her pillow.

39

THE FOLLOWING MORNING DAVIE arrived downtown and ran into Detective Striker at the front entrance of the Police Administration Building. As they walked up the steps, he told her that the DA's office had filed the case and issued an arrest warrant. They were waiting for it to officially appear in the system before arresting Brink.

Striker showed his ID to the officer at the front desk. "The surveillance team reported Brink left his Sherman Oaks apartment at about five p.m., carrying a large duffle bag. They followed him to a private shooting range in the Santa Monica Mountains. He stayed for a couple of hours. Then he drove back to the apartment and didn't leave for the rest of the night."

Davie also flashed her ID and followed Striker to the elevator. "Did they question anybody at the range?"

Striker pushed the UP button. "They interviewed the owner. He said Brink showed up about a month ago to shoot and has returned at least two or three times a week since then. Brink told him he was moving his company to L.A. and looking for office space."

"*His* company?"

"That's what he said. After a couple of sessions watching Brink shoot, the owner complimented him on his accuracy. That's when Brink told him he was a weapons instructor for a gun club. Brink seemed reluctant to name the group but finally did. The owner said he knew of them as anti-government survivalists."

"That explains a lot."

Striker continued briefing her as they stepped into the empty elevator car and rode to the sixth floor. "At 7:35 a.m. this morning, they followed his Mercedes into the parking garage of his office building. A member of the surveillance team verified he entered the suite and is still inside. He never went back to Topanga, so he doesn't know we were there unless Amber Johnson told him."

"I doubt she'd do that," Davie said. "She's too freaked out."

When they arrived in the squad room, Quintero hurried toward Striker's desk. "The warrant is in the system. Our team has eyes on Brink. Let's pick him up."

"He's got an elderly temp working for him," Davie said. "I don't want her to get hurt. Maybe we should wait until he leaves the office."

"He just drove out of the garage," Quintero said. "A black-and-white is following him. The blue-suits will stop the car for a traffic violation. He won't be expecting that. We'll arrest him and impound the car. I'm off to the Westside now. Vaughn, you come with me. Richards, you ride shotgun with Striker."

Davie was worried about Fern. She hoped Brink had cancelled her temp assignment and Fern was safe at home with her face plastered with cosmetic mud. She didn't want to think of what Brink might do to her if he found out she'd been talking to the police.

Striker adjusted the weapon in his shoulder holster. Davie pulled her raid jacket out of the desk drawer. Both jogged to the garage. Striker motioned her into the passenger seat. "Buckle up."

She assumed he was joking. She never wore a seatbelt unless she was in a high-speed chase. It limited her mobility. Striker was a competent driver so she felt little risk of a collision. Once they entered the freeway, Striker picked up the radio. He gave his personal ID to Dispatch and requested Code 3. Once he got a confirmation, he pulled down the light bar from under the windshield visor and activated the lights and siren. The car accelerated. The air was thick with tension as they sped to the location. Vaughn and Quintero were just ahead of them in an unmarked car.

Quintero's voice crackled over the radio. "Suspect's Mercedes is driving south on Westwood Boulevard. Chances are he'll be armed when we stop him, so everybody stay safe."

Davie heard another voice. This time it was one of the patrol officers. "Mercedes turning east on Olympic Boulevard, traveling in the inside lane. We'll stop him at Century Park East. Waiting for traffic to clear."

"Are they sure it's him?" Davie said.

Striker kept his eyes on the road ahead. "Life doesn't come with guarantees."

Once they got near Olympic Boulevard he turned off the siren. He eased into traffic but kept well behind the patrol car. All eyes were focused on the Mercedes as it approached the intersection of Olympic and Century Park East. Traffic was light so Davie had a clear view of Brink's car. The driver appeared to be alone in the front seat with a ball cap pulled down over his face, just like the person who'd left the scene of Zeke's murder.

Just ahead, the black-and-white pulled up behind the Mercedes and the siren chirped twice. Davie was relieved when Brink's vehicle slowed and then stopped. This would be over soon.

Striker inched the car closer. Davie saw one officer exit the vehicle and walk cautiously to the passenger-side window of the Mercedes. The other officer moved near the trunk of Brink's car, forming a triangular pattern to keep from hitting his partner if shots were fired.

Davie watched as the door of the Mercedes slowly opened and a shoe appeared. It was black and small. The rhinestone cats on the toe sparkled in the sun. *Fern.*

She turned to Striker. "We've been punked." She drew her weapon and bolted from the car. Striker followed.

Fern inched out of the front seat. The ball cap was tilted to the side of her head and she was clutching her chest. "Don't shoot me!"

Vaughn appeared behind Davie. "Jeez, she's having a heart attack. That's all we need."

Davie jogged toward the car but didn't holster her gun. For all she knew, Brink was hiding in the backseat or in the trunk. "Fern put your hands behind your head."

The woman seemed flustered and scared. "I can't. Bad shoulder."

"Okay. Hold them out to your sides."

"Anything you say. Just don't kill me."

"Is anybody in the car with you?"

"No. Just me."

Davie crept closer. "Do you have any weapons, Fern?"

"Of course not," she said in her nasally voice. "Who do you think I am? Ma Barker? What's going on here?"

Striker positioned himself near Davie at the Mercedes, his weapon drawn. The patrol officers opened each car door and the trunk to make sure nobody was inside as Davie patted Fern down. "Why are you driving Mr. Brink's car?"

"He asked me to pick up his dry cleaning. He offered me fifty bucks under the table, so I said yes."

"Why the hat?"

She pulled off the ball cap and patted her gray bob. "It was part of the deal. What did I care? For fifty bucks I'd wear a feather duster on my head. The guy's a little eccentric if you ask me." She leaned toward Davie and whispered, "He talks to himself, you know. He doesn't think I can hear him, but my ears are good."

Davie continued questioning Fern while Striker looked on. "Where is Mr. Brink now?"

"Back at the office, I guess."

"Do you have a key?"

"Temps don't have keys." Fern's complexion turned pale as she fanned her face with her hand. "Too much excitement. I need to sit down." Striker took her arm and gently eased her onto the front seat of Brink's Mercedes. She beamed him a look of fealty and adoration.

"We're going to tow the car, Fern," Davie said. "Somebody will drive you to our headquarters to take your statement. Then they'll see you get a ride home."

"Mr. Brink isn't going to like that. I don't want to leave him in the lurch."

"Fern, you're a temp."

"So what? I still have principles."

Davie helped Fern out of the Mercedes. "Don't worry. I'll explain when I see him. Meanwhile, your agency should find you another job."

Davie turned Fern over to one of the RHD detectives. Then she found her partner.

Vaughn was steamed. "What a screw up. Let's check Brink's office."

"He's not there," she said.

"At least he's got an active arrest warrant. Let's hope he gets stopped for speeding."

Davie was angry and no attempt by her partner to spin this screw-up into gold was going to change that. Brink was in the wind. She wouldn't rest until he was in custody.

40

ALDEN BRINK WAS NOWHERE to be found. Somehow he'd slipped out of the building without being seen. Fern claimed she didn't know anything about his plans or where he'd gone. After Quintero debriefed the team, Davie called Lunds to warn him Brink was on the run. Then she and Vaughn drove back to headquarters.

Davie spent the next few hours searching for evidence to strengthen the case against Brink—information about the BMW, credit card charges he may have made near the murder scenes, telephone calls, emails.

It had been a frustrating day and she didn't want to rehash the failed effort to arrest Brink with Quintero or anyone else. She'd been cooped up for hours at desks or in cars. Exercise is what she needed. She told her partner she was going home for a swim.

"I'm too wound up to go home," he said. "You want to grab something to eat? We could walk over to Luigi's."

"I thought you had a date."

"I cancelled. Again. I have a feeling that relationship is over."

The restaurant was several blocks away but walking was exactly what she needed, so she locked her desk and logged out. She and Vaughn had eaten at Luigi's before. The restaurant's wood-paneled bar was a favorite spot for people who worked downtown, theater patrons, and a few actual Italians. Vaughn's mother had given the Bolognese sauce her personal seal of approval. They snagged a small table near the kitchen and ordered a split of Chianti.

When the wine arrived, Vaughn raised his glass in a toast. "To next time."

Davie ignored him. She was in no mood to joke about failing to arrest a murder suspect. "We should call Dag Lunds again. He offered to help. Maybe he can lure Brink out."

Vaughn rolled the wine around in the glass and then lowered his nose to sniff the bouquet. "Brink knows we're onto him. Why would he fall for that?"

"What if he does? It's worth a try."

Vaughn set down the glass without tasting the wine. "We can't use a civilian as bait."

"Why not? We've done it before. Besides, Lunds is no normal civilian. He's a former US Army Ranger. Maybe he can offer to help Brink get out of the country. He might be willing to part with some cash for a deal like that."

He glanced at the menu and then motioned for the waiter. "Or he might use it as another opportunity to kill Lunds."

"We'll never let him get that close."

Vaughn ordered a tray of mini pizzas, his favorite. Ten minutes later the food arrived, but he seemed to have lost interest in eating. Even his wineglass sat on the table untouched. "You think Brink has already left the country?"

Davie thought about his question. People disappeared within the United States all the time. Gangster Whitey Bulger lived in plain sight in Santa Monica for years. Brink might do the same. If he planned to leave the country, his options were limited. He could drive across the border to Mexico or Canada, but that posed a high risk of being apprehended. Border agents would be watching. He might go to Hong Kong, where his uncle could help him disappear. Latham had created a new identity for himself. He would likely help his nephew do the same. If that was Brink's plan, the only way he could get there was by boat or air. A boat would take forever and would likely be intercepted by the US Coast Guard. So, he had to fly, but not on a commercial airline, that would be risky. It would have to be on a private plane.

Davie thought back to her conversation with Detective Giordano. "The key to Brink's behavior is hidden in his lies. Let's go over what we know."

"What good does that do? He lied about everything."

For the next few minutes they laid out all the evidence against Brink, including what they'd found during the search of the Topanga house. During a pause in the conversation, Vaughn plucked a pizza round from the tray.

As he raised it toward his mouth, he grimaced. "What kind of cheese is this? It smells like old man Latham's boxer shorts."

Davie winced. She thought about that day in Seattle, the smell, and the dingy Peregrine Aviation T-shirt Latham's father had been wearing. Then her stomach cramped as she realized what they'd missed. She fumbled for her cell and typed a name on the search line.

Vaughn leaned over the table to look at her phone. "What are you doing?"

"Checking a hunch."

Peregrine Aviation was a flight school in the San Fernando Valley. Midway through reading the text, a photo of the company's logo caught her eye. It was an angular winged insignia. It could have been a vintage hood ornament, as she had once thought, but it wasn't. It looked exactly like the logo on the pen clip Brink had been holding at his office the day she interviewed him.

Davie dialed the number. After waiting several agonizing moments, the company confirmed that Alden Brink was a licensed pilot who had rented an airplane from the company for at least one business trip.

The elder Mr. Latham suffered from dementia. In his muddled brain he'd thought his son had given him the T-shirt. Angela had been nervous as she tried to quiet her father because she knew it wasn't her brother who'd bought that shirt. It was her son, Alden Brink.

She pressed Dag Lunds's number into her phone as she bolted from the chair. "We need to move," she said to Vaughn. "Brink can fly out of here himself. I've alerted Peregrine to contact me if he shows up. We need to find out if TidePool used any other charter services. Call Quintero and let him know we're on our way back to headquarters. We need to contact all the private airports in the area."

Vaughn looked perplexed. Davie threw some bills on the table and ran toward the street. "I'll explain on the way."

She and Vaughn were breathing hard from exertion and stress by the time they reached the squad room and found Quintero, Striker, and two other RHD detectives.

"Jason just got off the phone with TidePool's CEO," she said. "A member of his board flew into town yesterday to sort out the mess Brink created. He arrived on a Gulfstream G650 corporate jet that's parked in a hangar at a private airport in the San Fernando Valley. An hour ago the owner of the facility saw Brink on the property. He wasn't the pilot, so he got suspicious and called the CEO to make sure he was authorized to be there. Brink is a pilot. I think he's going to steal the plane and fly it out of here."

"Any idea where he'd go?" Quintero said.

"The Gulfstream has a range of seven thousand nautical miles. Tide-Pool works with clients all over the world. Brink could have developed contacts in a lot of places, people who would be willing to help him."

"Let's roll," Quintero said.

Davie ran to the garage, along with her partner and two other RHD detectives. Striker motioned her into the backseat of the black-and-white he was driving. Vaughn scrambled into the front. She hadn't even closed the car door when Striker pulled out of the garage and sped toward the freeway, again requesting Code 3.

With sirens blasting and lights flashing, Striker pushed the car to its limits as they sped toward the Valley. Davie's heart raced. Adrenalin made the siren sound too loud, the menthol gel in Vaughn's pocket smell too pungent, and the leather on the seats feel too cold. Striker's hands gripped the wheel, but she still couldn't read the tattoo on his inner arm.

The drive seemed to take forever, but she knew they were close to the destination when Striker turned off the siren but didn't douse the lights or slow down. A few minutes later, he pulled onto a side road with a view of several helicopters parked on a slab near the runway. He braked, sending Davie slamming against the door. She felt nothing. That's when she realized the adrenaline had blocked the pain from her old injuries.

There were at least a dozen patrol cars already at the scene. Quintero and Lieutenant Repetto leaned against an unmarked city ride. Striker stopped next to them and all three piled out of the car.

"Brink drove up about fifteen minutes ago," Quintero told them. "He opened the hangar door so we assume he's planning to fly the plane. He's not going to get far. We've blocked his access to the runway. SWAT is on the way."

Davie scanned the area. It was dark outside but in the distance she saw what looked like a terminal or administration building and the control tower. A series of overhead lamps illuminated four rows of long buildings. Each had five enormous sliding doors, twenty hangars in all. The interior lights in the TidePool hangar weren't turned on, but ambient light spilled through the open door revealing a large jet. Barely visible in the shadows was a dark-colored BMW.

Davie turned to Quintero. "Did you see the car?"

"Yeah," he said. "We ran the plates. It's registered to a rental agency in Vegas."

A million questions cycled through Davie's mind. Where had he stored the car during the past ten days? Were there more weapons inside the trunk? Why did it have a Washington license plate? There was no time for answers now. She would find out eventually.

Striker put on his raid jacket and strapped his shoulder holster over it. "Does Brink know we're out here?"

Quintero trained his binoculars on the hangar. "We haven't tried to initiate dialogue, but I'm guessing he knows. We're pretty hard to miss."

Davie saw movement in the cockpit of the plane and then heard the sound of an engine roaring to life.

"They waited too long," Vaughn said. "We should have arrested him when he got out of the car."

Quintero grabbed a bullhorn and flipped a switch. "This is the Los Angeles Police Department. You're surrounded. Step out of the airplane and put your hands behind your head."

The jet crept forward until it cleared the hangar and turned toward the runway. A line of patrol cars with their spotlights blazing blocked the jet's path. Brink had two choices—give up or shoot it out. Either way, he wouldn't get away this time.

Quintero repeated the orders twice more. The plane stopped but the angle left most of the hangar in shadows. Davie focused on the cockpit but she could no longer see any movement through the window.

"Get out of the plane! Put your hands behind your head." Quintero's voice had become shrill.

Something seemed wrong. Brink was a killer who'd been willing to sacrifice Fern in order to escape. He was desperate and likely capable of much worse. He had to know the jet wasn't going anywhere. That's when she realized his only hope of escape was in the car. A moment later, the BMW streaked out of the hangar, headlights off, and raced for the runway. Davie bolted for the black-and-white. Striker got to the driver's seat first.

Striker rammed the accelerator to the floor before Davie landed on the seat. He pulled out his seatbelt and Davie clipped it into the slot so he could keep his hands on the wheel. Then she fastened her own. The patrol car barreled forward until it was within a foot of Brink's BMW. Behind her, the flashing lights of a dozen patrol cards reflected in the windshield. Striker stomped on the gas pedal, propelling the patrol into the BMW's bumper.

The collision threw her forward. Striker braked. Before her brain registered pain from the seatbelt cutting into her chest, her forward movement stopped and then reversed, sending her head banging against the headrest. Brink fought for control of the car, swerving wildly. Davie heard tires screech and metal grind against metal as the BMW came to an abrupt stop. Through plumes of smoke she saw the front of Brink's car caved in and the tangled remains of one of the helicopters that she'd seen parked at the edge of the runway.

Even before Striker put the car in park, Davie threw off her belt and tumbled out of the passenger door with her weapon drawn. She ran toward the wreck. Striker's shoes pounded the pavement behind her. When she got to the BMW, Brink was stunned but conscious. A trickle of blood rolled down his face from a cut near his eye and gray powder from the airbag explosion covered his clothes. He struggled as they pulled him out of the car and shoved him to the ground. Striker planted a knee in his back and pulled a Glock from Brink's waistband.

Davie grabbed the handcuffs from a pocket in the back of her gun belt, knelt on the ground, and slipped the restraints around Brink's wrists.

"Get off me!" he shouted. "You have no right! I know people. You'll pay for this."

"You tried to make me pay by the river," she said. "You failed."

Brink struggled to free his hands. His tone had grown raw and hysterical. "You have no authority over me. None! You're the cancer that corrupts this country. This fight is just beginning."

"You're right about that," she said. "Alden Brink, you're under arrest for the murder of Zeke Woodrow. You have the right to remain silent. Anything you say may be used against you in a court ... "

It felt good to say those words. Davie thought of all the people Brink had destroyed, not only the men he'd killed but also the families whose lives would never be the same.

Striker extended his hand toward her after she'd rattled off the Miranda warning. "You okay?"

She nodded and let him pull her to her feet.

Later that evening, Striker and Quintero flew to Seattle to have another chat with Angela Latham, this time in a SPD interview room. Davie and Vaughn stayed in L.A. and interrogated Alden Brink throughout the night. He blew off the Miranda warning to rage against the Army for scapegoating his uncle and ruining his whole family.

He told her Zeke had given him a copy of the letter he wrote to the Army, not knowing his relationship to John Latham. Once Brink saw that Zeke planned to expose his uncle, he had to act. First, he persuaded Zeke to hold off sending the letter. Instead, they would return to Hong Kong together and present the case to the local authorities with Guardian's help, in hopes of saving the business relationship. Davie could only assume Zeke agreed out of loyalty to TidePool. With Zeke silenced, at least for the moment, Brink lured Juno to Nevada with a fake job assignment and staged his suicide. After Zeke was dead, he went after Harlan Cormack. Brink told her his greatest regret was failing to kill Dag Lunds. He swore to remedy that as soon as he was released. Davie assured him that wasn't going to be any time soon.

Brink had assumed the original letter to the Army was on Zeke's computer. He had to destroy it. When he didn't find a laptop in Zeke's travel bag at the airport or in the Topanga house, he found it at the Santa Barbara cottage. It was clear to Davie that Brink confessed not because he felt remorse, but because he felt justified.

It was mid-morning the following day when Davie finally arrived home. Hootch was waiting for her by the front door. While he ate his breakfast, she told him Zeke's killer was in custody. She thought she saw him smile.

41

AFTER CATCHING SOME SLEEP, Davie drove to Pacific station later that day, planning to jog to the beach. She was about a half mile from the station when her cell phone rang. It was Detective Striker calling from the LAX substation. He and his partner had just returned from Seattle, where they'd questioned Angela Latham. Davie was eager to learn how the interview had gone so she offered to pick him up.

She was out of breath by the time she'd raced back to the station and fumbled in Giordano's desk drawer for the key to a detective car. She bolted from the squad room without bothering to speak to anyone or to change out of her sweaty running gear.

Striker was waiting for her at the curb. His blue suit and white shirt were both wrinkled from travel. His dark hair spiked at odd angles. He looked fatigued. She guessed he hadn't slept since leaving L.A. the previous night. He must have noticed her scrutiny because he ran his hand over his scalp until the hairs were mostly traveling in the same direction.

He threw his small duffle bag and a raincoat into the back and settled in next to her. "Anything happen while I was gone?"

She told him that techs had searched the BMW's navigation system and found programmed routes to Harlan Cormack's trailer and a motel in Nevada, not far from where Juno Karst's body was discovered. They also pulled Zeke's stolen computer from the trunk of the car, which she'd booked into evidence at SID.

He gave her a thumbs-up sign. "Good work, Detective."

His praise felt good. "So, what did you get out of Angela Latham?"

"It's a long story that requires coffee. You know someplace close?"

She did.

During the drive to Marina del Rey, Davie filled him in on Brink's confession and he told her about his conversation with Angela Latham. Striker's impression was that Brink had always been a piece of work and his mother was an enabler. He was smart enough to con his way through college and law school but was arrogant and compulsive, which got him in trouble everywhere he went. He was on the verge of getting fired from the real estate law firm where he worked when he found out TidePool was recruiting. They needed his expertise, so they hired him.

Ten minutes later, they sat in a small café in Fisherman's Village, gazing out the window at a cloudless blue sky. Boats cruised the main channel, back-dropped by high-rise apartment buildings that pierced the skyline. Davie heard the whoosh of milk frothing and the distant sound of a jet taking off from LAX. Striker had brought his duffle bag into the café and parked it on the floor by his feet.

She wrapped her hands around the cappuccino cup, inhaling the fragrance of cinnamon sprinkled on the foam. "Did Brink always know his uncle was alive?"

"He knew Latham was MIA. When he was about ten, Angela figured he was old enough to keep the family secret, so she started indoctrinating him with conspiracy theories. She told him his uncle was in hiding because the Army had manufactured bogus charges against him."

"That fits with what Brink told me. He thinks his uncle is a patriot who was betrayed by his country."

"Angela taught him to hate the military," Striker said, "and encouraged his obsession with guns. She said as a kid he fantasized about saving his uncle in some sort of commando raid. By the time he met Latham in person, he saw his uncle as a hero. Latham had no kids of his own, so he encouraged the relationship."

She noticed Striker's gaze sweeping over her body. Her hand flew to her head when she realized her hair had escaped the bun and hung in moist strings around her face and neck. She felt awkward knowing her form-fitting white top and black Spandex tights revealed every curve and straight line of her body. More than that, the getup was still damp from sweat and the synthetic fibers suddenly felt itchy against her skin. Striker didn't comment on her appearance—unlike Jason Vaughn, who would have had plenty to say.

She rethreaded the strands of hair into the stretchy band. "If Latham thought of his nephew as a son, it explains why he used Guardian to save Brink's job."

Striker looked down as he lifted the coffee cup to his lips. Sunlight spilled through the window, highlighting the stubble on his face. "When Latham recognized Zeke in Hong Kong he called to warn Brink about the possible fallout. Once Brink found out Zeke was the bogyman who'd destroyed his uncle's life, he turned his childhood commando fantasy into a reality."

"It's hard to believe Latham didn't know Zeke and Juno were part of the TidePool contingent."

Striker returned the cup to its saucer and lowered his voice. "Even if Latham had seen a list of TidePool employees, he wouldn't have made the connection—he didn't know Zeke's name. Remember, the massacre happened in the so-called fog of war. Everything was fluid before he disappeared. Latham goes to ground not knowing if any of the men survived the war. He figured he was safe."

She thought about that for a moment as she studied the sleeves of Striker's shirt, hoping to get a peek at the tattoo on his arm. But the cuffs were buttoned, blocking her view.

"You're staring at me," he said.

"Don't flatter yourself." Davie felt embarrassed that he'd noticed, so she deflected the awkwardness by wiping the sticky tabletop with a paper napkin dipped in water. "So, did Brink act alone?"

Striker looked skeptical, like he knew she was withholding something but he wasn't sure why. "Angela said her brother flew to Vancouver and planned to drive across the border from Canada, but when he found out Brink had already killed Zeke and Juno, he knew it was too dangerous. Latham claims he had nothing to do with the murders. He and his attorney have agreed to talk to us. Q and I are flying to Hong Kong in a day or two to question him."

Davie felt a twinge of regret that she wouldn't be in on that interrogation. Striker was a good detective. She would miss working with him, but once she transferred back to Pacific she would likely never see him again except in passing. It was the LAPD way. The department made vagabonds of its sworn personnel.

Striker loosened his tie. Silk, she guessed, with geometric shapes in shades of blue, including a sapphire tone that matched his eye color. She wondered if he'd figured that out by himself or if he'd had help. Salesperson? Wife? Girlfriend? It was a reminder of how little she knew about him. He eased his back into the chair and stretched out his legs, brushing his knee against hers.

She shot him a look.

He moved his leg. "Sorry."

"No problem." She wondered if his invasion of her personal space was inadvertent or intentional but was somewhat disappointed to see nothing in his expression that indicated the gesture was a come-on.

"I almost forgot," Striker said, reaching inside his duffle bag. "I bought this for you at the Seattle airport." He pulled out what looked like a compact umbrella. "You seem to have water issues. This won't help next time you fall in a river, but it'll definitely protect you from the rain, and it fits in a briefcase or even a pocket when you travel."

Davie remembered Striker watching her when she returned to RHD from Seattle, still damp from the downpour. He hadn't mentioned her appearance, but he must have noticed. She listened as he went on to point out the umbrella's unique engineering features that allowed it to fold up into its small sleeve. The umbrella was a thoughtful gesture and the technical lecture was … Davie wondered if it would be excessive to call it charming. She fumbled for an appropriate response, but a simple thank-you seemed inadequate.

"Can I ask you a personal question?" she asked.

Striker crossed his arms and frowned. "Depends on how personal."

"You have a tattoo on the inside of your right arm. What does it say?"

He didn't respond for what seemed like a long time. "Why are you asking?"

Davie leaned forward. "Because I hate not knowing things."

He nodded as if he understood the impulse and then his expression softened. "It's a story I don't share with many people."

"But you'll share it with me."

His lips pressed together in a noncommittal smile. "We'll see how it goes."

42

DAVIE LEFT THE PARKING lot and walked into the cemetery grounds, burdened by the weight of the heavy tote draped over her shoulder. Nearby, a gardener fired up a leaf blower. A moment later she realized the noise hadn't made her flinch. She paused when she saw all the white crosses—men and women who'd served in the military, many who had died for the cause. She thought of the oath she had taken when she'd graduated from the police academy, to protect and to serve. Her job was dangerous, but somehow, it wasn't the same as trading fire day after day in conflict zones in faraway countries. And yet, she had also killed to save lives. Twice.

She didn't presume to understand what happened between soldiers in war, but she and Lunds had shared a near-death experience that created a bond she would never forget. She hoped he felt the same. People processed emotions in different ways. Lunds had saved her life and she was grateful. Spencer Hall had never been able thank her for saving *his* life. The roses might have been his way of making amends. Maybe she'd ask him.

Shannon Woodrow had Zeke's body flown back to Iowa for burial in the family plot outside of Albia. Telling her about the circumstances surrounding her father's death was difficult, but watching Lynda Morrow's emotional meltdown was hard to watch. It was a trite notion, but maybe understanding the death and violence Zeke endured but never shared would finally allow her to move on. That seemed to already be happening. Zeke's Santa Barbara house was in Shannon's name, but Lynda and her husband offered to pay the insurance, taxes, and upkeep so her daughter could keep the house Zeke loved. In return, Shannon suggested they use the cottage for holidays and family get-togethers.

Harlan Cormack's cremated remains were scattered in a rose garden ossuary in St. Joseph, Missouri, near the graves of his parents and grandparents. Juno Karst had no family, at least none Davie had been able to find, so she had found a final resting place for his urn in a columbarian niche in the veteran's section of a cemetery in West L.A. She'd tried the Veteran's Cemetery on Wilshire, the one she'd seen from Alden Brink's office window the first time they'd met. It seemed like a fitting place for Juno, but the cemetery was full. It hadn't accepted new burials in forty years. *There should be a rule*, she thought. *When the cemeteries are full, all wars must end.*

A weight settled on her chest as she saw Dag Lunds sitting on a bench waiting for her. He wasn't Juno's biological brother, but he was a brother nonetheless, so together they would give Karst his final sendoff.

Lunds got up from the bench as she came closer. They embraced for a brief moment before she led him to the niche where Juno's ashes rested. She'd ordered a nameplate but it hadn't yet been installed, so yesterday she'd written some words on a post-it note and taped it to the metal so she could easily find the spot again.

Lunds ran his fingers over the niche and bowed his head. Grief had etched deep crevices in his face. His eyes seemed haunted with the violence he'd seen and the memories that would never go away. She wanted to reach out to him, touch his hand, but she held back.

She set the tote on the ground. "I'll leave you alone if you'd like."

He squeezed his eyes closed. "Stay."

Lunds remained quiet for a few moments, long enough to say his goodbyes. She didn't want to cry, not in front of him, so she redirected her focus toward the nearby chapel. The doors were open. About a hundred people dressed in black sat on benches and listened to a woman singing a capella—"Amazing Grace." Her voice was plaintive but comforting. Davie's breathing became deep and rhythmic until she regained control of her emotions.

"I never asked," she said. "Why did you call him Juno?"

A faint smile lifted the corners of his mouth. "It was a nickname we gave him back in basic training. Juno read everything he could get his hands on, from romance novels to *Popular Science* magazines. Factoids? He loved them and wanted to share everything with us, even when we didn't want him to. Didn't matter to him. He just laughed it off. He was always like 'Did you know that Saturn is the second biggest planet in our solar system?' Or 'Did you know only the female black widow's bite is dangerous to humans?' He'd get so excited about the telling that his words would run together. They came out sounding like 'Juno that Saturn' or 'Juno black widow spiders.' It got to be funny, so we started calling him Juno. He didn't seem to mind, so the name stuck."

Davie watched as the mourners filed out of the chapel. "You once told me you wouldn't go to Asia on assignment. Is that because of what happened with John Latham?"

He shook his head. "I went back once. A couple of years ago Tide-Pool sent me to Ho Chi Minh City. The war had been over for a long time and I thought it would be interesting to see the place again. There was an old man on the street selling pieces of fish from a bowl. He called to me in perfect English, so I went over to see what he wanted. He told me he worked for the US during the war. When Saigon fell, he didn't make it onto that last helicopter. The North Vietnamese Army arrested him and sent him to prison. He never saw his wife and child again. I'll never forget the way he looked at me—pure hate. Even after all those years, I think he would have killed me if he'd had the means. After that, I swore I'd never go back again. Ever."

Davie saw the pallbearers wheel the casket toward a waiting hearse. "I wish I could have saved Zeke's life. All their lives."

His face looked pinched and weary. "You saved mine. Zeke would have liked that."

"I'm sorry I never got to meet him."

"He was a good man," Lunds said. "They all were. All gone, except for me."

The LAPD had made Davie sit through enough therapy sessions with a department shrink to recognize survivor's guilt, but any attempt to counsel him would be playing shrink.

Davie watched the mourners walk along the road toward the gravesite, led by a woman who looked too young to be a widow. "I don't know why you survived and they didn't. I'm just glad you're still around."

"I'm alive because you saw a pattern and didn't take no for an answer."

"And I'm alive because you pulled me out of that river."

He put his callused hands on her shoulders, brushed a windblown red curl from her forehead, and planted a fatherly kiss in its place. "It's been great meeting you, Davie Richards. I just wish it had been under happier circumstances."

"Will you be okay?"

He removed his hands from her shoulders and stared at Juno's niche. "When I got home from Vietnam, I visited a guy in a hospital in Fort Campbell. He was suffering from PTSD and doing the Thorizine Shuffle. Every time he heard a door slam he'd hide under his bed. I thought he was weak and that it could never happen to me. After the Gulf War, I understood that PTSD can happen to anybody at any time."

"We call it The Limit. It's that last dead body you see before you can't take it anymore." She paused for a moment to think where she was on that spectrum but found her passion for the work still intact. "Where will you go now?"

"Oregon," Lunds said. "I'm going to spend a week or two with my son. When I get back this way, I hope it's okay to call you."

She picked up the new cat tote she'd bought and handed it to him. It was softer and easier to handle than the old one. "Thanks for adopting Hootch. I think Zeke would have wanted him to stay with family."

Lunds unzipped the top and draped Hootch over his shoulder. "He's a fine-looking animal." He buried his face in the cat's fur and stroked his back. "I'll take good care of him, don't you worry. And thanks for giving Juno a proper send off. I'll never forget it."

She watched as he slid the cat carrier into the back of his SUV and got into the front seat. She wasn't sure she was ready to see either one of them go, but it was too late now. Lunds gave her a final salute and drove out through the cemetery gates.

Striker was leaning against the city ride waiting for her, his arms crossed and his brow furrowed. The sun highlighted his long straight nose and the dusting of silver hair at his temples. "How did it go?"

She leaned next to him against the car and stared at the ground. "I've had better days."

"You having second thoughts about Hootch?"

She squeezed her eyes closed and thought about his question. Truth was she'd grown fond of the cat. She would miss him. But Lunds had just lost his three best friends and he was suffering. Hootch had been Zeke's cat and now he'd be Lunds's comfort cat. She hoped they'd help each other work through the pain.

Davie met Striker's gaze. "No second thoughts." It was a lie, but whether it was a big lie or a small one had yet to be determined.

Striker stared at the gravestones in the distance. "I thought you'd want to know. SID opened Zeke's computer with that code you found on Hootch's microchip. They confirmed Zeke's letter to the Army was stored on the hard drive."

Davie's phone pinged with an incoming text. It was Jason Vaughn, wondering where she was.

She centered herself and then turned to Striker. "Can you drop me off at Pacific?"

"Maybe your partner can pick you up on his horse."

She smiled. "He hasn't mentioned the Mounted Unit for a day or two. I think he's moved on."

Striker returned her smile and then folded himself into the driver's seat.

Before joining him in the car, Davie tapped a reply on her phone: ON MY WAY. SEE YOU THERE.

About the Author

Patricia Smiley (Los Angeles, CA) is a bestselling mystery author whose short fiction has appeared in *Ellery Queen Mystery Magazine* and *Two of the Deadliest*, an anthology edited by Elizabeth George. Patricia has taught writing classes at various conferences throughout the US and Canada, and she served on the board of directors of the Southern California Chapter of Mystery Writers of America and as president of Sisters in Crime / Los Angeles. Visit her online at www.PatriciaSmiley.com.